THE BURIAL OF THE RATS

and Other Tales of the Macabre
by Bram Stoker

THE
BURIAL OF
THE RATS

and Other Tales of the Macabre
by Bram Stoker

Edited by
XAVIER ALDANA REYES

THE BRITISH LIBRARY

This collection first published in 2023 by
The British Library
96 Euston Road
London NW1 2DB

Selection and introduction © 2023 Xavier Aldana Reyes
Volume copyright © 2023 The British Library Board

Cataloguing in Publication Data
A catalogue record for this publication is available from the British Library

ISBN 978 0 7123 5444 8

Frontispiece: illustration by William FitzGerald for 'The Castle of the King', from the Bram Stoker collection *Under the Sunset*, Sampson Low, London, 1881. Page 241: illustration by William FitzGerald for 'The Shadow Builder', from the same edition of *Under the Sunset*.

Cover design by Mauricio Villamayor with illustration by Mag Ruhig.
Original interior ornaments by Mag Ruhig.
Text design and typesetting by Tetragon, London
Printed in Czechia by Finidr

CONTENTS

I would like to dedicate this collection to Emma Liggins: wonderful friend, colleague and scholar. Thanks for many things, but especially for those long Covid walks that helped keep me sane.

'Perhaps at the end the little things may teach us most.'

INTRODUCTION

The last chapter in David J. Skal's *Something in the Blood: The Untold Story of Bram Stoker* (2016) is entitled "The Curse of Dracula". It is a poignant reminder that Bram Stoker's reputation and legacy rest primarily on the creation of the most famous vampire of all times. *Dracula* may have been outsold by Richard Marsh's *The Beetle* (1897) on the year of its publication, but it has never been out of print and remains, together with Mary Shelley's *Frankenstein* (1818) and Robert Louis Stevenson's *Strange Case of Dr. Jekyll and Mr. Hyde* (1886), one of the most adapted and influential of all Gothic texts. By contrast, the bulk of Stoker's incredibly varied oeuvre has never quite managed to emerge from the shadows cast by the Count's long, chameleonic cape. Horror fans will be familiar with the Egyptian mummy chiller *The Jewel of Seven Stars* (published in 1903 and revised in 1912) and *The Lair of the White Worm* (1911), about a snake-like creature who can transform into a woman. They may have sought out *The Mystery of the Sea* (1902), a novel about second sight, hidden treasure and secret codes that, like many of Stoker's writings, defies neat genre classifications. Eager readers may even have leapt at the chance of acquiring *The Snake's Pass* (1890), an earlier work steeped in Irish legend, and *The Lady of the Shroud* (1909), a spiritual companion to *Dracula* that "unwrites" the myth of the vampire, when they were reissued by Valancourt Books in 2006 and 2012, respectively. Yet some of Stoker's other novels, like *The Primrose Path* (1875), *The Shoulder of Shasta* (1895), *Miss Betty* (1898), *The Man* (1905) or *Lady Athlyne* (1908), are largely forgotten and hard to source. It is a shame, because they reveal an author who felt as comfortable penning romance novels and adventure stories as he did the more gruelling fiction for which he is remembered today.

Stoker was not just a consummate novelist but also a great writer of short stories. Perhaps as a result of the same vampiric curse, the only one of his collections to have had any repercussion is *Dracula's Guest and Other Weird Stories*. Published posthumously in 1914, it featured what Stoker's widow referred to as "an hitherto unpublished episode from 'Dracula,'" arguably the main selling point. The collection anthologised some of his strongest and most terrifying short stories, which had previously appeared in newspapers and magazines: "A Gipsy Prophecy" (1885), "The Judge's House" (1891), "The Secret of the Growing Gold" (1892), "The Squaw" (1893), "A Dream of Red Hands" (1894) and "The Burial of the Rats" (1896). These are classic stories that conjure up some of the most feverish nightmares ever conceived by the author's mind, including a murderous cat, an iron maiden, a vengeful portrait, a Poesque corpse whose ringlets keep growing after death, incriminating blood that simply will not wash away and rats with a taste for human blood. They are reproduced here and complemented with lesser-known stories from a variety of sources.

This collection opens with "The Crystal Cup", which was originally published in 1872 in the British magazine *London Society* but not anthologised until the 1980s. An example of Stoker's early writing bespeaking the influence of fantasy and fairy tales, it is a deeply evocative and poetic piece that plays with focalisation to tell a dark allegorical story about love and art. In the same magical vein, three stories are taken from Stoker's first collection, *Under the Sunset*, which was published in 1881 in an edition that included 33 illustrations by William FitzGerald and W. V. Cockburn and was aimed at a younger audience—the book was, in fact, dedicated to his son. Like the other five stories that accompany them, "The Invisible Giant" (1881), "The Shadow Builder" (1881) and "The

Castle of the King" (1876) are moralising tales that exhort Christian values of good, virtue and purity. The ones selected here are the grimmest, but interested readers might also want to check out "The Rose Prince" (1881) and "How 7 Went Mad" (1881). Although some could find the stories in *Under the Sunset* a little obvious, excessively cautionary in tone or even maudlin, they offer a good window into Stoker's vivid imagination and his fixation with mortality. They also show how versatile his style could be, shifting as it does from almost oneiric passages in "The Shadow Builder" to the more declarative prose of "The Invisible Giant".

In regard to the other stories that had initially appeared outside of the main Stoker collections, "Saved by a Ghost" is a fairly straightforward narrative of supernatural intervention recently unearthed by biographer David J. Skal and magazine and book editor Brian J. Showers. Believed to be only Stoker's second published piece of fiction, it appeared anonymously in 1873 in *The Irish Echo*, where he briefly worked as an editor. The story was reprinted for the first time in 2015 by the journal *The Green Book: Writings on Irish Gothic, Supernatural and Fantastic Literature*, along with a fascinating discussion on its origins. "The Dualitists; or, the Death Doom of the Double Born" was first published in *The Theatre Annual* in an issue dated 1887 but which came out in November of 1886. It is a compelling story that relishes in Gothic motifs (doppelgänger twins, serial killing, innate evil) and truly macabre tableaux. Unlike Stoker's other earlier works, it is not openly supernatural and seems less interested in putting forward a complex moral message than in exploring human depravity. As for "Old Hoggen: A Mystery", an odd but nevertheless engrossing story mixing mystery and comedy, it first appeared in the *Boston Herald* in 1893, was rescued from oblivion in 2012 by academic John Edgar Browning for his *The Forgotten Writings of Bram Stoker* and was subsequently given centre piece status in *Old Hoggen and Other Adventures* (2017), from Swan River Press. Apart from exhibiting Stoker's obsession with the nautical world, it features a skin-crawling moment that will ensure readers never look at crabs the same way. Finally, "The Man from Shorrox'" was first published in *Pall Mall Magazine* in 1894, accompanied by nine illustrations. One of his very few works set in Ireland, this sardonic tale of hubris and morbid games is marked by Stoker's distinctive flare for capturing linguistic idiosyncrasies, especially at play in his works set in Scotland. It hopefully offers a humorous counterpoint to the thrilling horrors of "The Burial of the Rats", which closes the collection. Taken together, these stories reflect how wildly varied Stoker's fiction was and celebrate his ability to adopt different registers and create diverse, sometimes diametrically opposite, moods. An ambivalence exists at the heart of his prose, where a deep preoccupation and desire to investigate the macabre, even indulge in its most blood-curdling and visceral jolts, cohabits seamlessly with a firm belief in ethical principles and the triumph of goodness. It may seem like a trite point to make, but Count Dracula encapsulates this duality perfectly as a seductive monster whose pervasive presence is felt throughout the novel yet is eventually expelled by stalwarts of propriety and their religious and scientific beliefs.

Stoker fans will notice the omission of three key stories from *Dracula's Guest and Other Weird Stories* that have been excluded only because they have already found their way into other collections published by the British Library. "Crooken Sands" (1894), first published in the magazine *Holly Leaves: The Christmas Number of the Illustrated Sporting and Dramatic News*, appeared in *Our Haunted Shores: Tales from the Coasts of the British Isles* (2022), edited by Emily Alder, Jimmy Packham and Joan Passey. A strange little tale about a peculiar double, it is perhaps most notable for its location: the Scottish coastline Stoker holidayed in and which inspired many of his writings. "The Coming of Abel Behenna" (1893), first published in *Lloyd's Weekly Newspaper* in the UK and *The New Haven Register* in the US, was part of *Cornish Horrors: Tales from the Land's End* (2021), edited by Joan Passey. Its plot revolves around a dead suitor staking his love claim from the grave. Finally, "Dracula's Guest" (1914) was already selected for *Visions of the Vampire: Two Centuries of Immortal Tales* (2020), edited by Sorcha Ní Fhlainn and me. Although necessarily open-ended, the story is incredibly atmospheric and a worthy companion to Stoker's masterpiece. The keen reader is encouraged to seek out these stories; they come as highly recommended as the collections in which they are hosted.

XAVIER ALDANA REYES, 2023

DR. XAVIER ALDANA REYES is Reader in English Literature and Film at Manchester Metropolitan University, where he co-leads the Manchester Centre for Gothic Studies. He is the author of several books on horror literature and cinema and the editor of six anthologies for the British Library, including *The Gothic Tales of Sheridan Le Fanu* (2020) and *The Weird Tales of William Hope Hodgson* (2019).

A NOTE FROM THE PUBLISHER

The original short stories reprinted in the British Library's classic fiction series were written and published in a period ranging across the nineteenth and twentieth centuries. There are many elements of these stories which continue to entertain modern readers; however, in some cases there are also uses of language, instances of stereotyping and some attitudes expressed by narrators or characters which may not be endorsed by the publishing standards of today. We acknowledge therefore that some elements in the stories selected for reprinting may continue to make uncomfortable reading for some of our audience. With this series British Library Publishing aims to offer a new readership a chance to read some of the rare material of the British Library's collections in an affordable paperback format, to enjoy their merits and to look back into the worlds of the past two centuries as portrayed by their writers. It is not possible to separate these stories from the history of their writing and as such the following stories are presented as they were originally published with the inclusion of minor edits made for consistency of style and sense. We welcome feedback from our readers, which can be sent to the following address:

British Library Publishing
The British Library
96 Euston Road
London, NW1 2DB
United Kingdom

THE CRYSTAL CUP

I

The Dream-Birth

THE blue waters touch the walls of the palace; I can hear their soft, lapping wash against the marble whenever I listen. Far out at sea I can see the waves glancing in the sunlight, ever-smiling, ever-glancing, ever-sunny. Happy waves!—happy in your gladness, thrice happy that ye are free!

I rise from my work and spring up the wall till I reach the embrasure. I grasp the corner of the stonework and draw myself up till I crouch in the wide window. Sea, sea, out away as far as my vision extends. There I gaze till my eyes grow dim; and in the dimness of my eyes my spirit finds its sight. My soul flies on the wings of memory away beyond the blue, smiling sea—away beyond the glancing waves and the gleaming sails, to the land I call my home. As the minutes roll by, my actual eye-sight seems to be restored, and I look round me in my old birth-house. The rude simplicity of the dwelling comes back to me as something new. There I see my old books and manuscripts and pictures, and there, away on their old shelves, high up above the door, I see my first rude efforts in art.

How poor they seem to me now! And yet, were I free, I would not give the smallest of them for all I now possess. Possess? How I dream.

The dream calls me back to waking life. I spring down from my window-seat and work away frantically, for every line I draw on paper, every new form that springs on the plaster, brings me nearer freedom. I will make a vase whose beauty will put to shame the glorious works of Greece in her golden prime! Surely a love like mine and a hope like mine must in time make some form of beauty spring to life! When He beholds it he will exclaim with rapture, and will order my instant freedom. I can forget my hate, and the deep debt of revenge which I owe him when I think of liberty—even from his hands. Ah! then on the wings of the morning shall I fly beyond the sea to my home—her home—and clasp her to my arms, never more to be separated!

But, oh Spirit of Day! if she should be—No, no, I cannot think of it, or I shall go mad. Oh Time, Time! maker and destroyer of men's fortunes, why hasten so fast for others whilst thou laggest so slowly for me? Even now my home may have become desolate, and she—my bride of an hour—may sleep calmly in the cold earth. Oh this suspense will drive me mad! Work, work! Freedom is before me; Aurora is the reward of my labour!

So I rush to my work; but to my brain and hand, heated alike, no fire or no strength descends. Half mad with despair, I beat myself against the walls of my prison, and then climb into the embrasure, and once more gaze upon the ocean, but find there no hope. And so I stay till night, casting its pall of blackness over nature, puts the possibility of effort away from me for yet another day.

So my days go on, and grow to weeks and months. So will they grow to years, should life so long remain an unwelcome guest within me; for what is man without hope? and is not hope nigh dead within this weary breast?

Last night, in my dreams, there came, like an inspiration from the Day-Spirit, a design for my vase.

All day my yearning for freedom—for Aurora, or news of her—had increased tenfold, and my heart and brain were on fire. Madly I beat myself, like a caged bird, against my prison-bars. Madly I leaped to my window-seat, and gazed with bursting eyeballs out on the free, open sea. And there I sat till my passion had worn itself out; and then I slept, and dreamed of thee, Aurora—of thee and freedom. In my ears I heard again the old song we used to sing together, when as children we wandered on the beach; when, as lovers, we saw the sun sink in the ocean, and I would see its glory doubled as it shone in thine eyes, and was mellowed against thy cheek; and when, as my bride, you clung to me as my arms went round you on that desert tongue of land whence rushed that band of sea-robbers that tore me away. Oh! how my heart curses those men—not men, but fiends! But one solitary gleam of joy remains from that dread encounter,—that my struggle stayed those hellhounds, and that, ere I was stricken down, this right hand sent one of them to his home. My spirit rises as I think of that blow that saved thee from a life worse than death. With the thought I feel my cheeks burning, and my forehead swelling with mighty veins. My eyes burn, and I rush wildly round my prison-house. "Oh! for one of my enemies, that I might dash out his brains against these marble walls, and trample his heart out as he lay before me!" These walls would spare him not. They are pitiless, alas! I know too well. "Oh, cruel mockery of kindness, to make a palace a prison, and to taunt a captive's aching heart with forms of beauty and sculptured marble!" Wondrous, indeed, are these sculptured walls! Men call them passing fair; but oh, Aurora! with thy beauty ever before my eyes, what form that men call lovely can be fair to me? Like him who gazes sun-wards, and then sees no light on earth, from the glory that dyes his iris, so thy beauty or its memory has turned the fairest things of earth to blackness and deformity.

In my dream last night, when in my ears came softly, like music stealing across the waters from afar, the old song we used to sing together, then to my brain, like a ray of light, came an idea whose grandeur for a moment struck me dumb. Before my eyes grew a vase of such beauty that I knew my hope was born to life, and that the Great Spirit had placed my foot on the ladder that leads from this my palace-dungeon to freedom and to thee. To-day I have got a block of crystal—for only in such pellucid substance can I body forth my dream—and have commenced my work.

I found at first that my hand had lost its cunning, and I was beginning to despair, when, like the memory of a dream, there came back in my ears the strains of the old song. I sang it softly to myself, and as I did so I grew calmer; but oh! how differently the song sounded to me when thy voice, Aurora, rose not in unison with my own! But what avails pining? To work! To work! Every touch of my chisel will bring me nearer thee.

My vase is daily growing nearer to completion. I sing as I work, and my constant song is the one I love so well. I can hear the echo of my voice in the vase; and as I end, the wailing song note is prolonged in sweet, sad music in the crystal cup. I listen, ear down, and sometimes I weep as I listen, so sadly comes the echo to my song. Imperfect though it be, my voice makes sweet music, and its echo in the cup guides my hand towards perfection as I work. Would that thy voice rose and fell with mine, Aurora, and then the world would behold a vase of such beauty as never before woke up the slumbering fires of man's love for what is fair; for if I do such work in sadness, imperfect as I am in my solitude and sorrow, what would I do in joy, perfect when with thee? I know that my work is good as an artist, and I feel that it is as a man; and the cup itself, as it daily grows in beauty, gives back a clearer echo. Oh! if I worked in joy how gladly would it give back our voices! *Then* would we hear an echo and music such as mortals seldom hear; but now the echo, like my song, seems imperfect. I grow daily weaker; but still I work on—work with my whole soul—for am I not working for freedom and for thee.

*

My work is nearly done. Day by day, hour by hour, the vase grows more finished. Ever clearer comes the echo whilst I sing; ever softer, ever more sad and heart-rending comes the echo of the wail at the end of the song. Day by day I grow weaker and weaker; still I work on with all my soul. At night the thought comes to me, whilst I think of thee, that I will never see thee more—that I breathe out my life into the crystal cup, and that it will last there when I am gone.

So beautiful has it become, so much do I love it, that I could gladly die to be maker of such a work, were it not for thee—for my love for thee, and my hope of thee, and my fear for thee, and my anguish for thy grief when thou knowest I am gone.

My work requires but few more touches. My life is slowly ebbing away, and I feel that with my last touch my life will pass out for ever into the cup. Till that touch is given I must not die—I will not die. My hate has passed away. So great are my wrongs that revenge of mine would be too small a compensation for my woe. I leave revenge to a juster and a mightier than I. Thee, oh Aurora, I will await in the land of flowers, where thou and I will wander, never more to part, never more! Ah, never more! Farewell, Aurora—Aurora—Aurora!

I I

The Feast of Beauty

The Feast of Beauty approaches rapidly, yet hardly so fast as my royal master wishes. He seems to have no other thought than to have this feast greater and better than any ever held before. Five summers ago his Feast of Beauty was nobler than all held in his sire's reign together; yet scarcely was it over, and the rewards given to the victors, when he conceived the giant project whose success is to be tested when the moon reaches her full. It was boldly chosen and boldly done; chosen and done as boldly as the project of a monarch should be. But still I cannot think that it will end well. This yearning after completeness must be unsatisfied in the end—this desire that makes a monarch fling his kingly justice to the winds, and strive to reach his Mecca over a desert of blighted hopes and lost lives. But hush! I must not dare to think ill of my master or his deeds; and besides, walls have ears. I must leave alone these dangerous topics, and confine my thoughts within proper bounds.

The moon is waxing quickly, and with its fulness comes the Feast of Beauty, whose success as a whole rests almost solely on my watchfulness and care; for if the ruler of the feast should fail in his duty, who could fill the void? Let me see what arts are represented, and what works compete. All the arts will have trophies: poetry in its various forms, and prose-writing; sculpture with carving in various metals, and glass, and wood, and ivory, and engraving gems, and setting jewels; painting on canvas, and glass, and wood, and stone and metal; music, vocal and instrumental; and dancing. If that woman will but sing, we will have a real triumph of music; but she appears sickly too. All our best artists either get ill or die, although we promise them freedom or rewards or both if they succeed.

Surely never yet was a Feast of Beauty so fair or so richly dowered as this which the full moon shall behold and hear; but ah! the crowning glory of the feast will be the crystal cup. Never yet have these eyes beheld such a form of beauty, such a wondrous mingling of substance and light. Surely some magic power must have helped to draw such loveliness from a cold block of crystal. I must be careful that no harm happens the vase. To-day when I touched it, it gave forth such a ringing sound that my heart jumped with fear lest it should sustain any injury. Henceforth, till I deliver it up to my master, no hand but my own shall touch it lest any harm should happen to it.

Strange story has that cup. Born to life in the cell of a captive torn from his artist home beyond the sea, to enhance the splendour of a feast by his labour—seen at work by spies, and traced and followed till a chance—cruel chance for him—gave him into the hands of the emissaries of my master. He too, poor moth, fluttered about the flame: the name of freedom spurred him on to exertion till he wore away his life. The beauty of that cup was dearly bought for him. Many a man would forget his captivity whilst he worked at such a piece of loveliness; but he appeared to have some sorrow at his heart, some sorrow so great that it quenched his pride.

How he used to rave at first! How he used to rush about his chamber, and then climb into the embrasure of his window, and gaze out away over the sea! Poor captive! perhaps over the sea some one waited for his coming who was dearer to him than many cups, even many cups as beautiful as this, if such could be on earth… Well, well, we must all die soon or late, and who dies first escapes the more sorrow, perhaps, who knows? How, when he had commenced the cup, he used to sing all day long, from the moment the sun shot its first fiery arrow into the retreating hosts of night-clouds, till the shades of evening advancing drove the lingering sunbeams into the west—and always the same song!

How he used to sing, all alone! Yet sometimes I could almost imagine I heard not one voice from his chamber, but two… No more will it echo again from the wall of a dungeon, or from a hillside in free air. No more will his eyes behold the beauty of his crystal cup.

It was well he lived to finish it. Often and often have I trembled to think of his death, as I saw him day by day grow weaker as he worked at the unfinished vase. Must his eyes never more behold the beauty that was born of his soul? Oh, never more! Oh Death, grim King of Terrors, how mighty is thy sceptre! All-powerful is the wave of thy hand that summons us in turn to thy kingdom away beyond the poles!

Would that thou, poor captive, hadst lived to behold thy triumph, for victory will be thine at the Feast of Beauty such as man never before achieved. Then thou mightst have heard the shout that hails the victor in the contest, and the plaudits that greet him as he passes out, a free man, through the palace gates. But now thy cup will come to light amid the smiles of beauty and rank and power, whilst thou liest there in thy lonely chamber, cold as the marble of its walls.

And, after all, the feast will be imperfect, since the victors cannot all be crowned. I must ask my master's direction as to how a blank place of a competitor, should he prove a victor, is to be filled up. So late? I must see him ere the noontide hour of rest be past.

Great Spirit! how I trembled as my master answered my question!

I found him in his chamber, as usual in the noontide. He was lying on his couch disrobed, half-sleeping; and the drowsy zephyr, scented with rich odours from the garden, wafted through the windows at either side by the fans, lulled him to complete repose. The darkened chamber was cool and silent. From the vestibule came the murmuring of many fountains, and the pleasant splash of falling waters. "Oh, happy," said I, in my heart, "oh, happy great King, that has such pleasures to enjoy!" The breeze from the fans swept over the strings of the Æolian harps, and a sweet, confused, happy melody arose like the murmuring of children's voices singing afar off in the valleys, and floating on the wind.

As I entered the chamber softly, with muffled footfall and pent-in breath, I felt a kind of awe stealing over me. To me who was born and have dwelt all my life within the precincts of the court—to me who talk daily with my royal master, and take his minutest directions as to the coming feast—to me who had all my life looked up to my king as to a spirit, and had venerated him as more than mortal—came a feeling of almost horror; for my master looked then, in his quiet chamber, half-sleeping amid the drowsy music of the harps and fountains, more like a common man than a God. As the thought came to me I shuddered in affright, for it seemed to me that I had been guilty of sacrilege. So much had my veneration for my royal master become a part of my nature, that but to think of him as another man seemed like the anarchy of my own soul.

I came beside the couch, and watched him in silence. He seemed to be half-listening to the fitful music; and as the melody swelled and died away his chest rose and fell as he breathed in unison with the sound.

After a moment or two he appeared to become conscious of the presence of some one in the room, although by no motion of his face could I see that he heard any sound, and his eyes were shut. He opened his eyes, and, seeing me, asked, "Was all right about the Feast of Beauty?" for that is the subject ever nearest to his thoughts. I answered that all was well, but that I had come to ask his royal pleasure as to how a vacant place amongst the competitors was to be filled up. He asked, "How vacant?" and on my telling him, "from death," he asked again, quickly, "Was the work finished?" When I told him that it was, he lay back again on his couch with a sigh of relief, for he had half arisen in his anxiety as he asked the question. Then he said, after a minute, "All the competitors must be present at the feast." "All?" said I. "All," he answered again, "alive or dead; for the old custom must be preserved, and the victors crowned." He stayed still for a minute more, and then said, slowly, "Victors or martyrs." And I could see that the kingly spirit was coming back to him.

Again he went on, "This will be my last Feast of Beauty; and all the captives shall be set free. Too much sorrow has sprung already from my ambition. Too much injustice has soiled the name of king."

He said no more, but lay still and closed his eyes. I could see by the working of his hands and the heaving of his chest that some violent emotion troubled him, and the thought arose, "He is a man, but he is yet a king; and, though a king as he is, still happiness is not for him. Great Spirit of Justice! thou metest out his pleasures and his woes to man, to king and slave alike! Thou lovest best to whom thou givest peace!"

Gradually my master grew more calm, and at length sunk into a gentle slumber; but even in his sleep he breathed in unison with the swelling murmur of the harps.

"To each is given," said I gently, "something in common with the world of actual things. Thy life, oh King, is bound by chains of sympathy to the voice of Truth, which is Music! Tremble, lest in the presence of a master-strain thou shouldst feel thy littleness, and die!" and I softly left the room.

III

The Story of the Moonbeam

Slowly I creep along the bosom of the waters.

Sometimes I look back as I rise upon a billow, and see behind me many of my kin sitting each upon a wave-summit as upon a throne. So I go on for long, a power that I wist not forcing me onward, without will or purpose of mine.

At length, as I rise upon a mimic wave, I see afar a hazy light that springs from a vast palace, through whose countless windows flame lamps and torches. But at the first view, as if my coming had been the signal, the lights disappear in an instant.

Impatiently I await what may happen; and as I rise with each heart-beat of the sea, I look forward to where the torches had gleamed. Can it be a deed of darkness that shuns the light?

The time has come when I can behold the palace without waiting to mount upon the waves. It is built of white marble, and rises steep from the brine. Its seafront is glorious with columns and statues; and from the portals the marble steps sweep down, broad and wide to the waters, and below them, down as deep as I can see.

No sound is heard, no light is seen. A solemn silence abounds, a perfect calm.

Slowly I climb the palace walls, my brethren following as soldiers up a breach. I slide along the roofs, and as I look behind me walls and roofs are glistening as with silver. At length I meet with something smooth and hard and translucent; but through it I pass and enter a vast hall, where for an instant I hang in mid-air and wonder.

My coming has been the signal for such a burst of harmony as brings back to my memory the music of the spheres as they rush through space; and in the full-swelling anthem of welcome I feel that I am indeed a sun-spirit, a child of light, and that this is homage to my master.

I look upon the face of a great monarch, who sits at the head of a banquet-table. He has turned his head upwards and backwards, and looks as if he had been awaiting my approach. He rises and fronts me with the ringing out of the welcome-song, and all the others in the great hall turn towards me as well. I can see their eyes gleaming. Down along the immense table, laden with plate and glass and flowers, they stand holding each a cup of ruby wine, with which they pledge the monarch when the song is ended, as they drink success to him and to the "Feast of Beauty."

I survey the hall. An immense chamber, with marble walls covered with bas-reliefs and frescoes and sculptured figures, and panelled by great columns that rise along the surface and support a dome-ceiling painted wondrously; in its centre the glass lantern by which I entered.

On the walls are hung pictures of various forms and sizes, and down the centre of the table stretches a raised platform on which are placed works of art of various kinds.

At one side of the hall is a dais on which sit persons of both sexes with noble faces and lordly brows, but all wearing the same expression— care tempered by hope. All these hold scrolls in their hands.

At the other side of the hall is a similar dais, on which sit others fairer to earthly view, less spiritual and more marked by surface-passion. They hold music-scores. All these look more joyous than those on the other platform, all save one, a woman, who sits with downcast face and dejected mien, as of one without hope. As my light falls at her feet she looks up, and I feel happy. The sympathy between us has called a faint gleam of hope to cheer that poor pale face.

Many are the forms of art that rise above the banquet-table, and all are lovely to behold. I look on all with pleasure one by one, till I see the last of them at the end of the table away from the monarch, and then all the others seem as nothing to me. What is this that makes other forms of beauty seem as nought when compared with it, when brought within the radius of its lustre? A crystal cup, wrought with such wondrous skill that light seems to lose its individual glory as it shines upon it and is merged in its beauty. "Oh Universal Mother, let me enter there. Let my life be merged in its beauty, and no more will I regret my sun-strength hidden deep in the chasms of my moon-mother. Let me live there and perish there, and I will be joyous whilst it lasts, and content to pass into the great vortex of nothingness to be born again when the glory of the cup has fled."

Can it be that my wish is granted, that I have entered the cup and become a part of its beauty? "Great Mother, I thank thee."

Has the cup life? or is it merely its wondrous perfectness that makes it tremble, like a beating heart, in unison with the ebb and flow, the great wave-pulse of nature? To me it feels as if it had life.

I look through the crystal walls and see at the end of the table, isolated from all others, the figure of a man seated. Are those cords that bind his limbs? How suits that crown of laurel those wide, dim eyes, and that pallid hue? It is passing strange. This Feast of Beauty holds some dread secrets, and sees some wondrous sights.

I hear a voice of strange, rich sweetness, yet wavering—the voice of one *almost* a king by nature. He is standing up; I see him through my palace-wall. He calls a name and sits down again.

Again I hear a voice from the platform of scrolls, the Throne of Brows; and again I look and behold a man who stands trembling yet flushed, as though the morning light shone bright upon his soul. He reads in cadenced measure a song in praise of my moon-mother, the Feast of Beauty, and the king. As he speaks, he trembles no more, but seems inspired, and his voice rises to a tone of power and grandeur, and rings back from walls and dome. I hear his words distinctly, though saddened in tone, in the echo from my crystal home. He concludes and sits down, half-fainting, amid a whirlwind of applause, every note, every beat of which is echoed as the words had been.

Again the monarch rises and calls "Aurora," that she may sing for freedom. The name echoes in the cup with a sweet, sad sound. So sad, so despairing seems the echo, that the hall seems to darken and the scene to grow dim.

"Can a sun-spirit mourn, or a crystal vessel weep?"

She, the dejected one, rises from her seat on the Throne of Sound, and all eyes turn upon her save those of the pale one, laurel-crowned. Thrice she essays to begin, and thrice nought comes from her lips but a dry, husky sigh, till an old man who has been moving round the hall settling all things, cries out, in fear lest she should fail, "Freedom!"

The word is re-echoed from the cup. She hears the sound, turns towards it and begins.

Oh, the melody of that voice! And yet it is not perfect alone; for after the first note comes an echo from the cup that swells in unison with the voice, and the two sounds together, seem as if one strain came ringing sweet from the lips of the All-Father himself. So sweet it is, that all throughout the hall sit spell-bound, and scarcely dare to breathe.

In the pause after the first verses of the song, I hear the voice of the old man speaking to a comrade, but his words are unheard by any other, "Look at the king. His spirit seems lost in a trance of melody. Ah! I fear me some evil: the nearer the music approaches to perfection the more rapt he becomes. I dread lest a perfect note shall prove his death-call." His voice dies away as the singer commences the last verse.

Sad and plaintive is the song; full of feeling and tender love, but love overshadowed by grief and despair. As it goes on the voice of the singer grows sweeter and more thrilling, more real; and the cup, my crystal time-home, vibrates more and more as it gives back the echo. The monarch looks like one entranced, and no movement is within the hall… The song dies away in a wild wail that seems to tear the heart of the singer in twain; and the cup vibrates still more as it gives back the echo. As the note, long-swelling, reaches its highest, the cup, the Crystal Cup, my wondrous home, the gift of the All-Father, shivers into millions of atoms, and passes away.

Ere I am lost in the great vortex I see the singer throw up her arms and fall, freed at last, and the King sitting, glory-faced, but pallid with the hue of Death.

SAVED BY A GHOST

"**D**o any of you believe in ghosts?"
The question was asked by Captain Merwin of the ship *Curlew*, as, standing with his back to the fire in the coffee-room of the Royal Hotel, Liverpool, he addressed an attentive group who had asked him to relate the particulars of a curious incident in his life. To this question there were various answers.

"The reason I ask," continued the captain, "is because a ghost was the principal cause of a sudden reformation, which has been the making of me. Seventeen years ago I was homeward bound from the East Indies in the old ship *Revere*, of Boston, since lost. We had for mate 'Brick Bracken', and for third mate a staunch chum and friend of mine, William P. McLellan. The captain and second officer's names I forget.

"I was just eighteen years old, and had shipped with an A.B. (able seaman). I had been with Bracken for three years and a harder or better master no one ever had. My father shipped me with him purposely to sicken me of a sailor's life, but, contrary to his expectation, I liked it so well that I never went near home for seven years. Thanks to Bracken's tuition, at eighteen I was a thorough sailor and a thorough drunkard.

"On this voyage we had before the mast an unusually hard crowd, all of them, except myself, being taken out of gaol and put on board the ship in irons. When we first got our beating down the gulf of Martaban, things worked pretty hard.

"About four weeks after we left Rangoon McLellan, the third mate, was taken with convulsions and died. I was just writing a letter for him—he didn't expect to live—when the convulsions seized him, and he died in my arms. This was the morning. At eight bells in the afternoon we buried him.

"That night there was a grand pow-wow held in the forecastle. Tom Leach—a well-educated man, and, of course, a sea lawyer—was spokesman. The gist of the matter was this: the ship was rice laden, and leaking badly, short-handed and poorly provisioned, and everybody was discontented. Leach reviewed all this speech, and wound up with the remark, 'One of them settled for, and if the old man don't put in somewhere soon, we can settle the rest; and I can navigate we can get along well enough without them.' As he finished, it flashed through my brain that my friend had met with foul play, but I had no time to think of it, for at that moment I was called aft. Obeying the summons, I was shown into the captain's private cabin.

"'Your name is Merwin, I believe?' said the old man.

"'Yes, sir,' I replied.

"'Mr. Bracken has recommended you to me for the position made vacant by the death of Mr. McLellan. Do you think you can fill it?'

"'Yes, sir.'

"'Then go and bring your things aft, at once.'

"Thus ended my interview with the captain, and I became mate of the good ship *Revere*.

"It was with some pride and considerable foreboding that I walked forward out of the cabin. I didn't know how they could take my promotion in the forecastle, but I made up my mind to go any length before I'd let them back me down; and I knew that if it came to any serious trouble on account of my elevation, I had a good backer in Bracken.

"When I got inside the forecastle, as I expected, I was asked what I was called aft for. I told them very briefly.

"'Are you going to take it?' demanded Leach.

"I answered that I was.

"'Are you going to play turn coat and give us away?'

"'I am going to stick by the end of the ship I belong to,' I replied.

"'Are you?' said the bully. 'Well, you will get stuck before you ever get to that end, you miserable sneak! Look here, Chuck Merwin' (Chuck was my nickname), 'when you step over this forecastle door to go aft,'—here he drew his knife—'I'll put this knife into your carcass, and commence the work of breaking up this cursed tyranny by killing you.'

"I had not time to reply, nor had Leach time to do anything, before the forecastle door was burst open, and he was dragged on deck. I was out in a second after him, and part of the watch followed me. Bracken had him by the throat, and after striking him several times, he flung him insensible on the deck then turning to a couple of the men, he told them to bring my things aft, and to obey me as being third officer; then he added—

"'After you have done that, fling a bucket of water over that preacher, and bring him to; and you, Mr. Merwin, come aft, and commence your duties at once.'

"This inaugural celebration on my promotion to the quarter deck passed off without any further disturbance, and matters went along very smoothly until off the Cape of Good Hope. One day all hands aft were suddenly taken sick with a terrible nausea and vomiting, which was unaccountable. The cook was called up and closely questioned, but as he was sick too, we could not derive much information from him. However, everybody recovered, and things went along their usual course. When off St. Helena, everybody aft was taken sick again, except myself, and with exactly the same symptoms, only much more violent. This confirmed the suspicion that some of our food for dinner had been poisoned, and as I was exempt from this last dose, of course the poisoned article must be one of which I had not eaten, and the only thing I had [not] partaken of was the pea soup; so the remainder of the pea soup—which fortunately had not been thrown away—was called up for examination. Our captain was something of a chemist, and soon discovered arsenic in the soup. This led to further investigation, and the captain's analysis was proved correct by our finding one of the tins of arsenic (which was kept in the paint-locker, and had never been opened) with a slit in the bottom of it made by a sheath knife.

"The whole mystery of our sickness was now explained. Some one or more of the crew had got the arsenic, and had attempted to poison every-body aft, so as to have the ship to put into some post in want of officers. As the two attempts were made—the first when in the longitude of Cape Town; and the second, just before getting up to the latitude of St. Helena, it looked as if some good calculator and navigator was at the bottom of it; so we hit upon Mr. Gentleman Leach—as we had nicknamed him—as being the criminal, but we could not prove anything against him.

"This positive proof that we had been poisoned set me to thinking, and after a careful review and consideration of everything, I came to the conclusion that my friend Billy McLellan had been poisoned, and by this man Leach. In the first place, you see he died in convulsions a short time after eating some gruel. Secondly, Leach was his bitter enemy. And then, again, thirdly, his words the night after McLellan's death. I put all these things together, and made up my mind that *he was the man*, and that night fell asleep with that thought in my head.

"I must have slept very sound, for three hours or a little over, when I suddenly awoke with a feeling as if some one was near me. Across the bunk there were curtains hung, and directly opposite the bunk was my chest. Opening my eyes wide, I could see nothing in the bunk. I then looked out the window, which was open, but could see no living thing on deck; then I settled myself down to sleep, but I couldn't get a wink. I still had that horrible feeling—a mysterious presence clinging to me. Unable to lie still with its oppressive sense, I started to get up, and drawing aside the curtains, which had been closed, I shoved one leg over the edge of the bunk; but there I stopped.

"Sitting on the chest in front of me was Billy McLellan.

"It did not frighten me, but I was considerably astonished. There he sat as natural as in life, with his usual dress on, and the right sleeve of his shirt rolled up above the elbow. His eyes were cast down, and he was occupied with his pocket-knife cutting a notch in the lid of my chest. I was so astonished that I was not sure whether I was asleep or awake; but after pinching myself several times, I concluded that I was in full and perfect possession of my senses. I then tried to speak, and asked, 'Is that you, Billy?' As soon as I had spoken the apparition looked up and full at me with a smiling face. This gave me more courage, and after a moment I asked, 'What do you want, Billy?' At this question the smile on the face of the apparition changed to a scowl, such as I had often seen on it in life when something had displeased him. Slowly closing the knife and putting it in his pocket, he arose to his full height, and pointing his bared right arm to the door, he walked through it, and disappeared in darkness. In a second I was out but before I reached the deck I heard a scuffle, and the cry of murder. I grabbed an iron heaver, and rushed along the deck.

"I saw at a glance, by the imperfect light of the binnacle lamp, that the second mate was engaged with Leach, who had been at the wheel, and that he was getting the worst of it. I seized hold of Leach, who was on top—both of them were down—and as I did so, I saw that he had stabbed the second mate and was just drawing the knife out. The instant I became aware of this, I struck him on the head with the heaver and knocked him senseless. All this didn't occupy more than five seconds, and by this time Bracken was round, tending to the second mate, and the captain had the wheel. On examining the second mate's wounds we found them to be slight; one through the fleshy part of the arm, and the other one on the cheek. There was no explanation asked as to the cause of the quarrel, such things too frequent to call for much talk. Mr. Gentleman Leach had fared worse than his victim. For two weeks he never left his bunk, and when he did, he was a dumb man. He was so enraged at not receiving any assistance from the rest of the crew that he never spoke to one of them for the remainder of the passage.

"Six weeks after this did the apparition of William Perry McLellan appear to me, and by exactly the same actions warn me of trouble on deck. This got to be so noticeable that Bracken once asked me if I ever slept, or if the devil always told me when there was going to be a row. At his questions I only laughed, and I kept the secret of my ghostly visitor. This I know, when we arrived at Hamburg, and I left the ship, there were seven distinct notches cut in the lid of my chest, and I was a firm believer in ghosts.

"After I left the old *Revere*, I kicked about everywhere for some ten years, going home but once during that period. All this time I had not once seen the apparition of McLellan.

"At last, one fine morning I found myself ashore in Bombay, out of employ, and a very few rupees in my pocket for ballast. I had been discharged from the ship I was mate of for drunkenness; and it wasn't the first time I had been served the same way. During the time I was ashore, I stayed at an hotel kept by an Irishman named Tracey. He had a daughter, an only child, who superintended the business, for his wife was dead. I need not describe her, because most of you have seen Mrs. Merwin. Well, during the time I was out of a ship I kept pretty straight, and fell in love with Mary Tracey; and I flattered myself that she reciprocated my affection. I was a pretty bold lover, and after a couple of weeks' wooing, I proposed, and was—rejected. She didn't deny but that she loved me; but knowing my failing she rightly felt that she couldn't trust her happiness in my hands.

"Well, I made all sorts of promises; I swore I would never drink another drop and all that sort of thing; and I was so persevering in my entreaties that at last I was put on probation. She promised to marry me if I would prove to her the sincereness of my good resolution by touching no kind of intoxicating liquor for a year. I promised readily and kept my promise for a couple of weeks.

"Just at this time I got a chance as mate of a native vessel, owned by some Chinamen in Maulmein, and commanded by a Spaniard. After being on board several days, the captain came off with a stranger and called me into his cabin. The stranger was introduced to me as the ship's agent. I had seen the man's face before, but could not tell where. It was an intelligent but evil-looking countenance, made more sinister by the carefully-waxed and jet-black Mephistophelean moustache which decorated his face. Liquors were put on the table, the doors closed, and the business I wanted for broached. I didn't drink. The captain asked me if I spoke Spanish. I told him I did not. 'Well, then, we must talk in English,' he said; and he then went on to state what he required of me.

"At this time, in Bombay, there was a great money panic, and all the banks were breaking. Captain Velarde had just collected his freight money—some twenty-seven thousand rupees—and didn't know what to do with it. He did not dare to leave it on shore, or change it into notes and keep it on his person, for fear of robbery; and the banks were all shaky, and on the verge of breaking: bills of exchange were worthless. Nor did he wish to leave it in his cabin, as he was away on ashore the most of his time; so he proposed to me to take care of it for him, I at first demurred, not wishing to undertake such a responsibility. But he argued with me no one would ever suspect me of having it, and consequently there was less danger of harm befalling it in my possession than in his. At last I consented to take charge of it, and that evening the money was brought off, all in silver rupees, in five large bags, and one small one. That night I slept on my chest, in which I stored the treasure, and dreamed that the devil was piling bags of silver on my stomach.

"Every thing went along smoothly, for two or three days, and every time Captain Velarde went on shore he would give me the keys of his private cabin, and told me to help myself out of his liquor case to anything I wanted. But I abstained, until one day I was left all alone, the steward and boy, the rest not being shipped, having gone on shore on 24 hours' liberty.

"Left to myself I became very lonesome, very blue, and very hot, and in a moment of weakness I thought that a bottle of 'Bass's Pale Ale' would be good company, and act as an antidote to the blues, and cool me off. I only thought twice of it before I got a bottle and drank it. It acted like a charm. My loneliness and the blues disappeared in company, and I didn't mind the heat a bit. In about ten or fifteen minutes I drank another pint, and a dim recollection entered my mind that there was a decanter of brandy somewhere on board. At this moment the captain came off, and I told him I had finished a couple of bottles of his ale. He made no comment on this, but presently called me into his cabin, and invited me to take some brandy with him. Nothing loth, I did so, and after this he jumped into his dingy and went on shore, and I went on shore, and I went for the brandy again.

"I don't know how many glasses I drank, but before dark I began to feel drowsy, and I went and laid down on my chest and fell asleep.

"For full five hours I laid this way. Suddenly I felt as if some one was moving me; then I heard a noise of wood breaking, when I awoke.

"The scene that met my gaze was startling. I was on my bunk, and standing alongside of it was McLellan, as I had last seen him, with his pocket knife open in his hand and pointing to a man who, with his back to me was wrenching open my chest with a hatchet, while Captain Velarde stood in the door way with a dark lantern. In moving I must have made a noise, for the man at the chest looked up. I recognised him at once—it was 'Gentleman Leach'. In an instant I jumped from my bunk and closed with him. The struggle was very short. I wrested the hatchet from his grasp, and struck him several violent blows on the head; at the same time I felt a sharp pain in my shoulder, then I heard the report of a pistol, and that was the last I knew for several weeks.

"When I returned to consciousness I found that I had lost my hair, for they had shaved my head, but I had gained in return the thanks of Young, Hai Inn and Company—the owners of the vessel—with a little present of two thousand rupees, and the offer of a command in their employ when I was able to get about.

"Then the whole affair was explained to me by Mr. Tracey, in whose hotel I lay sick.

"Captain Velarde, on the night of attempted robbery, had engaged a room at the hotel, and sent for the so-called-agent, who came, and the precious pair were closeted together several hours. What they were doing or talking about nobody knows. When they came down stairs it was after eleven o'clock, and there was nobody up except Mary.

"They settled their bill for the room and their refreshments with her, and then went out. Going after them to lock and bar the door, she found that they had stopped a few feet from it outside, and were conversing angrily in Spanish. She suspected something wrong, and as she understood the language, she listened, and found that Captain Velarde was arguing with the agent against using any violence, and explained to him that there would be no necessity for it, as it would be three or four hours before their victim would awake from the sleep into which he had been thrown by a powerful drug. This was all she heard; but with the quick instinct of a woman, she concluded that I was their victim, as I had informed her—when ashore a few minutes the day before—of the large amount of money under my care. She did not wait to alarm any one, or call the useless native police, but putting her father's revolver in her pocket, she hurried to the Apollo Bunda, and there hired a dingy, and put off for the ship to warn me of my danger. She arrived there just in time to save my life. Velarde had stabbed me once, and was raising his knife for a second blow, where she shot him. He didn't die, but recovered, and was sentenced to the chain gang in Pulo Penang for life.

"He had written to the owner telling them what he had done for the safe keeping of the money, with the intention of robbing me himself, with the assistance of his confederate, and then lay the blame on thieves. He had watched me some time, and knowing my failing, had shipped me as being best suited to carry out his rascally design. But, thank heaven; he was foiled by a determined little woman and the spirit of my friend.

"Leach—for it was he—died in a few hours after my wounding him. He wore a false full beard for a disguise, and as he had a natural one when on board the *Revere* ten years before, his disguise only served to help me remember his face.

"On the floor of my state-room was found a pocket-knife, which I recognised as belonging to McLellan; and when I recovered I saw the eighth notch cut into the lid of my chest. How the knife came there I can never tell, unless Leach had stolen it from McLellan before—McLellan—died, and dropped it in struggle that night; but that is not likely. I took command of one of Young, Hai Inn and Company's shops, and one year afterwards married.

"Not until I had fully established my reputation for sobriety did I tell my wife that I had drank liquor on that day; and as she had learned to trust me, it did not cause her much trouble then.

"I had never tasted liquor since, and poor Billy's ghost never appeared to me again. I am positive in my own mind that Leach poisoned him.

"Now, gentlemen, my story's told; you know how I was saved from the gutter, got command of a ship, and gained a wife—all through a ghost."

THE INVISIBLE GIANT

IME goes on in the Country Under the Sunset much as it does here.

Many years passed away: and they wrought much change. And now we find a time when the people that lived in good King Mago's time would hardly have known their beautiful Land if they had seen it again.

It had sadly changed indeed. No longer was there the same love or the same reverence towards the king,—no longer was there perfect peace. People had become more selfish and more greedy, and had tried to grasp all they could for themselves. There were some very rich and there were many poor. Most of the beautiful gardens were laid waste. Houses had grown up close round the palace; and in some of these dwelt many persons who could only afford to pay for part of a house.

All the beautiful Country was sadly changed, and changed was the life of the dwellers in it. The people had almost forgotten Prince Zaphir, who was dead many, many years ago; and no more roses were spread on the pathways. Those who lived now in the Country Under the Sunset laughed at the idea of more Giants, and they did not fear them because they did not see them. Some of them said,

"Tush! what can there be to fear? Even if there ever were giants there are none now."

And so the people sang and danced and feasted as before, and thought only of themselves. The Spirits that guarded the Land were very, very sad.

Their great white shadowy wings drooped as they stood at their posts at the Portals of the Land. They hid their faces, and their eyes were dim with continuous weeping, so that they heeded not if any evil thing went by them. They tried to make the people think of their evil-doing; but they could not leave their posts, and the people heard their moaning in the night season, and said,

"Listen to the sighing of the breeze; how sweet it is!"

So is it ever with us also, that when we hear the wind sighing and moaning and sobbing round our houses in the lonely nights, we do not think that our Angels may be sorrowing for our misdeeds, but only that there is a storm coming. The Angels wept evermore, and they felt the sorrow of dumbness—for though they could speak, those they spoke to would not hear.

Whilst the people laughed at the idea of Giants, there was one old old man who shook his head, and made answer to them, when he heard them, and said:

"Death has many children, and there are Giants in the marshes still. You may not see them, perhaps—but they are there, and the only bulwark of safety is in a land of patient, faithful hearts."

The name of this good old man was Knoal, and he lived in a house built of great blocks of stone, in the middle of a wild place far from the city.

In the city there were many great old houses, storey upon storey high; and in these houses lived much poor people. The higher you went up the great steep stairs the poorer were the people that lived there, so that in the garrets were some so poor, that when the morning came they did not know whether they should have anything to eat the whole long day. This was very, very sad, and gentle children would have wept if they had seen their pain.

In one of these garrets there lived all alone a little maiden called Zaya. She was an orphan, for her father had died many years before, and her poor mother, who had toiled long and wearily for her dear little daughter—her only child—had died also not long since.

Poor little Zaya had wept so bitterly when she saw her dear mother lying dead, and she had been so sad and sorry for a long time, that she quite forgot that she had no means of living. However, the poor people who lived in the house had given her part of their own food, so that she did not starve.

Then after a while she had tried to work for herself and earn her own living. Her mother had taught her to make flowers out of paper; so she made a lot of flowers, and when she had a full basket she took them into the street and sold them. She made flowers of many kinds, roses and lilies, and violets, and snowdrops, and primroses, and mignonette, and many beautiful sweet flowers that only grow in the Country Under the Sunset. Some of them she could make without any pattern, but others she could not, so when she wanted a pattern she took her basket of paper and scissors, and paste, and brushes, and all the things she used, and went into the garden which a kind lady owned, where there grew many beautiful flowers. There she sat down and worked away, looking at the flowers she wanted.

Sometimes she was very sad, and her tears fell thick and fast as she thought of her dear dead mother. Often she seemed to feel that her mother was looking down at her, and to see her tender smile in the sunshine on the water; then her heart was glad, and she sang so sweetly that the birds came around her and stopped their own singing to listen to her.

She and the birds grew great friends, and sometimes when she had sung a song they would all cry out together, as they sat round her in a ring, in a few notes that seemed to say quite plainly:

"Sing to us again. Sing to us again."

So she would sing again. Then she would ask them to sing, and they would sing till there was quite a concert. After a while the birds knew her so well that they would come into her room, and they even built their

nests there, and they followed her wherever she went. The people used
to say:

"Look at the girl with the birds; she must be half a bird herself, for see
how the birds know and love her." From so many people coming to say
things like this, some silly people actually believed that she was partly a bird,
and they shook their heads when wise people laughed at them, and said:

"Indeed she must be; listen to her singing; her voice is sweeter even
than the birds."

So a nickname was applied to her, and naughty boys called it after her
in the street, and the nickname was "Big Bird." But Zaya did not mind
the name; and although often naughty boys said it to her, meaning to
cause her pain, she did not dislike it, but the contrary, for she so gloried
in the love and trust of her little sweet-voiced pets that she wished to be
thought like them.

Indeed it would be well for some naughty little boys and girls if they
were as good and harmless as the little birds that work all day long for
their helpless baby birds, building nests and bringing food, and sitting so
patiently hatching their little speckled eggs.

One evening Zaya sat alone in her garret very sad and lonely. It was
a lovely summer's evening, and she sat in the window looking out over
the city. She could see over the many streets towards the great cathedral
whose spire towered aloft into the sky higher by far even than the great
tower of the king's palace. There was hardly a breath of wind, and the
smoke went up straight from the chimneys, getting fainter and fainter
till it was lost altogether.

Zaya was very sad. For the first time for many days her birds were
all away from her at once, and she did not know where they had gone.
It seemed to her as if they had deserted her, and she was so lonely, poor
little maid, that she wept bitter tears. She was thinking of the story which
long ago her dead mother had told her, how Prince Zaphir had slain the
Giant, and she wondered what the prince was like, and thought how

happy the people must have been when Zaphir and Bluebell were king and queen. Then she wondered if there were any hungry children in those good days, and if, indeed, as the people said, there were no more Giants. So she thought and thought, as she went on with her work before the open window.

Presently she looked up from her work and gazed across the city. There she saw a terrible thing—something so terrible that she gave a low cry of fear and wonder, and leaned out of the window, shading her eyes with her hand to see more clearly.

In the sky beyond the city she saw a vast shadowy Form with its arms raised. It was shrouded in a great misty robe that covered it, fading away into air so that she could only see the face and the grim, spectral hands.

The Form was so mighty that the city below it seemed like a child's toy. It was still far off the city.

The little maid's heart seemed to stand still with fear as she thought to herself, "The Giants, then, are not dead. This is another of them."

Quickly she ran down the high stairs and out into the street. There she saw some people, and cried to them,

"Look! look! the Giant, the Giant!" and pointed towards the Form which she still saw moving slowly onwards to the city.

The people looked up, but they could not see anything, and they laughed and said,

"The child is mad."

Then poor little Zaya was more than ever frightened, and ran down the street crying out still,

"Look! look! the Giant, the Giant!" But no one heeded her, and all said, "The child is mad," and they went on their own ways.

Then the naughty boys came around her and cried out,

"Big Bird has lost her mates. She sees a bigger bird in the sky, and she wants it." And they made rhymes about her, and sang them as they danced round.

Zaya ran away from them; and she hurried right through the city, and out into the country beyond it, for she still saw the great Form before her in the air.

As she went on, and got nearer and nearer to the Giant, it grew a little darker. She could see only the clouds; but still there was visible the form of a Giant hanging dimly in the air.

A cold mist closed around her as the Giant appeared to come onwards towards her. Then she thought of all the poor people in the city, and she hoped that the Giant would spare them, and she knelt down before him and lifted up her hands appealingly, and cried aloud:

"Oh, great Giant! spare them, spare them!"

But the Giant moved onwards still as though he never heard. She cried aloud all the more,

"Oh, great Giant! spare them, spare them!" And she bowed down her head and wept, and the Giant still, though very slowly, moved onward towards the city.

There was an old man not far off standing at the door of a small house built of great stones, but the little maid saw him not. His face wore a look of fear and wonder, and when he saw the child kneel and raise her hands, he drew nigh and listened to her voice. When he heard her say, "Oh, great Giant!" he murmured to himself,

"It is then even as I feared. There are more Giants, and truly this is another." He looked upwards, but he saw nothing, and he murmured again,

"I see not, yet this child can see; and yet I feared, for something told me that there was danger. Truly knowledge is blinder than innocence."

The little maid, still not knowing there was any human being near her, cried out again, with a great cry of anguish:

"Oh, do not, do not, great Giant, do them harm. If someone must suffer, let it be me. Take me. I am willing to die, but spare them. Spare them, great Giant; and do with me even as thou wilt." But the giant heeded not.

And Knoal—for he was the old man—felt his eyes fill with tears, and he said to himself,

"Oh, noble child, how brave she is, she would sacrifice herself!" And, coming closer to her, he put his hand upon her head.

Zaya, who was again bowing her head, started and looked round when she felt the touch. However, when she saw that it was Knoal, she was comforted, for she knew how wise and good he was, and felt that if any person could help her, he could. So she clung to him, and hid her face in his breast; and he stroked her hair and comforted her. But still he could see nothing.

The cold mist swept by, and when Zaya looked up, she saw that the Giant had passed by, and was moving onward to the city.

"Come with me, my child," said the old man; and the two arose, and went into the dwelling built of great stones.

When Zaya entered, she started, for lo! the inside was as a tomb. The old man felt her shudder, for he still held her close to him, and he said:

"Weep not, little one, and fear not. This place reminds me and all who enter it, that to the tomb we must all come at the last. Fear it not, for it has grown to be a cheerful home to me."

Then the little maid was comforted, and began to examine all around her more closely. She saw all sorts of curious instruments, and many strange and many common herbs and simples hung to dry in bunches on the walls. The old man watched her in silence till her fear was gone, and then he said:

"My child, saw you the features of the Giant as he passed?"

She answered, "Yes."

"Can you describe his face and form to me?" he asked again.

Whereupon she began to tell him all that she had seen. How the Giant was so great that all the sky seemed filled. How the great arms were outspread, veiled in his robe, till far away the shroud was lost in air.

31

How the face was as that of a strong man, pitiless, yet without malice; and that the eyes were blind.

The old man shuddered as he heard, for he knew that the Giant was a very terrible one; and his heart wept for the doomed city where so many would perish in the midst of their sin.

They determined to go forth and warn again the doomed people; and making no delay, the old man and the little maid hurried towards the city.

As they left the small house, Zaya saw the Giant before them, moving still towards the city. They hurried on; and when they had passed through the cold mist, Zaya looked back, and saw the Giant behind them.

Presently they came to the city.

It was a strange sight to see that old man and that little maid flying to tell the people of the terrible Plague that was coming upon them. The old man's long white beard and hair and the child's golden locks were swept behind them in the wind, so quick they came. The faces of both were white as death. Behind them, seen only to the eyes of the pure-hearted little maid when she looked back, came ever onward at slow pace the spectral Giant that hung a dark shadow in the evening air.

But those in the city never saw the Giant; and when the old man and the little maid warned them, still they heeded not, but scoffed and jeered at them, and said,

"Tush! there are no Giants now;" and they went on their way, laughing and jeering.

Then the old man came and stood on a raised place amongst them, on the lowest step of the great fountain with the little maid by his side, and he spake thus:

"Oh, people, dwellers in this Land, be warned in time. This pure-hearted child, round whose sweet innocence even the little birds that fear men and women gather in peace, has this night seen in the sky the form of a Giant that advances ever onward menacingly to our city. Believe, oh, believe; and be warned, whilst ye may. To myself even as to you the sky is a blank; and yet see that I believe. For listen to me: all unknowing that another Giant had invaded our land, I sat pensive in my dwelling; and, without cause or motive, there came into my heart a sudden fear for the safety of our city. I arose and looked north and south and east and west, and on high and below, but never a sign of danger could I see. So I said to myself,

"'Mine eyes are dim with a hundred years of watching and waiting, and so I cannot see.' And yet, oh people, dwellers in this land, though that century has dimmed mine outer eyes, still it has quickened mine inner eyes—the eyes of my soul. Again I went forth, and lo! this little maid knelt and implored a Giant, unseen by me, to spare the city; but he heard her not, or, if he heard, answered her not, and she fell prone. So hither we come to warn you. Yonder, says the maid, he passes onward to the city. Oh, be warned! be warned in time."

Still the people heeded not; but they scoffed and jeered the more, and said,

"Lo, the maid and the old man both are mad;" and they passed onwards to their homes—to dancing and feasting as before.

Then the naughty boys came and mocked them, and said that Zaya had lost her birds, and had gone mad; and they made songs, and sang them as they danced round.

Zaya was so sorely grieved for the poor people that she heeded not the cruel boys. Seeing that she did not heed them, some of them got still more rude and wicked; they went a little way off, and threw things at them, and mocked them all the more.

Then, sad of heart, the old man arose, and took the little maid by the hand, and brought her away into the wilderness; and lodged her with him in the house built with great stones. That night Zaya slept with the sweet smell of the drying herbs all around her; and the old man held her hand that she might have no fear.

In the morning Zaya arose betimes, and awoke the old man, who had fallen asleep in his chair.

She went to the doorway and looked out, and then a thrill of gladness came upon her heart; for outside the door, as though waiting to see her, sat all her little birds, and many many more. When the birds saw the little maid they sang a few loud joyous notes, and flew about foolishly for very joy—some of them fluttering their wings and looking so funny that she could not help laughing a little.

When Knoal and Zaya had eaten their frugal breakfast and given to their little feathered friends, they set out with sorrowful hearts to visit the city, and to try once more to warn the people. The birds flew around them as they went, and to cheer them sang as joyously as they could, although their little hearts were heavy.

As they walked they saw before them the great shadowy Giant; and he had now advanced to the very confines of the city.

Once again they warned the people, and great crowds came around them, but only mocked them more than ever; and naughty boys threw stones and sticks at the little birds and killed some of them. Poor Zaya wept bitterly, and Knoal's heart was very sad. After a time, when they had moved from the fountain, Zaya looked up and started with joyous surprise, for the great shadowy Giant was nowhere to be seen. She cried out in joy, and the people laughed, and said,

"Cunning child! she sees that we will not believe her, and she pretends that the Giant has gone."

They surrounded her, jeering, and some of them said,

"Let us put her under the fountain and duck her, as a lesson to liars who would frighten us." Then they approached her with menaces. She clung close to Knoal, who had looked terribly grave when she had said she did not see the Giant any longer, and who was now as if in a dream, thinking. But at her touch he seemed to wake up; and he spoke sternly to the people, and rebuked them. But they cried out on him also, and said that as he had aided Zaya in her lie he should be ducked also, and they advanced closer to lay hands on them both.

The hand of one who was a ringleader was already outstretched, when he gave a low cry, and pressed his hand to his side; and, whilst the others turned to look at him in wonder, he cried out in great pain, and screamed horribly. Even whilst the people looked, his face grew blacker and blacker, and he fell down before them, and writhed a while in pain, and then died.

All the people screamed out in terror, and ran away, crying aloud,

"The Giant! the Giant! he is indeed amongst us!" They feared all the more that they could not see him.

But before they could leave the market-place, in the centre of which was the fountain, many fell dead, and their corpses lay.

There in the centre knelt the old man and the little maid, praying; and the birds sat perched around the fountain, mute and still, and there was no sound heard save the cries of the people far off. Then their wailing sounded louder and louder, for the Giant—Plague—was amongst and around them, and there was no escaping, for it was now too late to fly.

Alas! in the Country Under the Sunset there was much weeping that day; and when the night came there was little sleep, for there was fear in some hearts and pain in others. None were still except the dead, who lay stark about the city, so still and lifeless that even the cold light of the moon and the shadows of the drifting clouds moving over them could not make them seem as though they lived.

And for many a long day there was pain and grief and death in the Country Under the Sunset.

Knoal and Zaya did all they could to help the poor people, but it was hard indeed to aid them, for the unseen Giant was amongst them, wandering through the city to and fro, so that none could tell where next he would lay his ice-cold hand.

Some people fled away out of the city; but it was little use, for go how they would and fly never so fast they were still within the grasp of the unseen Giant. Ever and anon he turned their warm hearts to ice with his breath and his touch, and they fell dead.

Some, like those within the city, were spared, and of these some perished of hunger, and the rest crept sadly back to the city and lived or died amongst their friends. And it was all, oh! so sad, for there was nothing but grief and fear and weeping from morn till night.

Now, see how Zaya's little bird friends helped her in her need.

They seemed to see the coming of the Giant when no one—not even the little maid herself—could see anything, and they managed to tell her when there was danger just as well as though they could talk.

At first Knoal and she went home every evening to the house built of great stones to sleep, and came again to the city in the morning, and stayed with the poor sick people, comforting them and feeding them, and giving them medicine which Knoal, from his great wisdom, knew would do them good. Thus they saved many precious human lives, and those who were rescued were very thankful, and henceforth ever after lived holier and more unselfish lives.

After a few days, however, they found that the poor sick people needed help even more at night than in the day, and so they came and lived in the city altogether, helping the stricken folk day and night.

At the earliest dawn Zaya would go forth to breathe the morning air; and there, just waked from sleep, would be her feathered friends waiting for her. They sang glad songs of joy, and came and perched on her shoulders and her head, and kissed her. Then, if she went to go towards any place where, during the night, the Plague had laid his deadly hand, they would flutter before her, and try to impede her, and scream out in their own tongue,

"Go back! go back!"

They pecked of her bread and drank of her cup before she touched them; and when there was danger—for the cold hand of the Giant was placed everywhere—they would cry,

"No, no!" and she would not touch the food, or let anyone else do so. Often it happened that, even whilst it pecked at the bread or drank of the cup, a poor little bird would fall down and flutter its wings and die; but all they that died, did so with a chirp of joy, looking at their little mistress, for whom they had gladly perished. Whenever the little birds found that the bread and the cup were pure and free from danger, they would look up at Zaya jauntily, and flap their wings and try to crow, and seemed so saucy that the poor sad little maiden would smile.

There was one old bird that always took a second, and often a great many pecks at the bread when it was good, so that he got quite a hearty meal; and sometimes he would go on feeding till Zaya would shake her finger at him and say,

"Greedy!" and he would hop away as if he had done nothing.

There was one other dear little bird—a robin, with a breast as red as the sunset—that loved Zaya more than one can think. When he tried the food and found that it was safe to eat, he would take a little tiny piece in his bill, and fly up and put it in her mouth.

Every little bird that drank from Zaya's cup and found it good raised its head to say grace; and ever since then the little birds do the same, and they never forget to say their grace—as some thankless children do.

Thus Knoal and Zaya lived, although many around them died, and the Giant still remained in the city. So many people died that one began to wonder that so many were left; for it was only when the town began to get thinned that people thought of the vast numbers that had lived in it.

Poor little Zaya had got so pale and thin that she looked like a shadow, and Knoal's form was bent more with the sufferings of a few weeks than it had been by his century of age. But although the two were weary and worn, they still kept on their good work of aiding the sick.

Many of the little birds were dead.

One morning the old man was very weak—so weak that he could hardly stand. Zaya got frightened about him, and said,

"Are you ill, father?" for she always called him father now.

He answered her in a voice alas! hoarse and low, but very, very tender:

"My child, I fear the end is coming: take me home, that there I may die."

At his words Zaya gave a low cry and fell on her knees beside him, and buried her head in his bosom and wept bitterly, whilst she hugged him close. But she had little time for weeping, for the old man struggled up to his feet, and, seeing that he wanted aid, she dried her tears and helped him.

The old man took his staff, and with Zaya helping to support him, got as far as the fountain in the midst of the market-place; and there, on the lowest step, he sank down as though exhausted. Zaya felt him grow cold as ice, and she knew that the chilly hand of the Giant had been laid upon him.

Then, without knowing why, she looked up to where she had last seen the Giant as Knoal and she had stood beside the fountain. And lo! as she looked, holding Knoal's hand, she saw the shadowy form of the terrible Giant who had been so long invisible growing more and more clearly out of the clouds.

His face was stern as ever, and his eyes were still blind.

Zaya cried to the Giant, still holding Knoal tightly by the hand:

"Not him, not him! Oh, mighty Giant! not him! not him!" and she bowed down her head and wept.

There was such anguish in her heart that to the blind eyes of the shadowy Giant came tears that fell like dew on the forehead of the old man. Knoal spake to Zaya:

"Grieve not, my child. I am glad that you see the Giant again, for I have hope that he will leave our city free from woe. I am the last victim, and I gladly die."

Then Zaya knelt to the Giant, and said:

"Spare him! oh! spare him and take me! but spare him! spare him!"

The old man raised himself upon his elbow as he lay, and spake to her:

"Grieve not, little one, and repine not. Sooth I know that you would gladly give your life for mine. But we must give for the good of others that which is dearer to us than our lives. Bless you, my little one, and be good. Farewell! farewell!"

As he spake the last word he grew cold as death, and his spirit passed away.

Zaya knelt down and prayed; and when she looked up she saw the shadowy Giant moving away.

The Giant turned as he passed on, and Zaya saw that his blind eyes looked towards her as though he were trying to see. He raised the great shadowy arms, draped still in his shroud of mist, as though blessing her; and she thought that the wind that came by her moaning bore the echo of the words:

"Innocence and devotion save the land."

Presently she saw far off the great shadowy Giant Plague moving away to the border of the Land, and passing between the Guardian Spirits out through the Portal into the deserts beyond—for ever.

THE SHADOW BUILDER

THE lonely Shadow Builder watches ever in his lonely abode. The walls are of cloud, and round and through them, changing ever as they come, pass the dim shades of all the things that have been.

This endless, shadowy, wheeling, moving circle is called The PROCESSION OF THE DEAD PAST. In it everything is just as it has been in the great world. There is no change in any part; for each moment, as it passes, sends its shade into this dim Procession. Here there are moving people and events—cares—thoughts—follies—crimes—joys—sorrows—places—scenes—hopes and fears, and all that make the sum of life with all its lights and shadows. Every picture in nature where shadow dwells—and that is every one—has here its dim phantom. Here are all pictures that are most fair and most sad to see—the passing gloom over a sunny cornfield when with the breeze comes the dark sway of the full ears as they bend and rise; the ripple on the glassy surface of a summer sea; the dark expanse that lies beyond and without the broad track of moonlight on the water; the lacework of glare and gloom that flickers over the road as one passes in autumn when the moonlight is falling through the naked branches of overhanging trees; the cool, restful shade under the thick trees in summer time when the sun is flaming down on the haymaker at work; the dark clouds that flit across the moon, hiding her light, which leaps out again hollowly and coldly; the gloom of violet and black that rises on the horizon when rain is near in summer time;

the dark recesses and gloomy caverns where the waterfall hurls itself shrieking into the pool below,—all these shadow pictures, and a thousand others that come by night and day, circle in the Procession among the things that have been.

Here, too, every act that any human being does, every thought—good and bad—every wish, every hope—everything that is secret—is pictured, and becomes a lasting record which cannot be blotted out; for at any time the Shadow Builder may summon with his spectral hand any one— sleeping or waking—to behold what is pictured of the Dead Past, in the dim, mysterious distance which encompasses his lonely abode.

In this ever-moving Procession of the Dead Past there is but one place where the circling phantoms are not, and where the cloudy walls are lost. There is here a great blackness, dense and deep, and full of gloom, and behind which lies the great real world without.

This blackness is called THE GATE OF DREAD.

The Procession afar off takes from it its course, and when passing on its way it circles again towards the darkness, the shadowy phantoms melt again into the mysterious gloom.

Sometimes the Shadow Builder passes through the vapoury walls of his abode and mingles in the ranks of the Procession; and sometimes a figure summoned by the wave of his spectral hand, with silent footfall stalks out of the mist and pauses beside him. Sometimes from a sleeping body the Shadow Builder summons a dreaming soul; then for a time the quick and the dead stand face to face, and men call it a dream of the Past. When this happens, friend meets friend or foe meets foe; and over the soul of the dreamer comes a happy memory long vanished, or the troubled agony of remorse. But no spectre passes through the misty wall, save to the Shadow Builder alone; and no human being—even in a dream—can enter the dimness where the Procession moves along.

So lives the lonely Shadow Builder amid his gloom; and his habitation is peopled by a spectral past.

His only people are of the past; for though he creates shadows they dwell not with him. His children go out at once to their homes in the big world, and he knows them no more till, in the fulness of time, they join the Procession of the Dead Past, and reach, in turn, the misty walls of his home.

For the Shadow Builder there is not night nor day, nor season of the year; but for ever round his lonely dwelling passes the silent Procession of the Dead Past.

Sometimes he sits and muses with eyes fixed and staring, and seeing nothing; and then out at sea there is a cloudless calm or the black gloom of night. Towards the far north or south for long months together he never looks, and then the stillness of the arctic night reigns alone. When the dreamy eyes again become conscious, the hard silence softens into the sounds of life and light.

Sometimes, with set frown on his face and a hard look in the eyes, which flash and gleam dark lightnings, the Shadow Builder sways resolute to his task, and round the world the shadows troop thick and fast. Over the sea sweeps the blackness of the tempest; the dim lights flicker in the cots away upon the lonely moors; and even in the palaces of kings dark shadows pass and fly and glide over all things—yea, through the hearts of the kings themselves—for the Shadow Builder is then dread to look upon.

Now and again, with long whiles between, the Shadow Builder as he completes his task lingers over the work as though he loves it. His heart yearns to the children of his will; and he fain would keep even one shadow to be a companion to him in his loneliness. But the voice of the Great Present is ever ringing in his ears at such times, enjoining him to haste. The giant voice booms out,

"Onwards, onwards."

Whilst the words ring in the ears of the Shadow Builder the completed shadow fades from beneath his hands, and passing unseen through the

Gate of Dread, mingles in the great world without, in which it is to play its part. When, in the fulness of time, this shadow comes into the ranks of the Procession of the Dead Past, the Shadow Builder knows it and remembers it; but in his dead heart there is no gleam of loving remembrance, for he can only love the Present, that slips ever from his grasp.

And oh! it is a lonely life which the Shadow Builder lives; and in the weird, sad, solemn, mysterious, silent gloom which encompasses him, he toils on ever at his lonely task.

But sometimes too the Shadow Builder has his joys. Baby shadows spring up, and sunny pictures, alight with sweetness and love, glide from under his touch, and are gone.

Before the Shadow Builder at his task lies a space wherein is neither light nor darkness, neither joy nor gloom. Whatsoever touches it fades away as sand heaps melt before the incoming tide, or like words writ on water. In it all things lose their being and become part of the great *Is-Not*; and this terrible line of mystery is called THE THRESHOLD. Whatsoever passes into it disappears; and whatsoever emerges from it is complete as it comes and passes into the great world as a thing to run its course. Before the Threshold the Shadow Builder himself is as naught; and in its absorbing might there is that which he cannot sway or rule.

When at his task he summons; and out of the impalpable nothingness of the Threshold there comes the object of his will. Sometimes the shadow bursts full and freshly and is suddenly lost in the gloom of the Gate of Dread; and sometimes it grows softly and faintly, getting fuller as it comes, and so melts away into the gloom.

The lonely Shadow Builder is working in his lonely abode; around him, beyond the vapoury walls, pressing onward as ever, is the circling Procession of the Dead Past. Storm and calm have each been summoned from the Threshold, and have gone; and now in this calm, wistful moment the Shadow Builder pauses at his task, and wishes and wishes till, to his lonely longing wistfulness, the nothingness of THE THRESHOLD sends an answer.

Forth from it grows the shadow of a Baby's foot, stepping with tottering gait out towards the world; then follows the little round body and the big head, and the Baby shadow moves onwards, swaying and balancing with uncertain step. Swift behind it come the Mother's hands stretched out in loving helpfulness, lest it should fall. One step—two—it totters, and is falling; but the Mother's arms are swift, and the gentle hands bear it firmly up. The Child turns and toddles again into its Mother's arms.

Again it strives to walk; and again the Mother's watchful hands are ready. This time it needs not the help; but when the race is over, the shadow Child turns again lovingly to its Mother's breast.

Once again it strives, and it walks boldly and firmly; but the Mother's hands quiver as they hang by her side, whilst a tear sweeps down the cheek, although that cheek is gladdened by a smile.

The Baby shadow turns, and goes a little way off. Then over the misty Nothing on which the shadows fall, flits the flickering shadow of a tiny hand waving; and onward, with firm tread, the shadow of the little feet moves out into the misty gloom of the Gate of Dread, and passes away.

But the Mother's shadow moves not. The hands are pressed to the heart, the loving face is upturned in prayer, and down the cheeks roll great tears. Then her head bows lower as the little feet pass beyond her ken; and lower and lower bends the weeping Mother till she lies prone. Even as he looks, the Shadow Builder sees the shadows fade away, away, and the terrible nothingness of the Threshold only is there.

Then presently in the Procession of the Dead Past circle round the misty walls the shadows that had been—the Mother and the Child.

Now from out the Threshold steps a Youth with brave and buoyant tread; and as on the misty veil his shadow falls, the dress and bearing proclaim him a sailor lad. Close to this shadow comes another—the

Mother's. Older and thinner she is, as if with watching, but still the same. The old loving hands array prettily the knotted kerchief hanging loosely on the open throat; and the Boy's hands reach out, take the Mother's face between them, and draw it forward for a kiss. The Mother's arms fly round her Son, and in a close embrace they cling.

The Mother kisses her Boy again and again; and together they stand, as though to part were impossible.

Suddenly the Boy turns as though he heard a call. The Mother clings closer. He seems to remonstrate tenderly; but the loving arms hold tighter, till with gentle force he tears himself away. The Mother takes a step forward, and holds out the thin hands trembling in an agony of grief. The Boy stops; to one knee he bends, then, dashing away his tears, he waves his cap, and hurries on, while once again the Mother sinks to her knees, and weeps.

And so, slowly, once again, the shadows of the Mother and the Child grown greater in the fulness of time, pass out through the Gate of Dread, and circle among the phantoms in the Procession of the Dead Past—the Mother following hard upon the speeding footsteps of her Son.

In the long pause that follows, whilst the Shadow Builder watches, all seems changed. Out from the Threshold comes a mist, such as hangs sometimes over the surface of a tropic sea.

By little and little the mist rolls away, and forth advances, black and great, the prow of a mighty vessel. The shadows of the great sails lie faintly in the cool depths of the sea, as the sails flap idly in the breezeless air. Over the bulwark lean listless figures waiting for a wind to come. The mist on the sea melts slowly away; and by the dark shadows of men sheltering from the sunny glare and fanning themselves with their broad sailor hats, it is plain that the heat is terrible.

Now from far off, behind the ship, comes up over the horizon a black cloud no bigger than a man's hand, but sweeping on with terrible speed. Also, from far away, before her course, rises the edge of a coral reef, scarcely seen above the glassy water, but darkling the depths below.

Those on board see neither of these things, for they shelter under their awnings, and sigh for cool breezes.

Quicker and quicker comes the dark cloud, sweeping faster and faster, and growing blacker and blacker and vaster and vaster as it comes.

Then those on board seem to know the danger. Hurried shadows fly along the decks; up the shadows of the ladders hurry shadows of men. The flapping of the great sails ceases as one by one the willing hands draw them in.

But quicker than the hands of men can work sweeps the tempest.

Onwards it rushes, and terrible things come close behind; black darkness—towering waves that break in fury and fly aloft—the spume of the sea swept heavenwards—the great clouds wheeling in fury;—and in the centre of these flying, whirling, maddening shadows, rocks the shadow of the ship.

As the black darkness of the heavens encompasses all, the rush of shadowy storm sweeps through the Gate of Dread.

As he waits and looks and sees the cyclone whirling amongst the shadows in the Procession of the Dead Past, the Shadow Builder, even in his dead heart, feels a weight of pain for the brave Sailor Boy tossed on the deep, and the anxious Mother sitting lonely at home.

Again from the Threshold passes a shadow, growing deeper as it comes, but very, very faint at first; for here the sun is strong, and there is but little room for shadows on the bare rock which seems to rise from the glare and the glitter of the sea deeps round.

On the lonely rock a Sailor Boy stands; thin and gaunt he is, and his clothing is but a few rags. Sheltering his eyes with his hand, he looks out to sea, where, afar off, the cloudless sky sinks to meet the burning sea; but no speck over the horizon—no distant glitter of a white sail—gives him a ray of hope.

Long, long he peers, till, wearied out, he sits down on the rock and bows his head as if in despair for a time. As the sea falls, he gathers from the rock the shellfish which has come during the tide.

So the day wears on, and the night comes; and in the tropic sky the stars hang like lamps.

In the cool silence of the night the forlorn Sailor Boy rests—sleeps, and dreams. His dreams are of home—of loving arms stretched out to meet him—of banquets spread—of green fields and waving branches, and the sheltering happiness of his mother's love. For in his sleep the Shadow Builder summons his dreaming soul, and shows him all these blessings passing ceaselessly in the Procession of the Dead Past, and so comforts him lest he should despair and die.

Thus wear on many weary days; and the sailor-boy lingers on the lonely rock.

Afar off he can just see a hill that seems to rise over the water. One morning when the blackening sky and the sultry air promise a storm, the distant mountain seems nearer; and he thinks that he will try to reach it by swimming.

Whilst he is thus resolving, the storm rushes up over the horizon and sweeps him from the lonely rock. He swims with a bold heart; but just as his strength is done, he is cast by the fury of the storm on a beach of soft sand. The storm passes on its way and the waves leave him high and dry. He goes inland, where, in a cave in the rock, he finds shelter, and sinks to sleep.

The Shadow Builder, as he sees all this happen in the shadows on the clouds, and land, and sea, rejoices in his dead heart that the lonely mother perhaps will not wait in vain.

So time wears on, and many, many weary days pass. The Boy becomes a young Man, living in the lonely island; his beard has grown, and he is clothed in a dress of leaves. All day long, save when he is not working to get food to eat, he watches from the mountain top for a ship to come. As he stands looking out over the sea, the sun casts his shadow down the hillside, so that at evening, as it sinks low in the waters, the shadow of the lonely Sailor grows longer and longer, till at the last it makes a dark streak down the hill side, even to the water's edge.

The lonely Man's heart grows heavier and heavier as he waits and watches, whilst the weary time passes and the countless days and nights come and go.

Time comes when he begins to get feebler and feebler. At last he grows sick to death, and lingers long a-dying.

Then these shadows pass away.

Out from the Threshold grows the shadow of an old woman, thin and worn, sitting in a lonely cottage on a jutting cliff. In the window a lamp burns in the night time to welcome the Lost One should he ever return, and to guide him to his Mother's home. By the lamp the Mother watches, till, wearied out, she sinks to sleep.

As she sleeps the Shadow Builder summons her sleeping soul with the wave of his spectral hand.

She stands beside him in the lonely abode, whilst round them through the misty walls passes onward the Procession of the Dead Past.

As she looks, the Shadow Builder lifts his spectral hand to point to the vision of her Son.

But the Mother's eyes are quicker than even the spectral hand that evokes all the shadows of the rushing storm, and ere the hand is raised she sees her Son among the Shadows of the Past. The Mother's heart is filled with unspeakable joy, as she sees him alive and hale, although a prisoner amongst the tropic seas.

But alas! she knows not that in the dim Procession pass only the things that have been; and that although in the past the lonely Sailor lived, in the present—even at the moment—he may be dying or dead.

The Mother stretches out her arms to her Boy; but even as she does, her sleeping soul loses sight of the dim Procession and vanishes from the Shadow Builder's lonely abode. For when she knows that her Boy is alive, there follows a great pain that he is lonely and waits and watches for help; and the quick heart of the Mother is overcome with grief, and she wakes with a bitter cry.

Then as she rises and looks past the dying lamp out into the dawn, the Mother feels that she has seen a vision of her son in sleep, and that he lives and waits for help; and her heart glows with a great resolve.

Quickly then from the threshold float many shadows.—

A lonely Mother speeding with flying feet to a distant city.

Grave men refusing, but not unkindly, a kneeling woman making an appeal with uplifted hands.

Hard men spurning a praying Mother from their doors.

A wild rabble of bad and thoughtless boys and girls hounding through the streets a hurrying woman.

A shadow of pain on a Mother's heart.

The upcoming of a black cloud of despair, but which hangs far off—for it cannot advance into the bright sunlight of the Mother's resolve.

Weary days with their own myriad shadows.

Lonely nights—black want—cold—hunger and pain; and through all these darkening shadows the swift moving shadow of the Mother's flying feet.

A long long line of such pictures come ever anigh in the Procession, till the dead heart of the Shadow Builder grows icy, and his burning eyes look out savagely on all who give pain and trial to the Mother's faithful heart.

And so all these shadows float out into a black mist, and are lost in the gloom of the Gate of Dread.

Another shadow grows out of the mist.—

An Old Man sits in his armchair. The firelight flickering throws his image, quaintly dancing, on the wall of the room. He is old, for the great shoulders are bowed, and the grand strong face is lined with years. There is another shadow in the room; it is the Mother's—she is standing by the table, and is telling her story; her thin hands point away where in the distance she knows her Son is a prisoner in the lonely seas.

The Old Man rises; the enthusiasm of the Mother's heart has touched him, and back to his memory rush the old love and energy and valour of his youth. The great hand rises, closes, and strikes the table with a mighty blow, as though declaring a binding promise. The Mother sinks to her knees,—she seizes the great hand and kisses it, and stands erect.

Other men come in—they receive orders—they hurry out.

Then come many shadows whose movement and swiftness and firm purpose mean life and hope.

At sunset, when the masts make long shadows on the harbour water, a big ship moves out on her journey to the tropic seas. Men's shadows quickly flit up and down the rigging and along the decks.

As the shadows wheel round the capstan bar the anchor rises; and into the sunset passes the great vessel.

In the bow, like a figure of Hope, stands the Mother, gazing with eager eyes on the far-off horizon.

Then this shadow fades.

A great ship sweeps along with white sails swelling to the breeze; at the bow stands the Mother, gazing ever out into the distance before her.

Storms come and the ship flies before the blast; but she swerves not, for the Mother, with outstretched hand, points the way, and the helmsman swaying beside his wheel obeys the hand.

So this shadow also passes.

The shadows of days and nights come on in quick succession; and the Mother seeks ever for her Son.

So the records of the prosperous journey melt into a faint, dim, misty shadow through which one figure alone stands clear—the watching Mother at the vessel's prow.

Now from the Threshold grow the shadows of the mountain island and of the ship drawing nigh. In the prow the Mother kneels, looking out and pointing. A boat is lowered. Men spring on board with eager feet; but before them all is the Mother. The boat nears the island; the water shallows, and on the hot white beach the men spring to land.

But in the boat's prow still the Mother sits. In her long anxious hours of agony she has seen in her dreams her Son standing afar off and watching; she has seen him wave his arms with a great joy as the ship rises over the horizon's edge; she has seen him standing on the beach waiting; she has seen him rushing through the surf so that the first thing that the lonely Sailor Boy should touch would be his Mother's loving hands.

But alas! for her dreams. No figure with joyous waving arms stands on the summit of the mountain—no eager figure stands at the water's edge or dashes to meet her through the surf. Her heart grows cold and chill with fear.

Has she indeed come too late?

The men leave the boat, comforting her as they go with shakings of the hand and kindly touches upon the shoulder. She motions them to haste and remains kneeling.

The time goes on. The men ascend the mountain; they search, but they find not the lost Sailor Boy, and with slow, halting feet they return to the boat.

The Mother hears them coming afar and rises to meet them. They hang their heads. The Mother's arms go up, tossed aloft in the anguish of despair, and she sinks swooning in the boat.

The Shadow Builder in an instant summons her spirit from her senseless clay, and points to a figure passing, without movement, in the Procession of the Dead Past.

Then quicker than light the Mother's soul flies back full of new-found joy.

She rises from the boat—she springs to land. The men follow wondering.

She rushes along the shore with flying feet; the sailors come close behind.

She stops opposite the entrance to a cave obscured with trailing brambles. Here, without turning, she motions to the men to wait. They pause and she passes within.

For a few moments grim darkness pours from the Threshold; and then one sad, sad vision grows and passes.—

A dim, dark cave—a worn man lying prone, and a Mother in anguish bending over the cold clay. On the icy breast she lays her hand; but alas! she cannot feel the beat of the heart she loves.

With a wild, heart-stricken gesture, she flings herself upon the body of her Son and holds it close, close—as though the clasp of a Mother were stronger than the grasp of Death.

The dead heart of the Shadow Builder is alive with pain as he turns away from the sad picture, and with anxious eyes looks where from behind the Gate of Dread, the Mother and Child must come to join the ever-swelling ranks of the Procession of the Dead Past.

Slowly, slowly comes the shadow of the clay cold Mariner passing on.

But swifter than light come the Mother's flying feet. The arms so strong with love are stretched out—the thin hands grasp the passing shadow of her Son and tear him back beyond the Gate of Dread—to life—and liberty—and love.

The lonely Shadow Builder knows now that the Mother's arms are stronger than the grasp of Death.

THE CASTLE OF THE KING

WHEN they told the poor Poet that the One he loved best was lying sick in the shadow of danger, he was nigh distraught.

For weeks past he had been alone; she, his Wife, having gone afar to her old home to see an aged grandsire ere he died.

The Poet's heart had for some days been oppressed with a strange sorrow. He did not know the cause of it; he only knew with the deep sympathy which is the poet's gift, that the One he loved was sick. Anxiously had he awaited tidings. When the news came, the shock, although he expected a sad message, was too much for him, and he became nigh distraught.

In his sadness and anxiety he went out into the garden which long years he had cultured for Her. There, amongst the bright flowers, where the old statues stood softly white against the hedges of yew, he lay down in the long uncut summer grass, and wept with his head buried low.

He thought of all the past—of how he had won his Wife and how they loved each other; and to him it seemed a sad and cruel thing that she was afar and in danger, and he not near to comfort her or even to share her pain.

Many many thoughts came back to him, telling the story of the weary years whose gloom and solitude he had forgotten in the brightness of his lovely home.—

How in youth they twain had met and in a moment loved. How his poverty and her greatness had kept them apart. How he had struggled and toiled in the steep and rugged road to fame and fortune.

How all through the weary years he had striven with the single idea of winning such a place in the history of his time, that he should be able to come and to her say, "I love you," and to her proud relations, "I am worthy, for I too have become great."

How amid all this dreaming of a happy time which might come, he had kept silent as to his love. How he had never seen her or heard her voice, or even known her habitation, lest, knowing, he should fail in the purpose of his life.

How time—as it ever does to those who work with honesty and singleness of purpose—crowned the labours and the patience of his life.

How the world had come to know his name and reverence and love it as of one who had helped the weak and weary by his example; who had purified the thoughts of all who listened to his words; and who had swept away baseness before the grandeur and simpleness of his noble thoughts.

How success had followed in the wake of fame.

How at length even to his heart, timorous with the doubt of love, had been borne the thought that he had at last achieved the greatness which justified him in seeking the hand of her he loved.

How he had come back to his native place, and there found her still free.

How when he had dared to tell her of his love she had whispered to him that she, too, had waited all the years, for that she knew that he would come to claim her at the end.

How she had come with him as his bride into the home which he had been making for her all these years. How, there, they had lived happily; and had dared to look into the long years to come for joy and content without a bar.

How he thought that even then, when though somewhat enfeebled in strength by the ceaseless toil of years and the care of hoping, he might look to the happy time to come.

But, alas! for hope; for who knoweth what a day may bring forth? Only a little while ago his Dear One had left him hale, departing in the cause of duty; and now she lay sick and he not nigh to help her.

All the sunshine of his life seemed passing away. All the long years of waiting and the patient continuance in well-doing which had crowned their years with love, seemed as but a passing dream, and was all in vain—all, all in vain.

Now with the shadow hovering over his Beloved One, the cloud seemed to be above and around them, and to hold in its dim recesses the doom of them both.

"Why, oh why," asked the poor Poet to the viewless air, "did love come to us? Why came peace and joy and happiness, if the darkening wings of peril shadow the air around her, and leave me to weep alone?"

Thus he moaned, and raved, and wept; and the bitter hours went by him in his solitude.

As he lay in the garden with his face buried in the long grass, they came to him and told him with weeping, that tidings—sad, indeed—had come.

As they spoke he lifted his poor head and gazed at them; and they saw in the great, dark, tender eyes that now he was quite distraught. He smiled at them sadly, as though not quite understanding the import of their words. As tenderly as they could they tried to tell him that the One he loved best was dead.

They said:—

"She has walked in the Valley of the Shadow;" but he seemed to understand them not.

They whispered,

"She has heard the Music of the Spheres," but still he comprehended not.

Then they spoke to him sorrowfully and said:

"She now abides in the Castle of the King."

He looked at them eagerly, as if to ask:

"What castle? What king?"

They bowed their heads; and as they turned away weeping they murmured to him softly—

"The Castle of the King of Death."

He spake no word; so they turned their weeping faces to him again. They found that he had risen and stood with a set purpose on his face. Then he said sweetly:

"I go to find her, that where she abideth, I too may there abide."

They said to him:

"You cannot go. Beyond the Portal she is, and in the Land of Death."

Set purpose shone in the Poet's earnest, loving eyes as he answered them for the last time:

"Where she has gone, there go I too. Through the Valley of the Shadow shall I wend my way. In these ears also shall ring the Music of the Spheres. I shall seek, and I shall find my Beloved in the Halls of the Castle of the King. I shall clasp her close—even before the dread face of the King of Death."

As they heard these words they bowed their heads again and wept, and said:

"Alas! alas!"

The poet turned and left them; and passed away. They fain would have followed; but he motioned them that they should not stir. So, alone, in his grief he went.

As he passed on he turned and waved his hand to them in farewell. Then for a while with uplifted hand he stood, and turned him slowly all around.

Suddenly his outstretched hand stopped and pointed. His friends looking with him saw, where, away beyond the Portal, the idle wilderness spread. There in the midst of desolation the mist from the marshes hung like a pall of gloom on the far off horizon.

As the Poet pointed there was a gleam of happiness—very very faint it was—in his poor sad eyes, distraught with loss, as if afar he beheld some sign or hope of the Lost One.

Swiftly and sadly the Poet fared on through the burning day.

The Rest Time came; but on he journeyed. He paused not for shade or rest. Never, even for an instant did he stop to cool his parched lips with an icy draught from the crystal springs.

The weary wayfarers resting in the cool shadows beside the fountains raised their tired heads and looked at him with sleepy eyes as he hurried. He heeded them not; but went ever onward with set purpose in his eyes, as though some gleam of hope bursting through the mists of the distant marshes urged him on.

So he fared on through all the burning day, and all the silent night. In the earliest dawn, when the promise of the still unrisen sun quickened the eastern sky into a pale light, he drew anigh the Portal. The horizon stood out blackly in the cold morning light.

There, as ever, stood the Angels who kept watch and ward, and oh, wondrous! although invisible to human eyes, they were seen of him.

As he drew nigh they gazed at him pityingly and swept their great wings out wide, as if to shelter him. He spake; and from his troubled heart the sad words came sweetly through the pale lips:

"Say, Ye who guard the Land, has my Beloved One passed hither on the journey to the Valley of the Shadow, to hear the Music of the Spheres, and to abide in the Castle of the King?"

The Angels at the Portal bowed their heads in token of assent; and they turned and looked outward from the Land to where, far off in the idle wilderness, the dank mists crept from the lifeless bosom of the marsh.

They knew well that the poor lonely Poet was in quest of his Beloved One; so they hindered him not, neither urged they him to stay. They pitied him much for that much he loved.

They parted wide, that through the Portal he might pass without let.

So, the Poet went onwards into the idle desert to look for his Beloved One in the Castle of the King.

For a time he went through gardens whose beauty was riper than the gardens of the Land. The sweetness of all things stole on the senses like the odours from the Isles of the Blest.

The subtlety of the King of Death, who rules in the Realms of Evil, is great. He has ordered that the way beyond the Portal be made full of charm. Thus those straying from the paths ordained for good see around them such beauty that in its joy the gloom and cruelty and guilt of the desert are forgotten.

But as the Poet passed onwards the beauty began to fade away.

The fair gardens looked as gardens do when the hand of care is taken off, and when the weeds in their hideous luxuriance choke, as they spring up, the choicer life of the flowers.

From cool alleys under spreading branches, and from crisp sward which touched as soft as velvet the Wanderer's aching feet, the way became a rugged stony path, full open to the burning glare. The flowers began to lose their odour, and to dwarf to stunted growth. Tall hemlocks rose on every side, infecting the air with their noisome odour.

Great fungi grew in the dark hollows where the pools of dank water lay. Tall trees, with branches like skeletons, rose—trees which had no leaves, and under whose shadow to pause were to die.

Then huge rocks barred the way. These were only passed by narrow, winding passages, overhung by the ponderous cliffs above, which ever threatened to fall and engulph the Sojourner.

Here the night began to fall; and the dim mist rising from the far-off marshes, took weird shapes of gloom. In the distant fastnesses of the mountains the wild beasts began to roar in their cavern lairs. The air became hideous with the fell sounds of the night season.

But the poor Poet heeded not ill sights or sounds of dread. Onward he went ever—unthinking of the terrors of the night. To him there was no dread of darkness—no fear of death—no consciousness of horror. He sought his Beloved One in the Castle of the King; and in that eager quest all natural terrors were forgot.

So fared he onward through the livelong night. Up the steep defiles he trod. Through the shadows of the huge rocks he passed unscathed. The wild animals came around him roaring fiercely—their great eyes flaming like fiery stars through the blackness of the night.

From the high rocks great pythons crawled and hung to seize their prey. From the crevices of the mountain steeps, and from cavernous rifts in the rocky way poisonous serpents glided and rose to strike.

But close though the noxious things came, they all refrained to attack; for they knew that the lonely Sojourner was bound for the Castle of their King.

Onward still, onward he went—unceasing—pausing not in his course—but pressing ever forward in his quest.

When daylight broke at last, the sun rose on a sorry sight. There toiling on the rocky way, the poor lonely Poet went ever onwards, unheeding of cold or hunger or pain.

His feet were bare, and his footsteps on the rock-strewn way were marked by blood. Around and behind him, and afar off keeping equal pace on the summits of the rocky ridges, came the wild beasts that looked on him as their prey, but that refrained from touching him because he sought the Castle of their King.

In the air wheeled the obscene birds who follow ever on the track of the dying and the lost. Hovered the bare-necked vultures with eager eyes, and hungry beaks. Their great wings flapped lazily in the idle air as they followed in the Wanderer's track. The vulture are a patient folk, and they await the falling of the prey.

From the cavernous recesses in the black mountain gorges crept, with silent speed, the serpents that there lurk. Came the python, with his colossal folds and endless coils, whence looked forth cunningly the small flat head. Came the boa and all his tribe, which seize their prey by force and crush it with the dread strictness of their embrace. Came the hooded snakes and all those which with their venom destroy their prey. Here, too, came those serpents most terrible of all to their quarry— which fascinate with eyes of weird magic and by the slow gracefulness of their approach.

Here came or lay in wait, subtle snakes, which take the colour of herb, or leaf, or dead branch, or slimy pool, amongst which they lurk, and so strike their prey unsuspecting.

Great serpents there were, nimble of body, which hang from rock or branch. These gripping tight to their distant hold, strike downward with the rapidity of light as they hurl their whip-like bodies from afar upon their prey.

Thus came forth all these noxious things to meet the Questing Man, and to assail him. But when they knew he was bound for the dread Castle of their King, and saw how he went onward without fear, they abstained from attack.

The deadly python and the boa towering aloft, with colossal folds, were passive, and for the nonce, became as stone. The hooded serpents drew in again their venomous fangs. The mild, deep earnest eyes of the fascinating snake became lurid with baffled spleen, as he felt his power to charm was without avail. In its deadly descent the hanging snake arrested its course, and hung a limp line from rock or branch.

Many followed the Wanderer onwards into the desert wilds, waiting and hoping for a chance to destroy.

Many other perils also were there for the poor Wanderer in the desert idleness. As he went onward the rocky way got steeper and darker. Lurid fogs and deadly chill mists arose.

Then in this path along the trackless wilderness were strange and terrible things.

Mandrakes—half plant, half man—shrieked at him with despairing cry, as, helpless for evil, they stretched out their ghastly arms in vain.

Giant thorns arose in the path; they pierced his suffering feet and tore his flesh as onward he trod. He felt the pain, but he heeded it not.

In all the long, terrible journey he had but one idea other than his eager search for his Beloved One. He thought that the children of men might learn much from the journey towards the Castle of the King, which began so fair, amidst the odorous gardens and under the cool shadow of the spreading trees. In his heart the Poet spake to the multitude of the children of men; and from his lips the words flowed like music, for he sang of the Golden Gate which the Angels call TRUTH.

"Pass not the Portal of the Sunset Land!
Pause where the Angels at their vigil stand.
Be warned! and press not though the gates lie wide,
But rest securely on the hither side.
Though odorous gardens and cool ways invite,
Beyond are darkest valleys of the night.
Rest! Rest contented.—Pause whilst undefiled,
Nor seek the horrors of the desert wild."

Thus treading down all obstacles with his bleeding feet, passed ever onwards, the poor distraught Poet, to seek his Beloved One in the Castle of the King.

Even as onward he went the life that is of the animals seemed to die away behind him. The jackals and the more cowardly savage animals slunk away. The lions and tigers, and bears, and wolves, and all the braver of the fierce beasts of prey which followed on his track even after the others had stopped, now began to halt in their career.

They growled low and then roared loudly with uplifted heads; the bristles of their mouths quivered with passion, and the great white teeth champed angrily together in baffled rage. They went on a little further; and stopped again roaring and growling as before. Then one by one they ceased, and the poor Poet went on alone.

In the air the vultures wheeled and screamed, pausing and halting in their flight, as did the savage beasts. These too ceased at length to follow in air the Wanderer in his onward course.

Longest of all kept up the snakes. With many a writhe and stealthy onward glide, they followed hard upon the footsteps of the Questing Man. In the blood marks of his feet upon the flinty rocks they found a joy and hope, and they followed ever.

But time came when the awful aspect of the places where the Poet passed checked even the serpents in their track—the gloomy defiles whence issue the poisonous winds that sweep with desolation even the dens of the beasts of prey—the sterile fastnesses which march upon the valleys of desolation. Here even the stealthy serpents paused in their course; and they too fell away. They glided back, smiling with deadliest rancour, to their obscene clefts.

Then came places where plants and verdure began to cease. The very weeds became more and more stunted and inane. Farther on they declined into the sterility of lifeless rock. Then the most noxious herbs that grew in ghastly shapes of gloom and terror lost even the power to harm, which outlives their living growth. Dwarfed and stunted even of evil, they were compact of the dead rock. Here even the deadly Upas tree could strike no root into the pestiferous earth.

Then came places where, in the entrance to the Valley of the Shadow, even solid things lost their substance, and melted in the dank and cold mists which swept along.

As he passed, the distraught Poet could feel not solid earth under his bleeding feet. On shadows he walked, and amid them, onward through the Valley of the Shadow to seek his Beloved One in the Castle of the King.

The Valley of the Shadow seemed of endless expanse. Circled by the teeming mist, no eye could pierce to where rose the great mountains between which the Valley lay.

Yet they stood there—Mount Despair on the one hand, and the Hill of Fear upon the other.

Hitherto the poor bewildered brain of the Poet had taken no note of all the dangers, and horrors, and pains which surrounded him—save only for the lesson which they taught. But now, lost as he was in the shrouding vapour of the Valley of the Shadow, he could not but think of the terrors of the way. He was surrounded by griesly phantoms that ever and anon arose silent in the mist, and were lost again before he could catch to the full their dread import.

Then there flashed across his soul a terrible thought—

Could it be possible that hither his Beloved One had travelled? Had there come to her the pains which shook his own form with agony? Was it indeed necessary that she should have been appalled by all these surrounding horrors?

At the thought of her, his Beloved One, suffering such pain and dread, he gave forth one bitter cry that rang through the solitude—that cleft the vapour of the Valley, and echoed in the caverns of the mountains of Despair and Fear.

The wild cry prolonged with the agony of the Poet's soul rang through the Valley, till the shadows that peopled it woke for the moment into life-in-death. They flitted dimly along, now melting away and anon springing again into life—till all the Valley of the Shadow was for once peopled with quickened ghosts.

Oh, in that hour there was agony to the poor distraught Poet's soul.

But presently there came a calm. When the rush of his first agony passed, the Poet knew that to the Dead came not the horrors of the journey that he undertook. To the Quick alone is the horror of the passage to the Castle of the King. With the thought came to him such peace that even there—in the dark Valley of the Shadow—stole soft music that sounded in the desert gloom like the Music of the Spheres.

Then the poor Poet remembered what they had told him; that his Beloved One had walked through the Valley of the Shadow, that she had known the Music of the Spheres, and that she abode in the Castle of the King. So he thought that as he was now in the Valley of the Shadow, and as he heard the Music of the Spheres, that soon he should see the Castle of the King where his Beloved One abode. Thus he went on in hope.

But alas! that very hope was a new pain that ere this he wot not of.

Hitherto he had gone on blindly, recking not of where he went or what came a-nigh him, so long as he pressed onward on his quest; but now the darkness and the peril of the way had new terrors, for he thought of how they might arrest his course. Such thoughts made the way long indeed, for the moments seemed an age with hoping. Eagerly he sought for the end to come, when, beyond the Valley of the Shadow through which he fared, he should see rising the turrets of the Castle of the King.

Despair seemed to grow upon him; and as it grew there rang out, ever louder, the Music of the Spheres.

Onward, ever onward, hurried in mad haste the poor distraught Poet. The dim shadows that peopled the mist shrank back as he passed, extending towards him warning hands with long gloomy fingers of deadly cold. In the bitter silence of the moment, they seemed to say:

"Go back! Go back!"

Louder and louder rang now the Music of the Spheres. Faster and faster in mad, feverish haste rushed the Poet, amid the shrinking Shadows of the gloomy valley. The peopling shadows as they faded away before him, seemed to wail in sorrowful warning:

"Go back! Go back!"

Still in his ears rang ever the swelling tumult of the music.

Faster and faster he rushed onward; till, at last, wearied nature gave way and he fell prone to earth, senseless, bleeding, and alone.

After a time—how long he could not even guess—he awoke from his swoon.

For awhile he could not think where he was; and his scattered senses could not help him.

All was gloom and cold and sadness. A solitude reigned around him, more deadly than aught he had ever dreamt of. No breeze was in the air; no movement of a passing cloud. No voice or stir of living thing in earth, or water, or air. No rustle of leaf or sway of branch—all was silent, dead, and deserted. Amid the eternal hills of gloom around, lay the valley devoid of aught that lived or grew.

The sweeping mists with their multitude of peopling shadows had gone by. The fearsome terrors of the desert even were not there. The Poet, as he gazed around him, in his utter loneliness, longed for the sweep of the storm or the roar of the avalanche to break the dread horror of the silent gloom.

Then the Poet knew that through the Valley of the Shadow had he come; that scared and maddened though he had been, he had heard the Music of the Spheres. He thought that now hard by the desolate Kingdom of Death he trod.

He gazed all around him, fearing lest he should see anywhere the dread Castle of the King, where his Beloved One abode; and he groaned as the fear of his heart found voice:

"Not here! oh not here, amid this awful solitude."

Then amid the silence around, upon distant hills his words echoed:

"Not here! oh not here," till with the echoing and re-echoing rock, the idle wilderness was peopled with voices.

Suddenly the echo voices ceased.

From the lurid sky broke the terrible sound of the thunder peal. Along the distant skies it rolled. Far away over the endless ring of the grey horizon it swept—going and returning—pealing—swelling—dying away. It traversed the æther, muttering now in ominous sound as of threats, and anon crashing with the voice of dread command.

In its roar came a sound as of a word:

"Onward."

To his knees the Poet sank and welcomed with tears of joy the sound of the thunder. It swept away as a Power from Above the silent desolation of the wilderness. It told him that in and above the Valley of the Shadow rolled the mighty tones of Heaven's command.

Then the Poet rose to his feet, and with new heart went onwards into the wilderness.

As he went the roll of the thunder died away, and again the silence of desolation reigned alone.

So time wore on; but never came rest to the weary feet. Onwards, still onwards he went, with but one memory to cheer him—the echo of the thunder roll in his ears, as it pealed out in the Valley of Desolation:

"Onward! Onward!"

Now the road became less and less rocky, as on his way he passed. The great cliffs sank and dwindled away, and the ooze of the fens crept upward to the mountain's feet.

At length the hills and hollows of the mountain fastnesses disappeared. The Wanderer took his way amid mere trackless wastes, where was nothing but quaking marsh and slime.

On, on he wandered; stumbling blindly with weary feet on the endless road.

Over his soul crept ever closer the blackness of despair. Whilst amid the mountain gorges he had been wandering, some small cheer came from the hope that at any moment some turn in the path might show him his journey's end. Some entry from a dark defile might expose to him, looming great in the distance—or even anigh him—the dread

Castle of the King. But now with the flat desolation of the silent marsh around him, he knew that the Castle could not exist without his seeing it.

He stood for a while erect, and turned him slowly round, so that the complete circuit of the horizon was swept by his eager eyes. Alas! never a sight did he see. Nought was there but the black line of the horizon, where the sad earth lay against the level sky. All, all was compact of a silent gloom.

Still on he tottered. His breath came fast and laboured. His weary limbs quivered as they bore him feebly up. His strength—his life—was ebbing fast.

On, on, he hurried, ever on, with one idea desperately fixed in his poor distraught mind—that in the Castle of the King he should find his Beloved One.

He stumbled and fell. There was no obstacle to arrest his feet; only from his own weakness he declined.

Quickly he arose and went onward with flying feet. He dreaded that should he fall he might not be able to arise again.

Again he fell. Again he rose and went on his way desperately, with blind purpose.

So for a while went he onwards, stumbling and falling; but arising ever and pausing not on his way. His quest he followed, of his Beloved One abiding in the Castle of the King.

At last so weak he grew that when he sank he was unable to rise again.

Feebler and feebler he grew as he lay prone; and over his eager eyes came the film of death.

But even then came comfort; for he knew that his race was run, and that soon he would meet his Beloved One in the Halls of the Castle of the King.

To the wilderness his thoughts he spoke. His voice came forth with a feeble sound, like the moaning before a storm of the wind as it passes through reeds in the grey autumn:

"A little longer. Soon I shall meet her in the Halls of the King; and we shall part no more. For this it is worth to pass through the Valley of the Shadow and to listen to the Music of the Spheres with their painful hope. What boots it though the Castle be afar? Quickly speed the feet of the dead. To the fleeting spirit all distance is but a span. I fear not now to see the Castle of the King; for there, within its chiefest Hall, soon shall I meet my Beloved—to part no more."

Even as he spoke he felt that the end was nigh.

Forth from the marsh before him crept a still, spreading mist. It rose silently, higher—higher—enveloping the wilderness for far around. It took deeper and darker shades as it arose. It was as though the Spirit of Gloom were hid within, and grew mightier with the spreading vapour.

To the eyes of the dying Poet the creeping mist was as a shadowy castle. Arose the tall turrets and the frowning keep. The gateway with its cavernous recesses and its beetling towers took shape as a skull. The distant battlements towered aloft into the silent air. From the very ground whereon the stricken Poet lay, grew, dim and dark, a vast causeway leading into the gloom of the Castle gate.

The dying Poet raised his head and looked. His fast failing eyes, quickened by the love and hope of his spirit, pierced through the dark walls of the keep and the gloomy terrors of the gateway.

There, within the great Hall where the grim King of Terrors himself holds his court, he saw her whom he sought. She was standing in the ranks of those who wait in patience for their Beloved to follow them into the Land of Death.

The Poet knew that he had but a little while to wait, and he was patient—stricken though he lay, amongst the Eternal Solitudes.

Afar off, beyond the distant horizon, came a faint light as of the dawn of a coming day.

As it grew brighter the Castle stood out more and more clearly; till in the quickening dawn it stood revealed in all its cold expanse.

The dying Poet knew that the end was at hand. With a last effort he raised himself to his feet, that standing erect and bold, as is the right of manhood, he might so meet face to face the grim King of Death before the eyes of his Beloved One.

The distant sun of the coming day rose over the horizon's edge.

A ray of light shot upward.

As it struck the summit of the Castle keep the Poet's Spirit in an instant of time swept along the causeway. Through the ghostly portal of the Castle it swept, and met with joy the kindred Spirit that it loved before the very face of the King of Death.

Quicker then than the lightning's flash the whole Castle melted into nothingness; and the sun of the coming day shone calmly down upon the Eternal Solitudes.

In the Land within the Portal rose the sun of the coming day. It shone calmly and brightly on a fair garden, where, among the long summer grass lay the Poet, colder than the marble statues around him.

A GIPSY PROPHECY

"I REALLY think," said the Doctor, "that, at any rate, one of us should go and try whether or not the thing is an imposture."

"Good!" said Considine. "After dinner we will take our cigars and stroll over to the camp."

Accordingly, when the dinner was over, and the *La Tour* finished, Joshua Considine and his friend, Dr. Burleigh, went over to the east side of the moor, where the gipsy encampment lay. As they were leaving, Mary Considine, who had walked as far as the end of the garden where it opened into the laneway, called after her husband:

"Mind, Joshua, you are to give them a fair chance, but don't give them any clue to a fortune—and don't you get flirting with any of the gipsy maidens—and take care to keep Gerald out of harm."

For answer Considine held up his hand, as if taking a stage oath, and whistled the air of the old song, "The Gipsy Countess." Gerald joined in the strain, and then, breaking into merry laughter, the two men passed along the laneway to the common, turning now and then to wave their hands to Mary, who leaned over the gate, in the twilight, looking after them.

It was a lovely evening in the summer; the very air was full of rest and quiet happiness, as though an outward type of the peacefulness and joy which made a heaven of the home of the young married folk. Considine's life had not been an eventful one. The only disturbing element which he had ever known was in his wooing of Mary Winston, and the long-continued objection of her ambitious parents, who expected a brilliant match for their only daughter. When Mr. and Mrs. Winston had discovered the attachment of the young barrister, they had tried to keep the young people apart by sending their daughter away for a long round of visits, having made her promise not to correspond with her lover during her absence. Love, however, had stood the test. Neither absence nor neglect seemed to cool the passion of the young man, and jealousy seemed a thing unknown to his sanguine nature; so, after a long period of waiting, the parents had given in, and the young folk were married.

They had been living in the cottage a few months, and were just beginning to feel at home. Gerald Burleigh, Joshua's old college chum, and himself a sometime victim of Mary's beauty, had arrived a week before, to stay with them for as long a time as he could tear himself away from his work in London.

When her husband had quite disappeared Mary went into the house, and, sitting down at the piano, gave an hour to Mendelssohn.

It was but a short walk across the common, and before the cigars required renewing the two men had reached the gipsy camp. The place was as picturesque as gipsy camps—when in villages and when business is good—usually are. There were some few persons round the fire, investing their money in prophecy, and a large number of others, poorer or more parsimonious, who stayed just outside the bounds, but near enough to see all that went on.

As the two gentlemen approached, the villagers, who knew Joshua, made way a little, and a pretty, keen-eyed gipsy girl tripped up and asked to tell their fortunes. Joshua held out his hand, but the girl, without seeming to see it, stared at his face in a very odd manner. Gerald nudged him:

"You must cross her hand with silver," he said. "It is one of the most important parts of the mystery." Joshua took from his pocket a half-crown and held it out to her, but, without looking at it, she answered:

"You must cross the gipsy's hand with gold."

74

Gerald laughed. "You are at a premium as a subject," he said. Joshua was of the kind of man—the universal kind—who can tolerate being stared at by a pretty girl; so, with some little deliberation, he answered:

"All right; here you are, my pretty girl; but you must give me a real good fortune for it," and he handed her a half sovereign, which she took, saying:

"It is not for me to give good fortune or bad, but only to read what the Stars have said." She took his right hand and turned it palm upward; but the instant her eyes met it she dropped it as though it had been red hot, and, with a startled look, glided swiftly away. Lifting the curtain of the large tent, which occupied the centre of the camp, she disappeared within.

"Sold again!" said the cynical Gerald. Joshua stood a little amazed, and not altogether satisfied. They both watched the large tent. In a few moments there emerged from the opening not the young girl, but a stately looking woman of middle age and commanding presence.

The instant she appeared the whole camp seemed to stand still. The clamour of tongues, the laughter and noise of the work were, for a second or two, arrested, and every man or woman who sat, or crouched, or lay, stood up and faced the imperial looking gipsy.

"The Queen, of course," murmured Gerald. "We are in luck to-night." The gipsy Queen threw a searching glance around the camp, and then, without hesitating an instant, came straight over and stood before Joshua.

"Hold out your hand," she said in a commanding tone.

Again Gerald spoke, *sotto voce*: "I have not been spoken to in that way since I was at school."

"Your hand must be crossed with gold."

"A hundred per cent. at this game," whispered Gerald, as Joshua laid another half sovereign on his upturned palm.

The gipsy looked at the hand with knitted brows; then suddenly looking up into his face, said:

"Have you a strong will—have you a true heart that can be brave for one you love?"

"I hope so; but I am afraid I have not vanity enough to say 'yes.'"

"Then I will answer for you; for I read resolution in your face—resolution desperate and determined if need be. You have a wife you love?"

"Yes," emphatically.

"Then leave her at once—never see her face again. Go from her now, while love is fresh and your heart is free from wicked intent. Go quick—go far, and never see her face again!"

Joshua drew away his hand quickly, and said: "Thank you!" stiffly but sarcastically, as he began to move away.

"I say!" said Gerald, "you're not going like that, old man; no use in being indignant with the Stars or their prophet—and, moreover, your sovereign—what of it? At least, hear the matter out."

"Silence, ribald!" commanded the Queen, "you know not what you do. Let him go—and go ignorant, if he will not be warned."

Joshua immediately turned back. "At all events, we will see this thing out," he said. "Now, madam, you have given me advice, but I paid for a fortune."

"Be warned!" said the gipsy. "The Stars have been silent for long; let the mystery still wrap them round."

"My dear madam, I do not get within touch of a mystery every day, and I prefer for my money knowledge rather than ignorance. I can get the latter commodity for nothing when I want any of it."

Gerald echoed the sentiment. "As for me I have a large and unsaleable stock on hand."

The gipsy Queen eyed the two men sternly, and then said. "As you wish. You have chosen for yourself, and have met warning with scorn, and appeal with levity. On your own heads be the doom!"

"Amen!" said Gerald.

With an imperious gesture the Queen took Joshua's hand again, and began to tell his fortune.

"I see here the flowing of blood; it will flow before long; it is running in my sight. It flows through the broken circle of a severed ring."

"Go on!" said Joshua, smiling. Gerald was silent.

"Must I speak plainer?"

"Certainly; we commonplace mortals want something definite. The Stars are a long way off, and their words get somewhat dulled in the message."

The gipsy shuddered, and then spoke impressively. "This is the hand of a murderer—the murderer of his wife!" She dropped the hand and turned away.

Joshua laughed. "Do you know," said he, "I think if I were you I should prophesy some jurisprudence into my system. For instance, you say 'this hand is the hand of a murderer.' Well, whatever it may be in the future—or potentially—it is at present not one. You ought to give your prophecy in such terms as 'the hand which will be a murderer's,' or, rather, 'the hand of one who will be the murderer of his wife.' The Stars are really not good on technical questions."

The gipsy made no reply of any kind, but, with drooping head and despondent mien, walked slowly to her tent, and, lifting the curtain, disappeared.

Without speaking the two men turned homewards, and walked across the moor. Presently, after some little hesitation, Gerald spoke.

"Of course, old man, this is all a joke; a ghastly one, but still a joke. But would it not be well to keep it to ourselves?"

"How do you mean?"

"Well, not to tell your wife. It might alarm her."

"Alarm her! My dear Gerald, what are you thinking of? Why, she would not be alarmed or afraid of me if all the gipsies that ever didn't come from Bohemia agreed that I was to murder her, or even to have a hard thought of her, whilst so long as she was saying 'Jack Robinson.'"

Gerald remonstrated. "Old fellow, women are superstitious—far more than we men are; and, also, they are blessed—or cursed—with a nervous system to which we are strangers. I see too much of it in my work not to realise it. Take my advice and do not let her know, or you will frighten her."

Joshua's lips unconsciously hardened as he answered: "My dear fellow, I would not have a secret from my wife. Why, it would be the beginning of a new order of things between us. We have no secrets from each other. If we ever have, then you may begin to look out for something odd between us."

"Still," said Gerald, "at the risk of unwelcome interference, I say again be warned in time."

"The gipsy's very words," said Joshua. "You and she seem quite of one accord. Tell me, old man, is this a put-up thing? You told me of the gipsy camp—did you arrange it all with Her Majesty?" This was said, with an air of bantering earnestness. Gerald assured him that he only heard of the camp that morning; but he made fun of every answer of his friend, and, in the process of this raillery, the time passed, and they entered the cottage.

Mary was sitting by the piano but not playing. The dim twilight had waked some very tender feelings in her breast, and her eyes were full of gentle tears. When the men came in she stole over to her husband's side and kissed him. Joshua struck a tragic attitude.

"Mary," he said in a deep voice, "before you approach me, listen to the words of Fate. The Stars have spoken and the doom is sealed."

"What is it, dear? Tell me the fortune, but do not frighten me."

"Not at all, my dear; but there is a truth which it is well that you should know. Nay, it is necessary so that all your arrangements can be made beforehand, and everything be decently done and in order."

"Go on, dear; I am listening."

"Mary Considine, your effigy may yet be seen at Madame Tussaud's. The juris-imprudent stars have announced their fell tidings that this hand is red with blood—your blood. Mary! Mary! my God!" He sprang forward, but too late to catch her as she fell fainting on the floor.

"I told you," said Gerald. "You don't know them as well as I do."

After a little while Mary recovered from her swoon, but only to fall into strong hysterics, in which she laughed and wept and raved and cried, "Keep him from me—from me, Joshua, my husband," and many other words of entreaty and of fear.

Joshua Considine was in a state of mind bordering on agony, and when at last Mary became calm he knelt by her and kissed her feet and hands and hair and called her all the sweet names and said all the tender things his lips could frame. All that night he sat by her bedside and held her hand. Far through the night and up to the early morning she kept waking from sleep and crying out as if in fear, till she was comforted by the consciousness that her husband was watching beside her.

Breakfast was late the next morning, but during it Joshua received a telegram which required him to drive over to Withering, nearly twenty miles. He was loth to go; but Mary would not hear of his remaining, and so before noon he drove off in his dog-cart alone.

When he was gone Mary retired to her room. She did not appear at lunch, but when afternoon tea was served on the lawn, under the great weeping willow, she came to join her guest. She was looking quite recovered from her illness of the evening before. After some casual remarks, she said to Gerald: "Of course it was very silly about last night, but I could not help feeling frightened. Indeed I would feel so still if I let myself think of it. But, after all, these people may only imagine things, and I have got a test that can hardly fail to show that the prediction is false—if indeed it be false," she added sadly.

"What is your plan?" asked Gerald.

"I shall go myself to the gipsy camp, and have my fortune told by the Queen."

"Capital. May I go with you?"

"Oh, no! That would spoil it. She might know you and guess at me, and suit her utterance accordingly. I shall go alone this afternoon."

When the afternoon was gone Mary Considine took her way to the gipsy encampment. Gerald went with her as far as the near edge of the common, and returned alone.

Half-an-hour had hardly elapsed when Mary entered the drawing-room, where he lay on a sofa reading. She was ghastly pale and was in a state of extreme excitement. Hardly had she passed over the threshold when she collapsed and sank moaning on the carpet. Gerald rushed to aid her, but by a great effort she controlled herself and motioned him to be silent. He waited, and his ready attention to her wish seemed to be her best help, for, in a few minutes, she had somewhat recovered, and was able to tell him what had passed.

"When I got to the camp," she said, "there did not seem to be a soul about. I went into the centre and stood there. Suddenly a tall woman stood beside me. 'Something told me I was wanted!' she said. I held out my hand and laid a piece of silver on it. She took from her neck a small golden trinket and laid it there also; and then, seizing the two, threw them into the stream that ran by. Then she took my hand in hers and spoke: 'Naught but blood in this guilty place,' and turned away. I caught hold of her and asked her to tell me more. After some hesitation, she said: 'Alas! alas! I see you lying at your husband's feet, and his hands are red with blood.'"

Gerald did not feel at all at ease, and tried to laugh it off. "Surely," he said, "this woman has a craze about murder."

"Do not laugh," said Mary, "I cannot bear it," and then, as if with a sudden impulse, she left the room.

Not long after Joshua returned, bright and cheery, and as hungry as a hunter after his long drive. His presence cheered his wife, who seemed much brighter, but she did not mention the episode of the visit to the gipsy camp, so Gerald did not mention it either. As if by tacit consent the subject was not alluded to during the evening. But there was a strange, settled look on Mary's face, which Gerald could not but observe.

In the morning Joshua came down to breakfast later than usual. Mary had been up and about the house from an early hour; but as the time drew on she seemed to get a little nervous, and now and again threw around an anxious look.

Gerald could not help noticing that none of those at breakfast could get on satisfactorily with their food. It was not altogether that the chops were tough, but that the knives were all so blunt. Being a guest, he, of course, made no sign; but presently saw Joshua draw his thumb across the edge of his knife in an unconscious sort of way. At the action Mary turned pale and almost fainted.

After breakfast they all went out on the lawn. Mary was making up a bouquet, and said to her husband, "Get me a few of the tea-roses, dear."

Joshua pulled down a cluster from the front of the house. The stem bent, but was too tough to break. He put his hand in his pocket to get his knife; but in vain. "Lend me your knife, Gerald," he said. But Gerald had not got one, so he went into the breakfast-room and took one from the table. He came out feeling its edge and grumbling. "What on earth has happened to all the knives—the edges seem all ground off?" Mary turned away hurriedly and entered the house.

Joshua tried to sever the stalk with the blunt knife as country cooks sever the necks of fowl—as school-boys cut twine. With a little effort he finished the task. The cluster of roses grew thick, so he determined to gather a great bunch.

He could not find a single sharp knife in the sideboard where the cutlery was kept, so he called Mary, and when she came, told her the state of things. She looked so agitated and so miserable that he could not help knowing the truth, and, as if astounded and hurt, asked her:

"Do you mean to say that *you* have done it?"

She broke in, "Oh, Joshua, I was so afraid."

He paused, and a set, white look came over his face. "Mary!" said he, "is this all the trust you have in me? I would not have believed it."

"Oh, Joshua! Joshua!" she cried entreatingly, "forgive me," and wept bitterly.

Joshua thought a moment and then said: "I see how it is. We shall better end this or we shall all go mad."

He ran into the drawing-room.

"Where are you going?" almost screamed Mary.

Gerald saw what he meant—that he would not be tied to blunt instruments by the force of a superstition, and was not surprised when he saw him come out through the French window, bearing in his hand a large Ghourka knife, which usually lay on the centre table, and which his brother had sent him from Northern India. It was one of those great hunting-knives which worked such havoc, at close quarters with the enemies of the loyal Ghourkas during the mutiny, of great weight but so evenly balanced in the hand as to seem light, and with an edge like a razor. With one of these knives a Ghourka can cut a sheep in two.

When Mary saw him come out of the room with the weapon in his hand she screamed in an agony of fright, and the hysterics of last night were promptly renewed.

Joshua ran toward her, and, seeing her falling, threw down the knife and tried to catch her.

However, he was just a second too late, and the two men cried out in horror simultaneously as they saw her fall upon the naked blade.

When Gerald rushed over he found that in falling her left hand had struck the blade, which lay partly upwards on the grass. Some of the small veins were cut through, and the blood gushed freely from the wound. As he was tying it up he pointed out to Joshua that the wedding ring was severed by the steel.

They carried her fainting to the house. When, after a while, she came out, with her arm in a sling, she was peaceful in her mind and happy. She said to her husband:

"The gipsy was wonderfully near the truth; too near for the real thing ever to occur now, dear."

Joshua bent over and kissed the wounded hand.

THE DUALITISTS;
OR, THE DEATH DOOM
OF THE DOUBLE BORN

CHAPTER I

Bis dat qui non cito dat

THERE was joy in the house of Bubb.

For ten long years had Ephraim and Sophonisba Bubb mourned in vain the loneliness of their life. Unavailingly had they gazed into the emporia of baby-linen, and fixed their searching glances on the basket-makers' warehouses where the cradles hung in tempting rows. In vain had they prayed, and sighed, and groaned, and wished, and waited, and wept, but never had even a ray of hope been held out by the family physician.

But now at last the wished-for moment had arrived. Month after month had flown by on leaden wings, and the destined days had slowly measured their course. The months had become weeks; the weeks had dwindled down to days; the days had been attenuated to hours; the hours had lapsed into minutes, the minutes had slowly died away, and but seconds remained.

Ephraim Bubb sat cowering on the stairs, and tried with high-strung ears to catch the strain of blissful music from the lips of his first-born.

There was silence in the house—silence as of the deadly calm before the cyclone. Ah! Ephraim Bubb, little thinkest thou that another moment may for ever destroy the peaceful, happy course of thy life, and open to thy too craving eyes the portals of that wondrous land where Childhood reigns supreme, and where the tyrant infant with the wave of his tiny hand and the imperious treble of his tiny voice sentences his parent to the deadly vault beneath the castle moat. As the thought strikes thee thou becomest pale. How thou tremblest as thou findest thyself upon the brink of the abyss! Wouldst that thou could recall the past!

But hark! the die is cast for good or ill. The long years of praying and hoping have found an end at last. From the chamber within comes a sharp cry, which shortly after is repeated. Ah! Ephraim, that cry is the feeble effort of childish lips as yet unused to the rough, worldly form of speech to frame the word Father. In the glow of thy transport all doubts are forgotten; and when the doctor cometh forth as the harbinger of joy he findeth thee radiant with new found delight.

"My dear sir, allow me to congratulate you—to offer twofold felicitations. Mr. Bubb, sir, you are the father of Twins!"

CHAPTER II

Halcyon Days

The twins were the finest children that ever were seen—so at least said the *cognoscenti*, and the parents were not slow to believe. The nurse's opinion was in itself a proof.

It was not, ma'am, that they was fine for twins, but they was fine for singles, and she had ought to know, for she had nussed a many in her time, both twins *and* singles. All they wanted was to have their dear little legs cut off and little wings on their dear little shoulders, for to be put one on each side of a white marble tombstone, cut beautiful, sacred to the relic of Ephraim Bubb, that they might, sir, if so be that missus was to survive the father of two such lovely twins—although she would make bold to say, and no offence intended, that a handsome gentleman, though a trifle or two older than his good lady, though for the matter of that she heerd that gentlemen was never too old at all, and for her own part she liked them the better for it: not like bits of boys that didn't know their own minds—that a gentleman what was the father of two such 'eavenly twins (God bless them!) couldn't be called anything but a boy; though for the matter of that she never knowed in her experience—which it was much—of a boy as had such twins, or any twins at all so much for the matter of that.

The twins were the idols of their parents, and at the same time their pleasure and their pain. Did Zerubbabel cough, Ephraim would start from his balmy slumbers with an agonised cry of consternation, for visions of innumerable twins black in the face from croup haunted his nightly pillow. Did Zacariah rail at æthereal expansion, Sophonisba with pallid hue and dishevelled locks would fly to the cradle of her offspring. Did pins torture or strings afflict, or flannel or flies tickle, or light dazzle, or darkness affright, or hunger or thirst assail the synchronous productions, the household of Bubb would be roused from quiet slumbers or the current of its manifold workings changed.

The twins grew apace; were weaned; teethed; and at length arrived at the stage of three years!

> "They grew in beauty side by side,
> They filled one home," etc.

CHAPTER III

Rumours of Wars

Harry Merford and Tommy Santon lived in the same range of villas as Ephraim Bubb. Harry's parents had taken up their abode in No. 25, No. 27 was happy in the perpetual sunshine of Tommy's smiles, and between these two residences Ephraim Bubb reared his blossoms, the number of his mansion being 26. Harry and Tommy had been accustomed from the earliest times to meet each other daily. Their primal method of communication had been by the housetops, till their respective sires had been obliged to pay compensation to Bubb for damages to his roof and dormer windows; and from that time they had been forbidden by the home authorities to meet, whilst their mutual neighbour had taken the precaution of having his garden walls pebble-dashed and topped with broken glass to prevent their incursions. Harry and Tommy, however, being gifted with daring souls, lofty ambitious, impetuous natures, and strong seats to their trousers, defied the rugged walls of Bubb and continued to meet in secret.

Compared with these two youths, Castor and Pollux, Damon and Pythias, Eloisa and Abelard are but tame examples of duality or constancy and friendship. All the poets from Hyginus to Schiller might sing of noble deeds done and desperate dangers held as naught for friendship's sake, but they would have been mute had they but known of the mutual affection of Harry and Tommy. Day by day, and often night by night, would these two brave the perils of nurse, and father, and mother, of whip and imprisonment, and hunger and thirst, and solitude and darkness to meet together. What they discussed in secret none other knew. What deeds of darkness were perpetrated in their symposia none could tell. Alone they met, alone they remained, and alone they departed to their several abodes. There was in the garden of Bubb a summer house overgrown with trailing plants, and surrounded by young poplars which the fond father had planted on his children's natal day, and whose rapid growth he had proudly watched. These trees quite obscured the summer house, and here Harry and Tommy, knowing after a careful observation that none ever entered the place, held their conclaves. Time after time they met in full security and followed their customary pursuit of pleasure. Let us raise the mysterious veil and see what was the great Unknown at whose shrine they bent the knee.

Harry and Tommy had each been given as a Christmas box a new knife; and for a long time—nearly a year—these knives, similar in size and pattern, were their chief delights. With them they cut and hacked in their respective homes all things which would not be likely to be noticed; for the young gentlemen were wary and had no wish that their moments of pleasure should be atoned for by moments of pain. The insides of drawers, and desks, and boxes, the underparts of tables and chairs, the backs of picture frames, even the floors, where corners of the carpets could surreptitiously be turned up, all bore marks of their craftsmanship; and to compare notes on these artistic triumphs was a source of joy. At length, however, a critical time came, some new field of action should be opened up, for the old appetites were sated, and the old joys had begun to pall. It was absolutely necessary that the existing schemes of destruction should be enlarged; and yet this could hardly be done without a terrible risk of discovery, for the limits of safety had long since been reached and passed. But, be the risk great or small, some new ground should be broken—some new joy found, for the old earth was barren, and the craving for pleasure was growing fiercer with each successive day.

The crisis had come: who could tell the issue?

CHAPTER IV

The Tucket Sounds

They met in the arbour, determined to discuss this grave question. The heart of each was big with revolution, the head of each was full of scheme and strategy, and the pocket of each was full of sweet-stuff, the sweeter for being stolen. After having despatched the sweets, the conspirators proceeded to explain their respective views with regard to the enlargement of their artistic operations. Tommy unfolded with much pride a scheme which he had in contemplation of cutting a series of holes in the sounding board of the piano, so as to destroy its musical properties. Harry was in no wise behind-hand in his ideas of reform. He had conceived the project of cutting the canvas at the back of his great grandfather's portrait, which his father held in high regard among his lares and penates, so that in time when the picture should be moved the skin of paint would be broken, the head fall bodily out from the frame.

At this point of the council a brilliant thought occurred to Tommy. "Why should not the enjoyment be doubled, and the musical instruments and family pictures of both establishments be sacrificed on the altar of pleasure?" This was agreed to *nem. con.*; and then the meeting adjourned for dinner. When they next met it was evident that there was a screw loose somewhere—that there was "something rotten in the state of Denmark." After a little fencing on both sides, it came out that all the schemes of domestic reform had been foiled by maternal vigilance, and that so sharp had been the reprimand consequent on a partial discovery of the schemes that they would have to be abandoned—till such time, at least, as increased physical strength would allow the reformers to laugh to scorn parental threats and injunctions.

Sadly the two forlorn youths took out their knives and regarded them; sadly, sadly they thought, as erst did Othello, of all the fair chances of honour and triumph and glory gone for ever. They compared knives with almost the fondness of doting parents. There they were—so equal in size and strength and beauty—dimmed by no corrosive rust, tarnished by no stain, and with unbroken edges of the keenness of Saladin's sword.

So like were the knives that but for the initials scratched in the handles neither boy could not have been sure which was his own. After a little while they began mutually to brag of the superior excellence of their respective weapons. Tommy insisted that his was the sharper, Harry asserted that his was the stronger of the two. Hotter and hotter grew the war of words. The tempers of Harry and Tommy got inflamed, and their boyish bosoms glowed with manly thoughts of daring and of hate. But there was abroad in that hour a spirit of a bygone age—one that penetrated even to that dim arbour in the grove of Bubb. The world-old scheme of ordeal was whispered by the spirit in the ear of each, and suddenly the tumult was allayed. With one impulse the boys suggested that they should test the quality of their knives by the ordeal of the Hack.

No sooner said than done. Harry held out his knife edge uppermost; and Tommy, grasping his firmly by the handle, brought down the edge of the blade crosswise on Harry's. The process was then reversed, and Harry became in turn the aggressor. Then they paused and eagerly looked for the result. It was not hard to see; in each knife were two great dents of equal depth; and so it was necessary to renew the contest, and seek a further proof.

What needs it to relate *seriatim* the details of that direful strife? The sun had long since gone down, and the moon with fair, smiling face had long risen over the roof of Bubb, when, wearied and jaded, Harry and Tommy sought their respective homes. Alas! the splendour of the knives was gone for ever. Ichabod!—Ichabod! the glory had departed and naught remained but two useless wrecks, with keen edges destroyed, and now like unto nothing save the serried hills of Spain.

But though they mourned for their fondly cherished weapons, the hearts of the boys were glad; for the bygone day had opened to their gaze a prospect of pleasure as boundless as the limits of the world.

CHAPTER V

The First Crusade

From that day a new era dawned in the lives of Harry and Tommy. So long as the resources of the parental establishments could hold out so long would their new amusement continue. Subtly they obtained surreptitious possession of articles of family cutlery not in general use, and brought them one by one to their rendezvous. These came fair and spotless from the sanctity of the butlers' pantry Alas! they returned not as they came.

But in course of time the stock of available cutlery became exhausted, and again the inventive faculties of the youths were called into requisition. They reasoned thus: "The knife game, it is true, is played out, but the excitement of the Hack is not to be dispensed with. Let us carry, then, this Great Idea into new worlds; let us still live in the sunshine of pleasure; let us continue to hack, but with objects other than knives."

It was done. Not knives now engaged the attention of the ambitious youths. Spoons and forks were daily flattened and beaten out of shape; pepper castor met pepper castor in combat, and both were borne dying from the field; candlesticks met in fray to part no more on this side of the grave; even épergnes were used as weapons in the crusade of Hack.

At last all the resources of the butler's pantry became exhausted, and then began a system of miscellaneous destruction that proved in a little time ruinous to the furniture of the respective homes of Harry and Tommy. Mrs. Santon and Mrs. Merford began to notice that the wear and tear in their households became excessive. Day after day some new domestic calamity seemed to have occurred. To-day a valuable edition of some book whose luxurious binding made it an object for public display would appear to have suffered some dire misfortune, for the edges were frayed and broken and the back loose if not altogether displaced; to-morrow the same awful fate would seem to have followed some miniature frame; the day following the legs of some chair or spider-table would show signs of extraordinary hardship. Even in the nursery the sounds of lamentation were heard. It was a thing of daily occurrence for the little girls to state that when going to bed at night they had laid their dear dollies in their beds with tender care, but that when again seeking them in the period of recess they had found them with all their beauty gone, with legs and arms amputated and faces beaten from all semblance of human form.

Then articles of crockery began to be missed. The thief could in no case be discovered, and the wages of the servants, from constant stoppages, began to be nominal rather than real. Mrs. Merford and Mrs. Santon mourned their losses, but Harry and Tommy gloated day after day over their spoils, which lay in an ever-increasing heap in the hidden grove of Bubb. To such an extent had the fondness of the Hack now grown that with both youths it was an infatuation—a madness—a frenzy.

At length one awful day arrived. The butlers of the houses of Merford and Santon, harassed by constant losses and complaints, and finding that their breakage account was in excess of their wages, determined to seek some sphere of occupation where, if they did not meet with a suitable reward or recognition of their services, they would, at least, not lose whatever fortune and reputation they had already acquired. Accordingly, before rendering up their keys and the goods entrusted to their charge, they proceeded to take a preliminary stock of their own accounts, to make sure of their accredited accuracy. Dire indeed was their distress when they knew to the full the havoc which had been wrought; terrible their anguish of the present, bitter their thoughts of the future. Their hearts, bowed down with weight of woe, failed them quite; reeled the strong brains that had erst overcome foes of deadlier spirit than grief; and fell their stalwart forms prone on the floors of their respective *sancta sanctorum*.

Late in the day when their services were required they were sought for in bower and hall, and at length discovered where they lay.

But alas for justice! They were accused of being drunk and for having, whilst in that degraded condition, deliberately injured all the property on which they could lay hands. Were not the evidences of their guilt patent to all in the hecatombs of the destroyed? Then they were charged with all the evils wrought in the houses, and on their indignant denial Harry and Tommy, each in his own home, according to their concerted scheme of action, stepped forward and relieved their minds of the deadly weight that had for long in secret borne them down. The story of each ran that time after time he had seen the butler, when he thought that nobody was looking, knocking knives together in the pantry, chairs and books and pictures in the drawing-room and study, dolls in the nursery, and plates in the kitchen. Then, indeed, was the master of each household stern and uncompromising in his demands for justice. Each butler was committed to the charge of myrmidons of the law under the double charge of drunk-enness and wilful destruction of property.

Softly and sweetly slept Harry and Tommy in their little beds that night. Angels seemed to whisper to them, for they smiled as though lost in pleasant dreams. The rewards given by proud and grateful parents lay in their pockets, and in their hearts the happy consciousness of having done their duty.

Truly sweet should be the slumbers of the just.

CHAPTER VI

"Let the Dead Past Bury Its Dead"

It might be supposed that now the operations of Harry and Tommy would be obliged to be abandoned.

Not so, however. The minds of these youths were of no common order, nor were their souls of such weak nature as to yield at the first summons of necessity. Like Nelson, they knew not fear; like Napoleon, they held "impossible" to be the adjective of fools; and they revelled in the glorious truth that in the lexicon of youth is no such word as "fail." Therefore on the day following the *eclaircissement* of the butlers' misdeeds, they met in the arbour to plan a new campaign.

In the hour when all seemed blackest to them, and when the narrowing walls of possibility hedged them in on every side, thus ran the deliberations of these dauntless youths:—

"We have played out the meaner things that are inanimate and inert; why not then trench on the domains of life? The dead have lapsed into the regions of the forgotten past—let the living look to themselves."

That night they met when all households had retired to balmy sleep, and naught but the amorous wailings of nocturnal cats told of the existence of life and sentience. Each bore into the arbour in his arms a pet rabbit and a piece of sticking-plaster. Then, in the peaceful, quiet moonlight, commenced a work of mystery, blood, and gloom. The proceedings began by the fixing of a piece of sticking-plaster over the mouth of each rabbit to prevent it making a noise, if so inclined. Then Tommy held up his rabbit by its scutty tail, and it hung wriggling, a white mass in the moonlight. Slowly Harry raised his rabbit holding it in the same manner, and when level with his head brought it down on Tommy's client.

But the chances had been miscalculated. The boys held firmly to the tails, but the chief portions of the rabbits fell to earth. Ere the doomed beasts could escape, however, the operators had pounced upon them, and this time holding them by the hind legs renewed the trial.

Deep into the night the game was kept up, and the Eastern sky began to show signs of approaching day as each boy bore triumphantly the dead corse of his favourite bunny and placed it within its sometime hutch.

Next night the same game was renewed with a new rabbit on each side, and for more than a week—so long as the hutches supplied the wherewithal—the battle was sustained. True that there were sad hearts and red eyes in the juveniles of Santon and Merford as one by one the beloved pets were found dead, but Harry and Tommy, with the hearts of heroes steeled to suffering and deaf to the pitiful cries of childhood, still fought the good fight on to the bitter end.

When the supply of rabbits was exhausted, other munition was not wanting, and for some days the war was continued with white mice, dormice, hedgehogs, guinea pigs, pigeons, lambs, canaries, parroqueets, linnets, squirrels, parrots, marmots, poodles, ravens, tortoises, terriers, and cats. Of these, as might be expected, the most difficult to manipulate were the terriers and the cats, and of these two classes the proportion of the difficulties in the way of terrier-hacking was, when compared with those of cat-hacking, about that which the simple *Lac* of the British Pharmacopoeia bears to water in the compound which dairymen palm off upon a too confiding public as milk. More than once when engaged in the rapturous delights of cat-hacking had Harry and Tommy wished that the silent tomb could ope its ponderous and massy jaws and engulf them, for the feline victims were not patient in their death agonies, and often broke the bonds in which the security of the artists rested, and turned fiercely on their executioners.

At last, however, all the animals available were sacrificed; but the passion for hacking still remained. How was it all to end?

CHAPTER VII

A Cloud with Golden Lining

Tommy and Harry sat in the arbour dejected and disconsolate. They wept like two Alexanders because there were no more worlds to conquer. At last the conviction had been forced upon them that the resources available for hacking were exhausted. That very morning they had had a desperate battle, and their attire showed the ravages of direful war. Their hats were battered into shapeless masses, their shoes were soleless and heelless and had the uppers broken, the ends of their braces, their sleeves, and their trousers were frayed, and had they indulged in the manly luxury of coat tails these too would have gone.

Truly, hacking had become an absorbing passion with them. Long and fiercely had they been swept onward on the wings of the demon of strife, and powerless at the best of times had been the promptings of good; but now, heated with combat, maddened by the equal success of arms, and with the lust for victory still unsated, they longed more fiercely than ever for some new pleasure: like tigers that have tasted blood they thirsted for a larger and more potent libation.

As they sat, with their souls in a tumult of desire and despair, some evil genius guided into the garden the twin blossoms of the tree of Bubb. Hand in hand Zacariah and Zerubbabel advanced from the back door; they had escaped from their nurses, and with the exploring instinct of humanity, advanced boldly into the great world—the *terra incognita*, the *Ultima Thule* of the paternal domain.

In the course of time they approached the hedge of poplars, from behind which the anxious eyes of Harry and Tommy looked for their approach, for the boys knew that where the twins were the nurses were accustomed to be gathered together, and they feared discovery if their retreat should be cut off.

It was a touching sight, these lovely babes, alike in form, feature, size, expression, and dress; in fact, so like each other that one "might not have told either from which." When the startling similarity was recognised by Harry and Tommy, each suddenly turned, and, grasping the other by the shoulder, spoke in a keen whisper:

"Hack! They are exactly equal! This is the very apotheosis of our art!"

With excited faces and trembling hands they laid their plans to lure the unsuspecting babes within the precincts of their charnel house, and they were so successful in their efforts that in a little time the twins had toddled behind the hedge and were lost to the sight of the parental mansion.

Harry and Tommy were not famed for gentleness within the immediate precincts of their respective homes, but it would have delighted the heart of any philanthropist to see the kindly manner in which they arranged for the pleasures of the helpless babes. With smiling faces and playful words and gentle wiles they led them within the arbour, and then, under pretence of giving them some of those sudden jumps in which infants rejoice, they raised them from the ground. Tommy held Zacariah across his arm with his baby moon-face smiling up at the cobwebs on the arbour roof, and Harry, with a mighty effort, raised the cherubic Zerubbabel aloft.

Each nerved himself for a great endeavour, Harry to give, Tommy to endure a shock, and then the form of Zerubbabel was seen whirling through the air round Harry's glowing and determined face. There was a sickening crash and the arm of Tommy yielded visibly.

The pasty face of Zerubbabel had fallen fair on that of Zacariah, for Tommy and Harry were by this time artists of too great experience to miss so simple a mark. The putty-like noses collapsed, the putty-like cheeks became for a moment flattened, and when in an instant more they parted, the faces of both were dabbled in gore. Immediately the firmament was rent with a series of such yells as might have awakened the dead. Forthwith from the house of Bubb came the echoes in parental cries and footsteps. As the sounds of scurrying feet rang through the mansion, Harry cried to Tommy:

"They will be on us soon. Let us cut to the roof of the stable and draw up the ladder."

Tommy answered by a nod, and the two boys, regardless of consequences, and bearing each a twin, ascended to the roof of the stable by means of a ladder which usually stood against the wall, and which they pulled up after them.

As Ephraim Bubb issued from his house in pursuit of his lost darlings, the sight which met his gaze froze his very soul. There, on the coping of the stable roof, stood Harry and Tommy renewing their game. They seemed like two young demons forging some diabolical implement, for each in turn the twins were lifted high in air and let fall with stunning force on the supine form of its fellow. How Ephraim felt none but a tender and imaginative father can conceive. It would be enough to wring the heart of even a callous parent to see his children, the darlings of his old age—his own beloved twins—being sacrificed to the brutal pleasure of unregenerate youths, without being made unconsciously and helplessly guilty of the crime of fratricide.

Loudly did Ephraim and also Sophonisba, who, with dishevelled locks, had now appeared upon the scene, bewail their unhappy lot and shriek in vain for aid; but by rare illchance no eyes save their own saw the work of butchery or heard the shrieks of anguish and despair. Wildly did Ephraim, mounting on the shoulders of his spouse, strive, but in vain, to scale the stable wall.

Baffled in every effort, he rushed into the house and appeared in a moment bearing in his hands a double-barrelled gun, into which he poured the contents of a shot pouch as he ran. He came anigh the stable and hailed the murderous youths:

"Drop them twins and come down here or I'll shoot you like a brace of dogs."

"Never!" exclaimed the heroic two with one impulse, and continued their awful pastime with a zest tenfold as they knew that the agonised eyes of parents wept at the cause of their joy.

"Then die!" shrieked Ephraim, as he fired both barrels, right-left, at the hackers.

But, alas! love for his darlings shook the hand that never shook before. As the smoke cleared off and Ephraim recovered from the kick of his gun, he heard a loud twofold laugh of triumph and saw Harry and Tommy, all unhurt, waving in the air the trunks of the twins—the fond father had blown the heads completely off his own offspring.

Tommy and Harry shrieked aloud in glee, and after playing catch with the bodies for some time, seen only by the agonised eyes of the infanticide and his wife, flung them high in the air. Ephraim leaped forward to catch what had once been Zacariah, and Sophonisba grabbed wildly for the loved remains of her Zerubbabel.

But the weight of the bodies and the height from which they fell were not reckoned by either parent, and from being ignorant of a simple dynamical formula each tried to effect an object which calm, common sense, united with scientific knowledge, would have told them was impossible. The masses fell, and Ephraim and Sophonisba were stricken dead by the falling twins, who were thus posthumously guilty of the crime of parricide.

An intelligent coroner's jury found the parents guilty of the crimes of infanticide and suicide, on the evidence of Harry and Tommy, who swore; reluctantly, that the inhuman monsters, maddened by drink, had killed their offspring by shooting them into the air out of a cannon—since stolen—whence like curses they had fallen on their own heads; and that then they had slain themselves *suis manibus* with their own hands.

Accordingly Ephraim and Sophonisba were denied the solace of Christian burial, and were committed to the earth with "maimed rites," and had stakes driven through their middles to pin them down in their unhallowed graves till the Crack of Doom.

Harry and Tommy were each rewarded with National honours and were knighted, even at their tender years.

Fortune seemed to smile upon them all the long after years, and they lived to a ripe old age, hale of body, and respected and beloved of all.

Often in the golden summer eves, when all nature seemed at rest, when the oldest cask was opened and the largest lamp was lit, when the chestnuts glowed in the embers and the kid turned on the spit, when their great-grandchildren pretended to mend fictional armour and to trim an imaginary helmet's plume, when the shuttles of the good wives of their grandchildren went flashing each through its proper loom, with shouting and with laughter they were accustomed to tell the tale of THE DUALITISTS; OR, THE DEATH-DOOM OF THE DOUBLE-BORN.

THE JUDGE'S HOUSE

WHEN the time for his examination drew near Malcolm Malcolmson made up his mind to go somewhere to read by himself. He feared the attractions of the seaside, and also he feared completely rural isolation, for of old he knew its charms, and so he determined to find some unpretentious little town where there would be nothing to distract him. He refrained from asking suggestions from any of his friends, for he argued that each would recommend some place of which he had knowledge, and where he had already acquaintances. As Malcolmson wished to avoid friends he had no wish to encumber himself with the attention of friends' friends, and so he determined to look out for a place for himself. He packed a portmanteau with some clothes and all the books he required, and then took ticket for the first name on the local time-table which he did not know.

When at the end of three hours' journey he alighted at Benchurch, he felt satisfied that he had so far obliterated his tracks as to be sure of having a peaceful opportunity of pursuing his studies. He went straight to the one inn which the sleepy little place contained, and put up for the night. Benchurch was a market town, and once in three weeks was crowded to excess, but for the remainder of the twenty-one days it was as attractive as a desert. Malcolmson looked around the day after his arrival to try to find quarters more isolated than even so quiet an inn as "The Good Traveller" afforded. There was only one place which took his fancy, and it certainly satisfied his wildest ideas regarding quiet; in fact, quiet was not the proper word to apply to it—desolation was the only term conveying any suitable idea of its isolation. It was an old rambling, heavy-built house of the Jacobean style, with heavy gables and windows, unusually small, and set higher than was customary in such houses, and was surrounded with a high brick wall massively built. Indeed, on examination, it looked more like a fortified house than an ordinary dwelling. But all these things pleased Malcolmson. "Here," he thought, "is the very spot I have been looking for, and if I can only get opportunity of using it I shall be happy." His joy was increased when he realised beyond doubt that it was not at present inhabited.

From the post-office he got the name of the agent, who was rarely surprised at the application to rent a part of the old house. Mr. Carnford, the local lawyer and agent, was a genial old gentleman, and frankly confessed his delight at anyone being willing to live in the house.

"To tell you the truth," said he, "I should be only too happy, on behalf of the owners, to let anyone have the house rent free for a term of years if only to accustom the people here to see it inhabited. It has been so long empty that some kind of absurd prejudice has grown up about it, and this can be best put down by its occupation—if only," he added with a sly glance at Malcolmson, "by a scholar like yourself, who wants its quiet for a time."

Malcolmson thought it needless to ask the agent about the "absurd prejudice"; he knew he would get more information, if he should require it, on that subject from other quarters. He paid his three months' rent, got a receipt, and the name of an old woman who would probably undertake to "do" for him, and came away with the keys in his pocket. He then went to the landlady of the inn, who was a cheerful and most kindly person, and asked her advice as to such stores and provisions as he would be likely to require. She threw up her hands in amazement when he told her where he was going to settle himself.

"Not in the Judge's House!" she said, and grew pale as she spoke. He explained the locality of the house, saying that he did not know its name. When he had finished she answered:

"Aye, sure enough—sure enough the very place! It is the Judge's House sure enough." He asked her to tell him about the place, why so called, and what there was against it. She told him that it was so called locally because it had been many years before—how long she could not say, as she was herself from another part of the country, but she thought it must have been a hundred years or more—the abode of a judge who was held in great terror on account of his harsh sentences and his hostility to prisoners at Assizes. As to what there was against the house itself she could not tell. She had often asked, but no one could inform her; but there was a general feeling that there was *something*, and for her own part she would not take all the money in Drinkwater's Bank and stay in the house an hour by herself. Then she apologised to Malcolmson for her disturbing talk.

"It is too bad of me, sir, and you—and a young gentleman, too—if you will pardon me saying it, going to live there all alone. If you were my boy—and you'll excuse me for saying it—you wouldn't sleep there a night, not if I had to go there myself and pull the big alarm bell that's on the roof!" The good creature was so manifestly in earnest, and was so kindly in her intentions, that Malcolmson, although amused, was touched. He told her kindly how much he appreciated her interest in him, and added:

"But, my dear Mrs. Witham, indeed you need not be concerned about me! A man who is reading for the Mathematical Tripos has too much to think of to be disturbed by any of these mysterious 'somethings,' and his work is of too exact and prosaic a kind to allow of his having any corner in his mind for mysteries of any kind. Harmonical Progression, Permutations and Combinations, and Elliptic Functions have sufficient mysteries for me!" Mrs. Witham kindly undertook to see after his commissions, and he went himself to look for the old woman who had been recommended to him. When he returned to the Judge's House with her, after an interval of a couple of hours, he found Mrs. Witham herself waiting with several men and boys carrying parcels, and an upholsterer's man with a bed in a cart, for she said, though tables and chairs might be all very well, a bed that hadn't been aired for mayhap fifty years was not proper for young bones to lie on. She was evidently curious to see the inside of the house; and though manifestly so afraid of the 'somethings' that at the slightest sound she clutched on to Malcolmson, whom she never left for a moment, went over the whole place.

After his examination of the house, Malcolmson decided to take up his abode in the great dining-room, which was big enough to serve for all his requirements; and Mrs. Witham, with the aid of the charwoman, Mrs. Dempster, proceeded to arrange matters. When the hampers were brought in and unpacked, Malcolmson saw that with much kind fore-thought she had sent from her own kitchen sufficient provisions to last for a few days. Before going she expressed all sorts of kind wishes; and at the door turned and said:

"And perhaps, sir, as the room is big and draughty it might be well to have one of those big screens put round your bed at night—though, truth to tell, I would die myself if I were to be so shut in with all kinds of—of 'things,' that put their heads round the sides, or over the top, and look on me!" The image which she had called up was too much for her nerves, and she fled incontinently.

Mrs. Dempster sniffed in a superior manner as the landlady disap-peared, and remarked that for her own part she wasn't afraid of all the bogies in the kingdom.

"I'll tell you what it is, sir," she said; "bogies is all kinds and sorts of things—except bogies! Rats and mice, and beetles; and creaky doors, and loose slates, and broken panes, and stiff drawer handles, that stay out when you pull them and then fall down in the middle of the night. Look at the wainscot of the room! It is old—hundreds of years old! Do you think there's no rats and beetles there! And do you imagine, sir, that you won't see none of them? Rats is bogies, I tell you, and bogies is rats; and don't you get to think anything else!"

"Mrs. Dempster," said Malcolmson gravely, making her a polite bow, "you know more than a Senior Wrangler! And let me say, that, as a mark of esteem for your indubitable soundness of head and heart, I shall, when I go, give you possession of this house, and let you stay here by yourself for the last two months of my tenancy, for four weeks will serve my purpose."

"Thank you kindly, sir!" she answered, "but I couldn't sleep away from home a night. I am in Greenhow's Charity, and if I slept a night away from my rooms I should lose all I have got to live on. The rules is very strict; and there's too many watching for a vacancy for me to run any risks in the matter. Only for that, sir, I'd gladly come here and attend on you altogether during your stay."

"My good woman," said Malcolmson hastily, "I have come here on purpose to obtain solitude; and believe me that I am grateful to the late Greenhow for having so organised his admirable charity—whatever it is—that I am perforce denied the opportunity of suffering from such a form of temptation! Saint Anthony himself could not be more rigid on the point!"

The old woman laughed harshly. "Ah, you young gentlemen," she said, "you don't fear for naught; and belike you'll get all the solitude you want here." She set to work with her cleaning; and by nightfall, when Malcolmson returned from his walk—he always had one of his books to study as he walked—he found the room swept and tidied, a fire burning in the old hearth, the lamp lit, and the table spread for supper with Mrs. Witham's excellent fare. "This is comfort, indeed," he said, as he rubbed his hands.

When he had finished his supper, and lifted the tray to the other end of the great oak dining-table, he got out his books again, put fresh wood on the fire, trimmed his lamp, and set himself down to a spell of real hard work. He went on without pause till about eleven o'clock, when he knocked off for a bit to fix his fire and lamp, and to make himself a cup of tea. He had always been a tea-drinker, and during his college life had sat late at work and had taken tea late. The rest was a great luxury to him, and he enjoyed it with a sense of delicious, voluptuous ease. The renewed fire leaped and sparkled, and threw quaint shadows through the great old room; and as he sipped his hot tea he revelled in the sense of isolation from his kind. Then it was that he began to notice for the first time what a noise the rats were making.

"Surely," he thought, "they cannot have been at it all the time I was reading. Had they been, I must have noticed it!" Presently, when the noise increased, he satisfied himself that it was really new. It was evident that at first the rats had been frightened at the presence of a stranger, and the light of fire and lamp; but that as the time went on they had grown bolder and were now disporting themselves as was their wont.

How busy they were! and hark to the strange noises! Up and down behind the old wainscot, over the ceiling and under the floor they raced, and gnawed, and scratched! Malcolmson smiled to himself as he recalled to mind the saying of Mrs. Dempster, "Bogies is rats, and rats is bogies!" The tea began to have its effect of intellectual and nervous stimulus, he saw with joy another long spell of work to be done before the night was past, and in the sense of security which it gave him, he allowed himself the luxury of a good look round the room. He took his lamp in one hand, and went all around, wondering that so quaint and beautiful an old house had been so long neglected. The carving of the oak on the panels of the wainscot was fine, and on and round the doors and windows it was beautiful and of rare merit. There were some old pictures on the walls, but they were coated so thick with dust and dirt that he could not distinguish any detail of them, though he held his lamp as high as he could over his head. Here and there as he went round he saw some crack or hole blocked for a moment by the face of a rat with its bright eyes glittering in the light, but in an instant it was gone, and a squeak and a scamper followed. The thing that most struck him, however, was the rope of the great alarm bell on the roof, which hung down in a corner of the room on the right-hand side of the fireplace. He pulled up close to the hearth a great high-backed carved oak chair, and sat down to his last cup of tea. When this was done he made up the fire, and went back to his work, sitting at the corner of the table, having the fire to his left. For a little while the rats disturbed him somewhat with their perpetual scampering, but he got accustomed to the noise as one does to the ticking of a clock or to the roar of moving water; and he became so immersed in his work that everything in the world, except the problem which he was trying to solve, passed away from him.

He suddenly looked up, his problem was still unsolved, and there was in the air that sense of the hour before the dawn, which is so dread to doubtful life. The noise of the rats had ceased. Indeed it seemed to him that it must have ceased but lately and that it was the sudden cessation which had disturbed him. The fire had fallen low, but still it threw out a deep red glow. As he looked he started in spite of his *sang froid*.

There on the great high-backed carved oak chair by the right side of the fireplace sat an enormous rat, steadily glaring at him with baleful eyes. He made a motion to it as though to hunt it away, but it did not stir. Then he made the motion of throwing something. Still it did not stir, but showed its great white teeth angrily, and its cruel eyes shone in the lamplight with an added vindictiveness.

Malcolmson felt amazed, and seizing the poker from the hearth ran at it to kill it. Before, however, he could strike it, the rat, with a squeak that sounded like the concentration of hate, jumped upon the floor, and, running up the rope of the alarm bell, disappeared in the darkness beyond the range of the green-shaded lamp. Instantly, strange to say, the noisy scampering of the rats in the wainscot began again.

By this time Malcolmson's mind was quite off the problem; and as a shrill cock-crow outside told him of the approach of morning, he went to bed and to sleep.

He slept so sound that he was not even waked by Mrs. Dempster coming in to make up his room. It was only when she had tidied up the place and got his breakfast ready and tapped on the screen which closed in his bed that he woke. He was a little tired still after his night's hard work, but a strong cup of tea soon freshened him up and, taking his book, he went out for his morning walk, bringing with him a few sandwiches lest he should not care to return till dinner time. He found a quiet walk between high elms some way outside the town, and here he spent the greater part of the day studying his Laplace. On his return he looked in to see Mrs. Witham and to thank her for her kindness. When she saw him coming through the diamond-paned bay window of her sanctum she came out to meet him and asked him in. She looked at him searchingly and shook her head as she said:

"You must not overdo it, sir. You are paler this morning than you should be. Too late hours and too hard work on the brain isn't good for any man! But tell me, sir, how did you pass the night? Well, I hope? But, my heart! sir, I was glad when Mrs. Dempster told me this morning that you were all right and sleeping sound when she went in."

"Oh, I was all right," he answered smiling, "the 'somethings' didn't worry me, as yet. Only the rats; and they had a circus, I tell you, all over the place. There was one wicked looking old devil that sat up on my own chair by the fire, and wouldn't go till I took the poker to him, and then he ran up the rope of the alarm bell and got to somewhere up the wall or the ceiling—I couldn't see where, it was so dark."

"Mercy on us," said Mrs. Witham, "an old devil, and sitting on a chair by the fireside! Take care, sir! take care! There's many a true word spoken in jest."

"How do you mean? 'Pon my word I don't understand."

"An old devil! The old devil, perhaps. There! sir, you needn't laugh," for Malcolmson had broken into a hearty peal. "You young folks thinks it easy to laugh at things that makes older ones shudder. Never mind, sir! never mind! Please God, you'll laugh all the time. It's what I wish you myself!" and the good lady beamed all over in sympathy with his enjoyment, her fears gone for a moment.

"Oh, forgive me!" said Malcolmson presently. "Don't think me rude; but the idea was too much for me—that the old devil himself was on the chair last night!" And at the thought he laughed again. Then he went home to dinner.

This evening the scampering of the rats began earlier; indeed it had been going on before his arrival, and only ceased whilst his presence by its freshness disturbed them. After dinner he sat by the fire for a while and had a smoke; and then, having cleared his table, began to work as before. To-night the rats disturbed him more than they had done on the previous night. How they scampered up and down and under and over! How they squeaked, and scratched, and gnawed! How they, getting bolder by degrees, came to the mouths of their holes and to the chinks and cracks and crannies in the wainscoting till their eyes shone like tiny lamps as the firelight rose and fell. But to him, now doubtless accustomed to them, their eyes were not wicked; only their playfulness touched him. Sometimes the boldest of them made sallies out on the floor or along the mouldings of the wainscot. Now and again as they disturbed him Malcolmson made a sound to frighten them, smiting the table with his hand or giving a fierce "Hsh, hsh," so that they fled straightway to their holes.

And so the early part of the night wore on; and despite the noise Malcolmson got more and more immersed in his work.

All at once he stopped, as on the previous night, being overcome by a sudden sense of silence. There was not the faintest sound of gnaw, or scratch, or squeak. The silence was as of the grave. He remembered the odd occurrence of the previous night, and instinctively he looked at the chair standing close by the fireside. And then a very odd sensation thrilled through him.

There, on the great old high-backed carved oak chair beside the fireplace sat the same enormous rat, steadily glaring at him with baleful eyes.

Instinctively he took the nearest thing to his hand, a book of logarithms, and flung it at it. The book was badly aimed and the rat did not stir, so again the poker performance of the previous night was repeated; and again the rat, being closely pursued, fled up the rope of the alarm bell. Strangely too, the departure of this rat was instantly followed by the renewal of the noise made by the general rat community. On this occasion, as on the previous one, Malcolmson could not see at what part of the room the rat disappeared, for the green shade of his lamp left the upper part of the room in darkness, and the fire had burned low.

On looking at his watch he found it was close on midnight; and, not sorry for the *divertissement*, he made up his fire and made himself his nightly pot of tea. He had got through a good spell of work, and thought himself entitled to a cigarette; and so he sat on the great carved oak chair before the fire and enjoyed it. Whilst smoking he began to think that he would like to know where the rat disappeared to, for he had certain ideas for the morrow not entirely disconnected with a rat-trap. Accordingly he lit another lamp and placed it so that it would shine well into the right-hand corner of the wall by the fireplace. Then he got all the books he had with him, and placed them handy to throw at the vermin. Finally he lifted the rope of the alarm bell and placed the end of it on the table, fixing the extreme end under the lamp. As he handled it he could not help noticing how pliable it was, especially for so strong a rope, and one not in use. "You could hang a man with it," he thought to himself. When his preparations were made he looked around, and said complacently:

"There now, my friend, I think we shall learn something of you this time!" He began his work again, and though as before somewhat disturbed at first by the noise of the rats, soon lost himself in his propositions and problems.

Again he was called to his immediate surroundings suddenly. This time it might not have been the sudden silence only which took his attention; there was a slight movement of the rope, and the lamp moved. Without stirring, he looked to see if his pile of books was within range, and then cast his eye along the rope. As he looked he saw the great rat drop from the rope on the oak armchair and sit there glaring at him. He raised a book in his right hand, and taking careful aim, flung it at the rat. The latter, with a quick movement, sprang aside and dodged the missile. He then took another book, and a third, and flung them one after another at the rat, but each time unsuccessfully. At last, as he stood with a book poised in his hand to throw, the rat squeaked and seemed afraid. This made Malcolmson more than ever eager to strike, and the book flew and struck the rat a resounding blow. It gave a terrified squeak, and turning on his pursuer a look of terrible malevolence, ran up the chair-back and made a great jump to the rope of the alarm bell and ran up it like lightning. The lamp rocked under the sudden strain, but it was a heavy one and did not topple over. Malcolmson kept his eyes on the rat, and saw it by the light of the second lamp leap to a moulding of the wainscot and disappear through a hole in one of the great pictures which hung on the wall, obscured and invisible through its coating of dirt and dust.

"I shall look up my friend's habitation in the morning," said the student, as he went over to collect his books. "The third picture from the fireplace; I shall not forget." He picked up the books one by one, commenting on them as he lifted them. "*Conic Sections* he does not mind, nor *Cycloidal Oscillations*, nor the *Principia*, nor *Quaternions*, nor *Thermodynamics*. Now for the book that fetched him!" Malcolmson took it up and looked at it. As he did so he started, and a sudden pallor overspread his face. He looked round uneasily and shivered slightly, as he murmured to himself:

"The Bible my mother gave me! What an odd coincidence." He sat down to work again, and the rats in the wainscot renewed their gambols. They did not disturb him, however; somehow their presence gave him a sense of companionship. But he could not attend to his work, and after striving to master the subject on which he was engaged gave it up in despair, and went to bed as the first streak of dawn stole in through the eastern window.

He slept heavily but uneasily, and dreamed much; and when Mrs. Dempster woke him late in the morning he seemed ill at ease, and for a few minutes did not seem to realise exactly where he was. His first request rather surprised the servant.

"Mrs. Dempster, when I am out to-day I wish you would get the steps and dust or wash those pictures—specially that one the third from the fireplace—I want to see what they are."

Late in the afternoon Malcolmson worked at his books in the shaded walk, and the cheerfulness of the previous day came back to him as the day wore on, and he found that his reading was progressing well. He had worked out to a satisfactory conclusion all the problems which had as yet baffled him, and it was in a state of jubilation that he paid a visit to Mrs. Witham at "The Good Traveller." He found a stranger in the cosy sitting-room with the landlady, who was introduced to him as Dr. Thornhill. She was not quite at ease, and this, combined with the doctor's plunging at once into a series of questions, made Malcolmson come to the conclusion that his presence was not an accident, so without preliminary he said:

"Dr. Thornhill, I shall with pleasure answer you any question you may choose to ask me if you will answer me one question first."

The doctor seemed surprised, but he smiled and answered at once, "Done! What is it?"

"Did Mrs. Witham ask you to come here and see me and advise me?"

Dr. Thornhill for a moment was taken aback, and Mrs. Witham got fiery red and turned away; but the doctor was a frank and ready man, and he answered at once and openly:

"She did: but she didn't intend you to know it. I suppose it was my clumsy haste that made you suspect. She told me that she did not like the idea of your being in that house all by yourself, and that she thought you took too much strong tea. In fact, she wants me to advise you if possible to give up the tea and the very late hours. I was a keen student in my time, so I suppose I may take the liberty of a college man, and without offence, advise you not quite as a stranger."

Malcolmson with a bright smile held out his hand. "Shake! as they say in America," he said. "I must thank you for your kindness and Mrs. Witham too, and your kindness deserves a return on my part. I promise to take no more strong tea—no tea at all till you let me—and I shall go to bed to-night at one o'clock at latest. Will that do?"

"Capital," said the doctor. "Now tell us all that you noticed in the old house," and so Malcolmson then and there told in minute detail all that had happened in the last two nights. He was interrupted every now and then by some exclamation from Mrs. Witham, till finally when he told of the episode of the Bible the landlady's pent-up emotions found vent in a shriek; and it was not till a stiff glass of brandy and water had been administered that she grew composed again. Dr. Thornhill listened with a face of growing gravity, and when the narrative was complete and Mrs. Witham had been restored he asked:

"The rat always went up the rope of the alarm bell?"

"Always."

"I suppose you know," said the Doctor after a pause, "what the rope is?"

"No!"

"It is," said the Doctor slowly, "the very rope which the hangman used for all the victims of the Judge's judicial rancour!" Here he was interrupted by another scream from Mrs. Witham, and steps had to be taken for her recovery. Malcolmson having looked at his watch, and found that it was close to his dinner hour, had gone home before her complete recovery.

When Mrs. Witham was herself again she almost assailed the Doctor with angry questions as to what he meant by putting such horrible ideas into the poor young man's mind. "He has quite enough there already to upset him," she added. Dr. Thornhill replied.

"My dear madam, I had a distinct purpose in it! I wanted to draw his attention to the bell rope, and to fix it there. It may be that he is in a highly overwrought state, and has been studying too much, although I am bound to say that he seems as sound and healthy a young man, mentally and bodily, as ever I saw—but then the rats—and that suggestion of the devil." The doctor shook his head and went on. "I would have offered to go and stay the first night with him but that I felt sure it would have been a cause of offence. He may get in the night some strange fright or hallucination; and if he does I want him to pull that rope. All alone as he is it will give us warning, and we may reach him in time to be of service. I shall be sitting up pretty late to-night and shall keep my ears open. Do not be alarmed if Benchurch gets a surprise before morning."

"Oh, Doctor, what do you mean? What do you mean?"

"I mean this; that possibly—nay, more probably—we shall hear the great alarm bell from the Judge's House to-night," and the Doctor made about as effective an exit as could be thought of.

When Malcolmson arrived home he found that it was a little after his usual time, and Mrs. Dempster had gone away—the rules of Greenhow's Charity were not to be neglected. He was glad to see that the place was bright and tidy with a cheerful fire and a well-trimmed lamp. The evening was colder than might have been expected in April, and a heavy wind was blowing with such rapidly-increasing strength that there was every promise of a storm during the night. For a few minutes after his entrance the noise of the rats ceased; but so soon as they became accustomed to his presence they began again. He was glad to hear them, for he felt once more the feeling of companionship in their noise, and his mind ran back to the strange fact that they only ceased to manifest themselves when that other—the great rat with the baleful eyes—came upon the scene. The reading-lamp only was lit and its green shade kept the ceiling and the upper part of the room in darkness, so that the cheerful light from the hearth spreading over the floor and shining on the white cloth laid over the end of the table was warm and cheery. Malcolmson sat down to his dinner with a good appetite and a buoyant spirit. After his dinner and a cigarette he sat steadily down to work, determined not to let anything disturb him, for he remembered his promise to the doctor, and made up his mind to make the best of the time at his disposal.

For an hour or so he worked all right, and then his thoughts began to wander from his books. The actual circumstances around him, the calls on his physical attention, and his nervous susceptibility were not to be denied. By this time the wind had become a gale, and the gale a storm. The old house, solid though it was, seemed to shake to its foundations, and the storm roared and raged through its many chimneys and its queer old gables, producing strange, unearthly sounds in the empty rooms and corridors. Even the great alarm bell on the roof must have felt the force of the wind, for the rope rose and fell slightly, as though the bell were moved a little from time to time, and the limber rope fell on the oak floor with a hard and hollow sound.

As Malcolmson listened to it he bethought himself of the doctor's words, "It is the rope which the hangman used for the victims of the Judge's judicial rancour," and he went over to the corner of the fireplace and took it in his hand to look at it. There seemed a sort of deadly interest in it, and as he stood there he lost himself for a moment in speculation as to who these victims were, and the grim wish of the Judge to have such a ghastly relic ever under his eyes. As he stood there the swaying of the bell on the roof still lifted the rope now and again; but presently there came a new sensation—a sort of tremor in the rope, as though something was moving along it.

Looking up instinctively Malcolmson saw the great rat coming slowly down towards him, glaring at him steadily. He dropped the rope and started back with a muttered curse, and the rat turning ran up the rope again and disappeared, and at the same instant Malcolmson became conscious that the noise of the rats, which had ceased for a while, began again.

All this set him thinking, and it occurred to him that he had not investigated the lair of the rat or looked at the pictures, as he had intended. He lit the other lamp without the shade, and, holding it up, went and stood opposite the third picture from the fireplace on the right-hand side where he had seen the rat disappear on the previous night.

At the first glance he started back so suddenly that he almost dropped the lamp, and a deadly pallor overspread his face. His knees shook, and heavy drops of sweat came on his forehead, and he trembled like an aspen. But he was young and plucky, and pulled himself together, and after the pause of a few seconds stepped forward again, raised the lamp, and examined the picture which had been dusted and washed, and now stood out clearly.

It was of a judge dressed in his robes of scarlet and ermine. His face was strong and merciless, evil, crafty, and vindictive, with a sensual mouth, hooked nose of ruddy colour, and shaped like the beak of a bird of prey. The rest of the face was of a cadaverous colour. The eyes were of peculiar brilliance and with a terribly malignant expression. As he looked at them, Malcolmson grew cold, for he saw there the very counterpart of the eyes of the great rat. The lamp almost fell from his hand, he saw the rat with its baleful eyes peering out through the hole in the corner of the picture, and noted the sudden cessation of the noise of the other rats. However, he pulled himself together, and went on with his examination of the picture.

The Judge was seated in a great high-backed carved oak chair, on the right-hand side of a great stone fireplace where, in the corner, a rope hung down from the ceiling, its end lying coiled on the floor. With a feeling of something like horror, Malcolmson recognised the scene of the room as it stood, and gazed around him in an awestruck manner as though he expected to find some strange presence behind him. Then he looked over to the corner of the fireplace—and with a loud cry he let the lamp fall from his hand.

There, in the Judge's armchair, with the rope hanging behind, sat the rat with the Judge's baleful eyes, now intensified and with a fiendish leer. Save for the howling of the storm without there was silence.

The fallen lamp recalled Malcolmson to himself. Fortunately it was of metal, and so the oil was not spilt. However, the practical need of attending to it settled at once his nervous apprehensions. When he had turned it out, he wiped his brow and thought for a moment.

"This will not do," he said to himself. "If I go on like this I shall become a crazy fool. This must stop! I promised the doctor I would not take tea. Faith, he was pretty right! My nerves must have been getting into a queer state. Funny I did not notice it. I never felt better in my life. However, it is all right now, and I shall not be such a fool again."

Then he mixed himself a good stiff glass of brandy and water and resolutely sat down to his work.

It was nearly an hour when he looked up from his book, disturbed by the sudden stillness. Without, the wind howled and roared louder than ever, and the rain drove in sheets against the windows, beating like hail on the glass; but within there was no sound whatever save the echo of the wind as it roared in the great chimney, and now and then a hiss as a few raindrops found their way down the chimney in a lull of the storm. The fire had fallen low and had ceased to flame, though it threw out a red glow. Malcolmson listened attentively, and presently heard a thin, squeaking noise, very faint. It came from the corner of the room where the rope hung down, and he thought it was the creaking of the rope on the floor as the swaying of the bell raised and lowered it. Looking up, however, he saw in the dim light the great rat clinging to the rope and gnawing it. The rope was already nearly gnawed through—he could see the lighter colour where the strands were laid bare. As he looked the job was completed, and the severed end of the rope fell clattering on the oaken floor, whilst for an instant the great rat remained like a knob or tassel at the end of the rope, which now began to sway to and fro. Malcolmson felt for a moment another pang of terror as he thought that now the possibility of calling the outer world to his assistance was cut off, but an intense anger took its place, and seizing the book he was reading he hurled it at the rat. The blow was well aimed, but before the missile could reach him the rat dropped off and struck the floor with a soft thud. Malcolmson instantly rushed over towards him, but it darted away and disappeared in the darkness of the shadows of the room. Malcolmson felt that his work was over for the night, and determined then and there to vary the monotony of the proceedings by a hunt for the rat, and took off the green shade of the lamp so as to insure a wider spreading light. As he did so the gloom of the upper part of the room was relieved, and in the new flood of light, great by comparison with the previous darkness, the pictures on the wall stood out boldly. From where he stood, Malcolmson saw right opposite to him the third picture on the wall from the right of the fireplace. He rubbed his eyes in surprise, and then a great fear began to come upon him.

In the centre of the picture was a great irregular patch of brown canvas, as fresh as when it was stretched on the frame. The background was as before, with chair and chimney-corner and rope, but the figure of the Judge had disappeared.

Malcolmson, almost in a chill of horror, turned slowly round, and then he began to shake and tremble like a man in a palsy. His strength seemed to have left him, and he was incapable of action or movement, hardly even of thought. He could only see and hear.

There, on the great high-backed carved oak chair sat the Judge in his robes of scarlet and ermine, with his baleful eyes glaring vindictively, and a smile of triumph on, the resolute, cruel mouth, as he lifted with his hands a *black cap*. Malcolmson felt as if the blood was running from his heart, as one does in moments of prolonged suspense. There was a singing in his ears. Without, he could hear the roar and howl of the tempest, and through it, swept on the storm, came the striking of midnight by the great chimes in the market place. He stood for a space of time that seemed to him endless still as a statue, and with wide-open, horror-struck eyes, breathless. As the clock struck, so the smile of triumph on the Judge's face intensified, and at the last stroke of midnight he placed the black cap on his head.

Slowly and deliberately the Judge rose from his chair and picked up the piece of the rope of the alarm bell which lay on the floor, drew it through his hands as if he enjoyed its touch, and then deliberately began to knot one end of it, fashioning it into a noose. This he tightened and tested with his foot, pulling hard at it till he was satisfied and then making a running noose of it, which he held in his hand. Then he began to move along the table on the opposite side to Malcolmson keeping his eyes on him until he had passed him, when with a quick movement he stood in front of the door. Malcolmson then began to feel that he was trapped, and tried to think of what he should do. There was some fascination in the Judge's eyes, which he never took off him, and he had, perforce, to look. He saw the Judge approach—still keeping between him and the door—and raise the noose and throw it towards him as if to entangle him. With a great effort he made a quick movement to one side, and saw the rope fall beside him, and heard it strike the oaken floor. Again the Judge raised the noose and tried to ensnare him, ever keeping his baleful eyes fixed on him, and each time by a mighty effort the student just managed to evade it. So this went on for many times, the Judge seeming never discouraged nor discomposed at failure, but playing as a cat does with a mouse. At last in despair, which had reached its climax, Malcolmson cast a quick glance round him. The lamp seemed to have blazed up, and there was a fairly good light in the room. At the many rat-holes and in the chinks and crannies of the wainscot he saw the rats' eyes; and this aspect, that was purely physical, gave him a gleam of comfort. He looked around and saw that the rope of the great alarm bell was laden with rats. Every inch of it was covered with them, and more and more were pouring through the small circular hole in the ceiling whence it emerged, so that with their weight the bell was beginning to sway.

Hark! it had swayed till the clapper had touched the bell. The sound was but a tiny one, but the bell was only beginning to sway, and it would increase.

At the sound the Judge, who had been keeping his eyes fixed on Malcolmson, looked up, and a scowl of diabolical anger overspread his face. His eyes fairly glowed like hot coals, and he stamped his foot with a sound that seemed to make the house shake. A dreadful peal of thunder broke overhead as he raised the rope again, whilst the rats kept running up and down the rope as though working against time. This time, instead of throwing it, he drew close to his victim, and held open the noose as he approached. As he came closer there seemed something paralysing in his very presence, and Malcolmson stood rigid as a corpse. He felt the Judge's icy fingers touch his throat as he adjusted the rope. The noose tightened—tightened. Then the Judge, taking the rigid form of the student in his arms, carried him over and placed him standing in the oak chair, and stepping up beside him, put his hand up and caught the end of the swaying rope of the alarm bell. As he raised his hand the rats fled squeaking, and disappeared through the hole in the ceiling. Taking the end of the noose which was round Malcolmson's neck he tied it to the hanging-bell rope, and then descending pulled away the chair.

When the alarm bell of the Judge's House began to sound a crowd soon assembled. Lights and torches of various kinds appeared, and soon a silent crowd was hurrying to the spot. They knocked loudly at the door, but there was no reply. Then they burst in the door, and poured into the great dining-room, the doctor at the head.

There at the end of the rope of the great alarm bell hung the body of the student, and on the face of the Judge in the picture was a malignant smile.

THE SECRET OF
THE GROWING GOLD

WHEN Margaret Delandre went to live at Brent's Rock the whole neighbourhood awoke to the pleasure of an entirely new scandal. Scandals in connection with either the Delandre family or the Brents of Brent's Rock, were not few; and if the secret history of the county had been written in full both names would have been found well represented. It is true that the status of each was so different that they might have belonged to different continents—or to different worlds for the matter of that—for hitherto their orbits had never crossed. The Brents were accorded by the whole section of the country an unique social dominance, and had ever held themselves as high above the yeoman class to which Margaret Delandre belonged, as a blue-blooded Spanish hidalgo out-tops his peasant tenantry.

The Delandres had an ancient record and were proud of it in their way as the Brents were of theirs. But the family had never risen above yeomanry; and although they had been once well-to-do in the good old times of foreign wars and protection, their fortunes had withered under the scorching of the free trade sun and the "piping times of peace." They had, as the elder members used to assert, "stuck to the land," with the result that they had taken root in it, body and soul. In fact, they, having chosen the life of vegetables, had flourished as vegetation does—blossomed and thrived in the good season and suffered in the bad. Their holding, Dander's Croft, seemed to have been worked out, and to be typical of the family which had inhabited it. The latter had declined generation after generation, sending out now and again some abortive shoot of unsatisfied energy in the shape of a soldier or sailor, who had worked his way to the minor grades of the services and had there stopped, cut short either from unheeding gallantry in action or from that destroying cause to men without breeding or youthful care—the recognition of a position above them which they feel unfitted to fill. So, little by little, the family dropped lower and lower, the men brooding and dissatisfied, and drinking themselves into the grave, the women drudging at home, or marrying beneath them—or worse. In process of time all disappeared, leaving only two in the Croft, Wykham Delandre and his sister Margaret. The man and woman seemed to have inherited in masculine and feminine form respectively the evil tendency of their race, sharing in common the principles, though manifesting them in different ways, of sullen passion, voluptuousness and recklessness.

The history of the Brents had been something similar, but showing the causes of decadence in their aristocratic and not their plebeian forms. They, too, had sent their shoots to the wars; but their positions had been different, and they had often attained honour—for without flaw they were gallant, and brave deeds were done by them before the selfish dissipation which marked them had sapped their vigour.

The present head of the family—if family it could now be called when one remained of the direct line—was Geoffrey Brent. He was almost a type of a worn-out race, manifesting in some ways its most brilliant qualities, and in others its utter degradation. He might be fairly compared with some of those antique Italian nobles whom the painters have preserved to us with their courage, their unscrupulousness, their refinement of lust and cruelty—the voluptuary actual with the fiend potential. He was certainly handsome, with that dark, aquiline, commanding beauty which women so generally recognise as dominant. With men he was distant and cold; but such a bearing never deters womankind. The inscrutable laws of sex have so arranged that even a timid woman is not afraid of a fierce and haughty man. And so it was that there was hardly a woman of any kind or degree, who lived within view of Brent's Rock, who did not cherish some form of secret admiration for the handsome wastrel. The category was a wide one, for Brent's Rock rose up steeply from the midst of a level region and for a circuit of a hundred miles it lay on the horizon, with its high old towers and steep roofs cutting the level edge of wood and hamlet, and far-scattered mansions.

So long as Geoffrey Brent confined his dissipations to London and Paris and Vienna—anywhere out of sight and sound of his home—opinion was silent. It is easy to listen to far off echoes unmoved, and we can treat them with disbelief, or scorn, or disdain, or whatever attitude of coldness may suit our purpose. But when the scandal came close home it was another matter; and the feelings of independence and integrity which is in people of every community which is not utterly spoiled, asserted itself and demanded that condemnation should be expressed. Still there was a certain reticence in all, and no more notice was taken of the existing facts than was absolutely necessary. Margaret Delandre bore herself so fearlessly and so openly—she accepted her position as the justified companion of Geoffrey Brent so naturally that people came to believe that she was secretly married to him, and therefore thought it wiser to hold their tongues lest time should justify her and also make her an active enemy.

The one person who, by his interference, could have settled all doubts was debarred by circumstances from interfering in the matter. Wykham Delandre had quarrelled with his sister—or perhaps it was that she had quarrelled with him—and they were on terms not merely of armed neutrality but of bitter hatred. The quarrel had been antecedent to Margaret going to Brent's Rock. She and Wykham had almost come to blows. There had certainly been threats on one side and on the other; and in the end Wykham overcome with passion, had ordered his sister to leave his house. She had risen straightway, and, without waiting to pack up even her own personal belongings, had walked out of the house. On the threshold she had paused for a moment to hurl a bitter threat at Wykham that he would rue in shame and despair to the last hour of his life his act of that day. Some weeks had since passed; and it was understood in the neighbourhood that Margaret had gone to London, when she suddenly appeared driving out with Geoffrey Brent, and the entire neighbourhood knew before nightfall that she had taken up her abode at the Rock. It was no subject of surprise that Brent had come back unexpectedly, for such was his usual custom. Even his own servants never knew when to expect him, for there was a private door, of which he alone had the key, by which he sometimes entered without anyone in the house being aware of his coming. This was his usual method of appearing after a long absence.

Wykham Delandre was furious at the news. He vowed vengeance— and to keep his mind level with his passion drank deeper than ever. He tried several times to see his sister, but she contemptuously refused to meet him. He tried to have an interview with Brent and was refused by him also. Then he tried to stop him in the road, but without avail, for Geoffrey was not a man to be stopped against his will. Several actual encounters took place between the two men, and many more were threatened and avoided. At last Wykham Delandre settled down to a morose, vengeful acceptance of the situation.

Neither Margaret nor Geoffrey was of a pacific temperament, and it was not long before there began to be quarrels between them. One thing would lead to another, and wine flowed freely at Brent's Rock. Now and again the quarrels would assume a bitter aspect, and threats would be exchanged in uncompromising language that fairly awed the listening servants. But such quarrels generally ended where domestic altercations do, in reconciliation, and in a mutual respect for the fighting qualities proportionate to their manifestation. Fighting for its own sake is found by a certain class of persons, all the world over, to be a matter of absorbing interest, and there is no reason to believe that domestic conditions minimise its potency. Geoffrey and Margaret made occasional absences from Brent's Rock, and on each of these occasions Wykham Delandre also absented himself; but as he generally heard of the absence too late to be of any service, he returned home each time in a more bitter and discontented frame of mind than before.

At last there came a time when the absence from Brent's Rock became longer than before. Only a few days earlier there had been a quarrel, exceeding in bitterness anything which had gone before; but this, too, had been made up, and a trip on the Continent had been mentioned before the servants. After a few days Wykham Delandre also went away, and it was some weeks before he returned. It was noticed that he was full of some new importance—satisfaction, exaltation—they hardly knew how to call it. He went straightway to Brent's Rock, and demanded to see Geoffrey Brent, and on being told that he had not yet returned, said, with a grim decision which the servants noted:

"I shall come again. My news is solid—it can wait!" and turned away. Week after week went by, and month after month; and then there came a rumour, certified later on, that an accident had occurred in the Zermatt valley. Whilst crossing a dangerous pass the carriage containing an English lady and the driver had fallen over a precipice, the gentleman of the party, Mr. Geoffrey Brent, having been fortunately saved as he had been walking up the hill to ease the horses. He gave information, and search was made. The broken rail, the excoriated roadway, the marks where the horses had struggled on the decline before finally pitching over into the torrent—all told the sad tale. It was a wet season, and there had been much snow in the winter, so that the river was swollen beyond its usual volume, and the eddies of the stream were packed with ice. All search was made, and finally the wreck of the carriage and the body of one horse were found in an eddy of the river. Later on the body of the driver was found on the sandy, torrent-swept waste near Täsch; but the body of the lady, like that of the other horse, had quite disappeared, and was—what was left of it by that time—whirling amongst the eddies of the Rhone on its way down to the Lake of Geneva.

Wykham Delandre made all the enquiries possible, but could not find any trace of the missing woman. He found, however, in the books of the various hotels the name of "Mr. and Mrs. Geoffrey Brent." And he had a stone erected at Zermatt to his sister's memory, under her married name, and a tablet put up in the church at Bretten, the parish in which both Brent's Rock and Dander's Croft were situated.

There was a lapse of nearly a year, after the excitement of the matter had worn away, and the whole neighbourhood had gone on its accustomed way. Brent was still absent, and Delandre more drunken, more morose, and more revengeful than before.

Then there was a new excitement. Brent's Rock was being made ready for a new mistress. It was officially announced by Geoffrey himself in a letter to the Vicar, that he had been married some months before to an Italian lady, and that they were then on their way home. Then a small army of workmen invaded the house; and hammer and plane sounded, and a general air of size and paint pervaded the atmosphere. One wing of the old house, the south, was entirely re-done; and then the great body of the workmen departed, leaving only materials for the doing of the old hall when Geoffrey Brent should have returned, for he had directed that the decoration was only to be done under his own eyes. He had brought with him accurate drawings of a hall in the house of his bride's father, for he wished to reproduce for her the place to which she had been accustomed. As the moulding had all to be re-done, some scaffolding poles and boards were brought in and laid on one side of the great hall, and also a great wooden tank or box for mixing the lime, which was laid in bags beside it.

When the new mistress of Brent's Rock arrived the bells of the church rang out, and there was a general jubilation. She was a beautiful creature, full of the poetry and fire and passion of the South; and the few English words which she had learned were spoken in such a sweet and pretty broken way that she won the hearts of the people almost as much by the music of her voice as by the melting beauty of her dark eyes.

Geoffrey Brent seemed more happy than he had ever before appeared; but there was a dark, anxious look on his face that was new to those who knew him of old, and he started at times as though at some noise that was unheard by others.

And so months passed and the whisper grew that at last Brent's Rock was to have an heir. Geoffrey was very tender to his wife, and the new bond between them seemed to soften him. He took more interest in his tenants and their needs than he had ever done; and works of charity on his part as well as on his sweet young wife's were not lacking. He seemed to have set all his hopes on the child that was coming, and as he looked deeper into the future the dark shadow that had come over his face seemed to die gradually away.

All the time Wykham Delandre nursed his revenge. Deep in his heart had grown up a purpose of vengeance which only waited an opportunity to crystallise and take a definite shape. His vague idea was somehow centred in the wife of Brent, for he knew that he could strike him best through those he loved, and the coming time seemed to hold in its womb the opportunity for which he longed. One night he sat alone in the living-room of his house. It had once been a handsome room in its way, but time and neglect had done their work and it was now little better than a ruin, without dignity or picturesqueness of any kind. He had been drinking heavily for some time and was more than half stupefied. He thought he heard a noise as of someone at the door and looked up. Then he called half savagely to come in; but there was no response. With a muttered blasphemy he renewed his potations. Presently he forgot all around him, sank into a daze, but suddenly awoke to see standing before him some one or something like a battered, ghostly edition of his sister. For a few moments there came upon him a sort of fear. The woman before him, with distorted features and burning eyes seemed hardly human, and the only thing that seemed a reality of his sister, as she had been, was her wealth of golden hair, and this was now streaked with grey. She eyed her brother with a long, cold stare; and he, too, as he looked and began to realise the actuality of her presence, found the hatred of her which he had had, once again surging up in his heart. All the brooding passion of the past year seemed to find a voice at once as he asked her:—

"Why are you here? You're dead and buried."

"I am here, Wykham Delandre, for no love of you, but because I hate another even more than I do you!" A great passion blazed in her eyes.

"Him?" he asked, in so fierce a whisper that even the woman was for an instant startled till she regained her calm.

"Yes, him!" she answered. "But make no mistake, my revenge is my own; and I merely use you to help me to it." Wykham asked suddenly:

"Did he marry you?"

The woman's distorted face broadened out in a ghastly attempt at a smile. It was a hideous mockery, for the broken features and seamed scars took strange shapes and strange colours, and queer lines of white showed out as the straining muscles pressed on the old cicatrices.

"So you would like to know! It would please your pride to feel that your sister was truly married! Well, you shall not know. That was my revenge on you, and I do not mean to change it by a hair's breadth. I have come here to-night simply to let you know that I am alive, so that if any violence be done me where I am going there may be a witness."

"Where are you going?" demanded her brother.

"That is my affair! and I have not the least intention of letting you know!" Wykham stood up, but the drink was on him and he reeled and fell. As he lay on the floor he announced his intention of following his sister; and with an outburst of splenetic humour told her that he would follow her through the darkness by the light of her hair, and of her beauty. At this she turned on him, and said that there were others beside

132

him that would rue her hair and her beauty too. "As he will," she hissed; "for the hair remains though the beauty be gone. When he withdrew the lynch-pin and sent us over the precipice into the torrent, he had little thought of my beauty. Perhaps his beauty would be scarred like mine were he whirled, as I was, among the rocks of the Visp, and frozen on the ice pack in the drift of the river. But let him beware! His time is coming!" and with a fierce gesture she flung open the door and passed out into the night.

Later on that night, Mrs. Brent, who was but half-asleep, became suddenly awake and spoke to her husband:

"Geoffrey, was not that the click of a lock somewhere below our window?"

But Geoffrey—though she thought that he, too, had started at the noise—seemed sound asleep, and breathed heavily. Again Mrs. Brent dozed; but this time awoke to the fact that her husband had arisen and was partially dressed. He was deadly pale, and when the light of the lamp which he had in his hand fell on his face, she was frightened at the look in his eyes.

"What is it, Geoffrey? What dost thou?" she asked.

"Hush! little one," he answered, in a strange, hoarse voice. "Go to sleep. I am restless, and wish to finish some work I left undone."

"Bring it here, my husband," she said; "I am lonely and I fear when thou art away."

For reply he merely kissed her and went out, closing the door behind him. She lay awake for awhile, and then nature asserted itself, and she slept.

Suddenly she started broad awake with the memory in her ears of a smothered cry from somewhere not far off. She jumped up and ran to the door and listened, but there was no sound. She grew alarmed for her husband, and called out: "Geoffrey! Geoffrey!"

After a few moments the door of the great hall opened, and Geoffrey appeared at it, but without his lamp.

"Hush!" he said, in a sort of whisper, and his voice was harsh and stern. "Hush! Get to bed! I am working, and must not be disturbed. Go to sleep, and do not wake the house!"

With a chill in her heart—for the harshness of her husband's voice was new to her—she crept back to bed and lay there trembling, too frightened to cry, and listened to every sound. There was a long pause of silence, and then the sound of some iron implement striking muffled blows! Then there came a clang of a heavy stone falling, followed by a muffled curse. Then a dragging sound, and then more noise of stone on stone. She lay all the while in an agony of fear, and her heart beat dreadfully. She heard a curious sort of scraping sound; and then there was silence. Presently the door opened gently, and Geoffrey appeared. His wife pretended to be asleep; but through her eyelashes she saw him wash from his hands something white that looked like lime.

In the morning he made no allusion to the previous night, and she was afraid to ask any question.

From that day there seemed some shadow over Geoffrey Brent. He neither ate nor slept as he had been accustomed, and his former habit of turning suddenly as though someone were speaking from behind him revived. The old hall seemed to have some kind of fascination for him. He used to go there many times in the day, but grew impatient if anyone, even his wife, entered it. When the builder's foreman came to inquire about continuing his work Geoffrey was out driving; the man went into the hall, and when Geoffrey returned the servant told him of his arrival and where he was. With a frightful oath he pushed the servant aside and hurried up to the old hall. The workman met him almost at the door; and as Geoffrey burst into the room he ran against him. The man apologised:

"Beg pardon, sir, but I was just going out to make some enquiries. I directed twelve sacks of lime to be sent here, but I see there are only ten."

"Damn the ten sacks and the twelve too!" was the ungracious and incomprehensible rejoinder.

The workman looked surprised, and tried to turn the conversation.

"I see, sir, there is a little matter which our people must have done; but the governor will of course see it set right at his own cost."

"What do you mean?"

"That 'ere 'arth-stone, sir: Some idiot must have put a scaffold pole on it and cracked it right down the middle, and it's thick enough you'd think to stand hanythink." Geoffrey was silent for quite a minute, and then said in a constrained voice and with much gentler manner:

"Tell your people that I am not going on with the work in the hall at present. I want to leave it as it is for a while longer."

"All right sir. I'll send up a few of our chaps to take away these poles and lime bags and tidy the place up a bit."

"No! No!" said Geoffrey, "leave them where they are. I shall send and tell you when you are to get on with the work." So the foreman went away, and his comment to his master was:

"I'd send in the bill, sir, for the work already done. 'Pears to me that money's a little shaky in that quarter."

Once or twice Delandre tried to stop Brent on the road, and, at last, finding that he could not attain his object rode after the carriage, calling out:

"What has become of my sister, your wife." Geoffrey lashed his horses into a gallop, and the other, seeing from his white face and from his wife's collapse almost into a faint that his object was attained, rode away with a scowl and a laugh.

That night when Geoffrey went into the hall he passed over to the great fireplace, and all at once started back with a smothered cry. Then with an effort he pulled himself together and went away, returning with a light. He bent down over the broken hearth-stone to see if the moonlight falling through the storied window had in any way deceived him. Then with a groan of anguish he sank to his knees.

There, sure enough, through the crack in the broken stone were protruding a multitude of threads of golden hair just tinged with grey!

He was disturbed by a noise at the door, and looking round, saw his wife standing in the doorway. In the desperation of the moment he took action to prevent discovery, and lighting a match at the lamp, stooped down and burned away the hair that rose through the broken stone. Then rising nonchalantly as he could, he pretended surprise at seeing his wife beside him.

For the next week he lived in an agony; for, whether by accident or design, he could not find himself alone in the hall for any length of time. At each visit the hair had grown afresh through the crack, and he had to watch it carefully lest his terrible secret should be discovered. He tried to find a receptacle for the body of the murdered woman outside the house, but someone always interrupted him; and once, when he was coming out of the private doorway, he was met by his wife, who began to question him about it, and manifested surprise that she should not have before noticed the key which he now reluctantly showed her. Geoffrey dearly and passionately loved his wife, so that any possibility of her discovering his dread secrets, or even of doubting him, filled him with anguish; and after a couple of days had passed, he could not help coming to the conclusion that, at least, she suspected something.

That very evening she came into the hall after her drive and found him there sitting moodily by the deserted fireplace. She spoke to him directly.

"Geoffrey, I have been spoken to by that fellow Delandre, and he says horrible things. He tells to me that a week ago his sister returned to his house, the wreck and ruin of her former self, with only her golden hair as of old, and announced some fell intention. He asked me where she is—and oh, Geoffrey, she is dead, she is dead! So how can she have returned? Oh! I am in dread, and I know not where to turn!"

For answer, Geoffrey burst into a torrent of blasphemy which made her shudder. He cursed Delandre and his sister and all their kind, and in especial he hurled curse after curse on her golden hair.

"Oh, hush! hush!" she said, and was then silent, for she feared her husband when she saw the evil effect of his humour. Geoffrey in the torrent of his anger stood up and moved away from the hearth; but suddenly stopped as he saw a new look of terror in his wife's eyes. He followed their glance, and then he, too, shuddered—for there on the broken hearth-stone lay a golden streak as the points of the hair rose through the crack.

"Look, look!" she shrieked. "Is it some ghost of the dead! Come away—come away!" and seizing her husband by the wrist with the frenzy of madness, she pulled him from the room.

That night she was in a raging fever. The doctor of the district attended her at once, and special aid was telegraphed for to London. Geoffrey was in despair, and in his anguish at the danger of his young wife almost forgot his own crime and its consequences. In the evening the doctor had to leave to attend to others; but he left Geoffrey in charge of his wife. His last words were:

"Remember, you must humour her till I come in the morning, or till some other doctor has her case in hand. What you have to dread is another attack of emotion. See that she is kept warm. Nothing more can be done."

Late in the evening, when the rest of the household had retired, Geoffrey's wife got up from her bed and called to her husband.

"Come!" she said. "Come to the old hall! I know where the gold comes from! I want to see it grow!"

Geoffrey would fain have stopped her, but he feared for her life or reason on the one hand, and lest in a paroxysm she should shriek out her terrible suspicion, and seeing that it was useless to try to prevent her, wrapped a warm rug around her and went with her to the old hall. When they entered, she turned and shut the door and locked it.

"We want no strangers amongst us three to-night!" she whispered with a wan smile.

"We three! nay we are but two," said Geoffrey with a shudder; he feared to say more.

"Sit here," said his wife as she put out the light. "Sit here by the hearth and watch the gold growing. The silver moonlight is jealous! See it steals along the floor towards the gold—our gold!" Geoffrey looked with growing horror, and saw that during the hours that had passed the golden hair had protruded further through the broken hearth-stone. He tried to hide it by placing his feet over the broken place; and his wife, drawing her chair beside him, leant over and laid her head on his shoulder.

"Now do not stir, dear," she said; "let us sit still and watch. We shall find the secret of the growing gold!" He passed his arm round her and sat silent; and as the moonlight stole along the floor she sank to sleep.

He feared to wake her; and so sat silent and miserable as the hours stole away.

Before his horror-struck eyes the golden hair from the broken stone grew and grew; and as it increased, so his heart got colder and colder, till at last he had not power to stir, and sat with eyes full of terror watching his doom.

In the morning when the London doctor came, neither Geoffrey nor his wife could be found. Search was made in all the rooms, but without avail. As a last resource the great door of the old hall was broken open, and those who entered saw a grim and sorry sight.

There by the deserted hearth Geoffrey Brent and his young wife sat cold and white and dead. Her face was peaceful, and her eyes were closed in sleep; but his face was a sight that made all who saw it shudder, for there was on it a look of unutterable horror. The eyes were open and stared glassily at his feet, which were twined with tresses of golden hair, streaked with grey, which came through the broken hearth-stone.

THE SQUAW

NURNBERG at the time was not so much exploited as it has been since then. Irving had not been playing *Faust*, and the very name of the old town was hardly known to the great bulk of the travelling public. My wife and I being in the second week of our honeymoon, naturally wanted someone else to join our party, so that when the cheery stranger, Elias P. Hutcheson, hailing from Isthmian City, Bleeding Gulch, Maple Tree County, Neb., turned up at the station at Frankfort, and casually remarked that he was going on to see the most all-fired old Methusaleh of a town in Yurrup, and that he guessed that so much travelling alone was enough to send an intelligent, active citizen into the melancholy ward of a daft house, we took the pretty broad hint and suggested that we should join forces. We found, on comparing notes afterwards, that we had each intended to speak with some diffidence or hesitation so as not to appear too eager, such not being a good compliment to the success of our married life; but the effect was entirely marred by our both beginning to speak at the same instant—stopping simultaneously and then going on together again. Anyhow, no matter how, it was done; and Elias P. Hutcheson became one of our party. Straightway Amelia and I found the pleasant benefit; instead of quarrelling, as we had been doing, we found that the restraining influence of a third party was such that we now took every opportunity of spooning in odd corners. Amelia declares that ever since she has, as the result of that experience, advised all her friends to take a friend on the honeymoon. Well, we "did" Nurnberg together, and much enjoyed the racy remarks of our Transatlantic friend, who, from his quaint speech and his wonderful stock of adventures, might have stepped out of a novel. We kept for the last object of interest in the city to be visited the Burg, and on the day appointed for the visit strolled round the outer wall of the city by the eastern side.

The Burg is seated on a rock dominating the town, and an immensely deep fosse guards it on the northern side. Nurnberg has been happy in that it was never sacked; had it been it would certainly not be so spick and span perfect as it is at present. The ditch has not been used for centuries, and now its base is spread with tea-gardens and orchards, of which some of the trees are of quite respectable growth. As we wandered round the wall, dawdling in the hot July sunshine, we often paused to admire the views spread before us, and in especial the great plain covered with towns and villages and bounded with a blue line of hills, like a landscape of Claude Lorraine. From this we always turned with new delight to the city itself, with its myriad of quaint old gables and acre-wide red roofs dotted with dormer windows, tier upon tier. A little to our right rose the towers of the Burg, and nearer still, standing grim, the Torture Tower, which was, and is, perhaps, the most interesting place in the city. For centuries the tradition of the Iron Virgin of Nurnberg has been handed down as an instance of the horrors of cruelty of which man is capable; we had long looked forward to seeing it; and here at last was its home.

In one of our pauses we leaned over the wall of the moat and looked down. The garden seemed quite fifty or sixty feet below us, and the sun pouring into it with an intense, moveless heat like that of an oven. Beyond rose the grey, grim wall seemingly of endless height, and losing itself right and left in the angles of bastion and counterscarp. Trees and bushes crowned the wall, and above again towered the lofty houses on whose massive beauty Time has only set the hand of approval. The sun was hot and we were lazy; time was our own, and we lingered, leaning on the wall.

Just below us was a pretty sight—a great black cat lying stretched in the sun, whilst round her gambolled prettily a tiny black kitten. The mother would wave her tail for the kitten to play with, or would raise her feet and push away the little one as an encouragement to further play. They were just at the foot of the wall, and Elias P. Hutcheson, in order to help the play, stooped and took from the walk a moderate sized pebble.

"See!" he said, "I will drop it near the kitten, and they will both wonder where it came from."

"Oh, be careful," said my wife; "you might hit the dear little thing!"

"Not me, ma'am," said Elias P. "Why, I'm as tender as a Maine cherry-tree. Lor, bless ye, I wouldn't hurt the poor pooty little critter more'n I'd scalp a baby. An' you may bet your variegated socks on that! See, I'll drop it fur away on the outside so's not to go near her!" Thus saying, he leaned over and held his arm out at full length and dropped the stone. It may be that there is some attractive force which draws lesser matters to greater; or more probably that the wall was not plumb but sloped to its base—we not noticing the inclination from above; but the stone fell with a sickening thud that came up to us through the hot air, right on the kitten's head, and shattered out its little brains then and there. The black cat cast a swift upward glance, and we saw her eyes like green fire fixed an instant on Elias P. Hutcheson; and then her attention was given to the kitten, which lay still with just a quiver of her tiny limbs, whilst a thin red stream trickled from a gaping wound. With a muffled cry, such as a human being might give, she bent over the kitten, licking its wound and moaning. Suddenly she seemed to realise that it was dead, and again threw her eyes up at us. I shall never forget the sight, for she looked the perfect incarnation of hate. Her green eyes blazed with lurid fire, and the white, sharp teeth seemed to almost shine through the blood which dabbled her mouth and whiskers. She gnashed her teeth, and her claws stood out stark and at full length on every paw. Then she made a wild rush up the wall as if to reach us, but when the momentum ended fell back, and further added to her horrible appearance for she fell on the kitten, and rose with her black fur smeared with its brains and blood. Amelia turned quite faint, and I had to lift her back from the wall. There was a seat close by in shade of a spreading plane-tree, and here I placed her whilst she composed herself. Then I went back to Hutcheson, who stood without moving, looking down on the angry cat below.

As I joined him, he said:

"Wall, I guess that air the savagest beast I ever see—'cept once when an Apache squaw had an edge on a half-breed what they nicknamed 'Splinters' 'cos of the way he fixed up her papoose which he stole on a raid just to show that he appreciated the way they had given his mother the fire torture. She got that kinder look so set on her face that it jest seemed to grow there. She followed Splinters more'n three year till at last the braves got him and handed him over to her. They did say that no man, white or Injun, had ever been so long a-dying under the tortures of the Apaches. The only time I ever see her smile was when I wiped her out. I kem on the camp just in time to see Splinters pass in his checks, and he wasn't sorry to go either. He was a hard citizen, and though I never could shake with him after that papoose business—for it was bitter bad, and he should have been a white man, for he looked like one—I see he had got paid out in full. Durn me, but I took a piece of his hide from one of his skinnin' posts an' had it made into a pocketbook. It's here now!" and he slapped the breast pocket of his coat.

Whilst he was speaking the cat was continuing her frantic efforts to get up the wall. She would take a run back and then charge up, sometimes reaching an incredible height. She did not seem to mind the heavy fall which she got each time but started with renewed vigour; and at every tumble her appearance became more horrible. Hutcheson was a kind-hearted man—my wife and I had both noticed little acts of kindness to animals as well as to persons—and he seemed concerned at the state of fury to which the cat had wrought herself.

"Wall, now!" he said, "I du declare that that poor critter seems quite desperate. There! there! poor thing, it was all an accident—though that won't bring back your little one to you. Say! I wouldn't have had such a thing happen for a thousand! Just shows what a clumsy fool of a man can do when he tries to play! Seems I'm too darned slipperhanded to even play with a cat. Say Colonel!" it was a pleasant way he had to bestow titles freely—"I hope your wife don't hold no grudge against me on account of this unpleasantness? Why, I wouldn't have had it occur on no account."

He came over to Amelia and apologised profusely, and she with her usual kindness of heart hastened to assure him that she quite understood that it was an accident. Then we all went again to the wall and looked over.

The cat missing Hutcheson's face had drawn back across the moat, and was sitting on her haunches as though ready to spring. Indeed, the very instant she saw him she did spring, and with a blind unreasoning fury, which would have been grotesque, only that it was so frightfully real. She did not try to run up the wall, but simply launched herself at him as though hate and fury could lend her wings to pass straight through the great distance between them. Amelia, womanlike, got quite concerned, and said to Elias P. in a warning voice:

"Oh! you must be very careful. That animal would try to kill you if she were here; her eyes look like positive murder."

He laughed out jovially. "Excuse me, ma'am," he said, "but I can't help laughin'. Fancy a man that has fought grizzlies an' Injuns bein' careful of bein' murdered by a cat!"

When the cat heard him laugh, her whole demeanour seemed to change. She no longer tried to jump or run up the wall, but went quietly over, and sitting again beside the dead kitten began to lick and fondle it as though it were alive.

"See!" said I, "the effect of a really strong man. Even that animal in the midst of her fury recognises the voice of a master, and bows to him!"

"Like a squaw!" was the only comment of Elias P. Hutcheson, as we moved on our way round the city fosse. Every now and then we looked over the wall and each time saw the cat following us. At first she had kept going back to the dead kitten, and then as the distance grew greater took it in her mouth and so followed. After a while, however, she abandoned this, for we saw her following all alone; she had evidently hidden the body somewhere. Amelia's alarm grew at the cat's persistence, and more than once she repeated her warning; but the American always laughed with amusement, till finally, seeing that she was beginning to be worried, he said:

"I say, ma'am, you needn't be skeered over that cat. I go heeled, I du!" Here he slapped his pistol pocket at the back of his lumbar region. "Why sooner'n have you worried, I'll shoot the critter, right here, an' risk the police interferin' with a citizen of the United States for carryin' arms contrairy to reg'lations!" As he spoke he looked over the wall, but the cat, on seeing him, retreated, with a growl, into a bed of tall flowers, and was hidden. He went on: "Blest if that ar critter ain't got more sense of what's good for her than most Christians. I guess we've seen the last of her! You bet, she'll go back now to that busted kitten and have a private funeral of it, all to herself!"

Amelia did not like to say more, lest he might, in mistaken kindness to her, fulfil his threat of shooting the cat: and so we went on and crossed the little wooden bridge leading to the gateway whence ran the steep paved roadway between the Burg and the pentagonal Torture Tower. As we crossed the bridge we saw the cat again down below us. When she saw us her fury seemed to return, and she made frantic efforts to get up the steep wall. Hutcheson laughed as he looked down at her, and said:

"Good-bye, old girl. Sorry I in-jured your feelin's, but you'll get over it in time! So long!" And then we passed through the long, dim archway and came to the gate of the Burg.

When we came out again after our survey of this most beautiful old place which not even the well-intentioned efforts of the Gothic restorers of forty years ago have been able to spoil—though their restoration was then glaring white—we seemed to have quite forgotten the unpleasant episode of the morning. The old lime tree with its great trunk gnarled with the passing of nearly nine centuries, the deep well cut through the heart of the rock by those captives of old, and the lovely view from the city wall whence we heard, spread over almost a full quarter of an hour, the multitudinous chimes of the city, had all helped to wipe out from our minds the incident of the slain kitten.

We were the only visitors who had entered the Torture Tower that morning—so at least said the old custodian—and as we had the place all to ourselves were able to make a minute and more satisfactory survey than would have otherwise been possible. The custodian, looking to us as the sole source of his gains for the day, was willing to meet our wishes in any way. The Torture Tower is truly a grim place, even now when many thousands of visitors have sent a stream of life, and the joy that follows life, into the place; but at the time I mention it wore its grimmest and most gruesome aspect. The dust of ages seemed to have settled on it, and the darkness and the horror of its memories seem to have become sentient in a way that would have satisfied the Pantheistic souls of Philo or Spinoza. The lower chamber where we entered was seemingly, in its normal state, filled with incarnate darkness; even the hot sunlight streaming in through the door seemed to be lost in the vast thickness of the walls, and only showed the masonry rough as when the builder's scaffolding had come down, but coated with dust and marked here and there with patches of dark stain which, if walls could speak, could have given their own dread memories of fear and pain. We were glad to pass up the dusty wooden staircase, the custodian leaving the outer door open to light us somewhat on our way; for to our eyes the one long-wick'd, evil-smelling candle stuck in a sconce on the wall gave an inadequate light. When we came up through the open trap in the corner of the chamber overhead, Amelia held on to me so tightly that I could actually feel her heart beat. I must say for my own part that I was not surprised at her fear, for this room was even more gruesome than that below. Here there was certainly more light, but only just sufficient to realise the horrible surroundings of the place. The builders of the tower had evidently intended that only they who should gain the top should have any of the joys of light and prospect. There, as we had noticed from below, were ranges of windows, albeit of mediæval smallness, but elsewhere in the tower were only a very few narrow slits such as were habitual in places of mediæval defence. A few of these only lit the chamber, and these so high up in the wall that from no part could the sky be seen through the thickness of the walls. In racks, and leaning in disorder against the walls, were a number of headsmen's swords, great double-handed weapons with broad blade and keen edge. Hard by were several blocks whereon the necks of the victims had lain, with here and there deep notches where the steel had bitten through the guard of flesh and shored into the wood. Round the chamber, placed in all sorts of irregular ways, were many implements of torture which made one's heart ache to see—chairs full of spikes which gave instant and excruciating pain; chairs and couches with dull knobs whose torture was seemingly less, but which, though slower, were equally efficacious; racks, belts, boots, gloves, collars, all made for compressing at will; steel baskets in which the head could be slowly crushed into a pulp if necessary; watchmen's hooks with long handle and knife that cut at resistance—this a speciality of the old Nurnberg police system; and many, many other devices for man's injury to man. Amelia grew quite pale with the horror of the things, but fortunately did not faint, for being a little overcome she sat down on a torture chair, but jumped up again with a shriek, all tendency to faint gone. We both pretended that it was the injury done to her dress by the dust of the chair, and the rusty spikes which had upset her, and Mr. Hutcheson acquiesced in accepting the explanation with a kind-hearted laugh.

But the central object in the whole of this chamber of horrors was the engine known as the Iron Virgin, which stood near the centre of the room. It was a rudely-shaped figure of a woman, something of the bell order, or, to make a closer comparison, of the figure of Mrs. Noah in the children's Ark, but without that slimness of waist and perfect *rondeur* of hip which marks the æsthetic type of the Noah family. One would hardly have recognised it as intended for a human figure at all had not the founder shaped on the forehead a rude semblance of a woman's face. This machine was coated with rust without, and covered with dust; a rope was fastened to a ring in the front of the figure, about where the waist should have been, and was drawn through a pulley, fastened on the wooden pillar which sustained the flooring above. The custodian pulling this rope showed that a section of the front was hinged like a door at one side; we then saw that the engine was of considerable thickness, leaving just room enough inside for a man to be placed. The door was of equal thickness and of great weight, for it took the custodian all his strength, aided though he was by the contrivance of the pulley, to open it. This weight was partly due to the fact that the door was of manifest purpose hung so as to throw its weight downwards, so that it might shut of its own accord when the strain was released. The inside was honeycombed with rust—nay more, the rust alone that comes through time would hardly have eaten so deep into the iron walls; the rust of the cruel stains was deep indeed! It was only, however, when we came to look at the inside of the door that the diabolical intention was manifest to the full. Here were several long spikes, square and massive, broad at the base and sharp at the points, placed in such a position that when the door should close the upper ones would pierce the eyes of the victim, and the lower ones his heart and vitals. The sight was too much for poor Amelia, and this time she fainted dead off, and I had to carry her down the stairs, and place her on a bench outside till she recovered. That she felt it to the quick was afterwards shown by the fact that my eldest son bears to this day a rude birthmark on his breast, which has, by family consent, been accepted as representing the Nurnberg Virgin.

When we got back to the chamber we found Hutcheson still opposite the Iron Virgin; he had been evidently philosophising, and now gave us the benefit of his thought in the shape of a sort of exordium.

"Wall, I guess I've been learnin' somethin' here while madam has been gettin' over her faint. 'Pears to me that we're a long way behind the times on our side of the big drink. We uster think out on the plains that the Injun could give us points in tryin' to make a man oncomfortable; but I guess your old mediæval law-and-order party could raise him every time. Splinters was pretty good in his bluff on the squaw, but this here young miss held a straight flush all high on him. The points of them spikes air sharp enough still, though even the edges air eaten out by what uster be on them. It'd be a good thing for our Indian section to get some specimens of this here play-toy to send round to the Reservations jest to knock the stuffin' out of the bucks, and the squaws too, by showing them as how old civilisation lays over them at their best. Guess but I'll get in that box a minute jest to see how it feels!"

"Oh no! no!" said Amelia. "It is too terrible!"

"Guess, ma'am, nothin's too terrible to the explorin' mind. I've been in some queer places in my time. Spent a night inside a dead horse while a prairie fire swept over me in Montana Territory—an' another time slept inside a dead buffler when the Comanches was on the war path an' I didn't keer to leave my kyard on them. I've been two days in a caved-in tunnel in the Billy Broncho gold mine in New Mexico, an' was one of the four shut up for three parts of a day in the caisson what slid over on her side when we was settin' the foundations of the Buffalo Bridge. I've not funked an odd experience yet, an' I don't propose to begin now!"

We saw that he was set on the experiment, so I said: "Well, hurry up, old man, and get through it quick?"

"All right, General," said he, "but I calculate we ain't quite ready yet. The gentlemen, my predecessors, what stood in that thar canister, didn't volunteer for the office—not much! And I guess there was some ornamental tyin' up before the big stroke was made. I want to go into this thing fair and square, so I must get fixed up proper first. I dare say this old galoot can rise some string and tie me up accordin' to sample?"

This was said interrogatively to the old custodian, but the latter, who understood the drift of his speech, though perhaps not appreciating to the full the niceties of dialect and imagery, shook his head. His protest was, however, only formal and made to be overcome. The American thrust a gold piece into his hand, saying, "Take it, pard! it's your pot; and don't be skeer'd. This ain't no necktie party that you're asked to assist in!" He produced some thin frayed rope and proceeded to bind our companion with sufficient strictness for the purpose. When the upper part of his body was bound, Hutcheson said:

"Hold on a moment, Judge. Guess I'm too heavy for you to tote into the canister. You jest let me walk in, and then you can wash up regardin' my legs!"

Whilst speaking he had backed himself into the opening which was just enough to hold him. It was a close fit and no mistake. Amelia looked on with fear in her eyes, but she evidently did not like to say anything. Then the custodian completed his task by tying the American's feet together so that he was now absolutely helpless and fixed in his voluntary prison. He seemed to really enjoy it, and the incipient smile which was habitual to his face blossomed into actuality as he said:

"Guess this here Eve was made out of the rib of a dwarf! There ain't much room for a full-grown citizen of the United States to hustle. We uster make our coffins more roomier in Idaho territory. Now, Judge, you jest begin to let this door down, slow, on to me. I want to feel the same pleasure as the other jays had when those spikes began to move toward their eyes!"

"Oh no! no! no!" broke in Amelia hysterically. "It is too terrible! I can't bear to see it!—I can't! I can't!"

But the American was obdurate. "Say, Colonel," said he, "Why not take Madame for a little promenade? I wouldn't hurt her feelin's for the world; but now that I am here, havin' kem eight thousand miles, wouldn't it be too hard to give up the very experience I've been pinin' an' pantin' fur? A man can't get to feel like canned goods every time! Me and the Judge here'll fix up this thing in no time, an' then you'll come back, an' we'll all laugh together!"

Once more the resolution that is born of curiosity triumphed, and Amelia stayed holding tight to my arm and shivering whilst the custodian began to slacken slowly inch by inch the rope that held back the iron door. Hutcheson's face was positively radiant as his eyes followed the first movement of the spikes.

"Wall!" he said, "I guess I've not had enjoyment like this since I left Noo York. Bar a scrap with a French sailor at Wapping—an' that warn't much of a picnic neither—I've not had a show fur real pleasure in this dod-rotted Continent, where there ain't no b'ars nor no Injuns, an' wheer nary man goes heeled. Slow there, Judge! Don't you rush this business! I want a show for my money this game—I du!"

The custodian must have had in him some of the blood of his predecessors in that ghastly tower, for he worked the engine with a deliberate and excruciating slowness which after five minutes, in which the outer edge of the door had not moved half as many inches, began to overcome Amelia. I saw her lips whiten, and felt her hold upon my arm relax. I looked around an instant for a place whereon to lay her, and when I looked at her again found that her eye had become fixed on the side of the Virgin. Following its direction I saw the black cat crouching out of sight. Her green eyes shone like danger lamps in the gloom of the place, and their colour was heightened by the blood which still smeared her coat and reddened her mouth. I cried out:

"The cat! look out for the cat!" for even then she sprang out before the engine. At this moment she looked like a triumphant demon. Her eyes blazed with ferocity, her hair bristled out till she seemed twice her normal size, and her tail lashed about as does a tiger's when the quarry is before it. Elias P. Hutcheson when he saw her was amused, and his eyes positively sparkled with fun as he said:

"Darned if the squaw hain't got on all her war paint! Jest give her a shove off if she comes any of her tricks on me, for I'm so fixed everlastingly by the boss, that durn my skin if I can keep my eyes from her if she wants them! Easy there, Judge! don't you slack that ar rope or I'm euchered!"

At this moment Amelia completed her faint, and I had to clutch hold of her round the waist or she would have fallen to the floor. Whilst attending to her I saw the black cat crouching for a spring, and jumped up to turn the creature out.

But at that instant, with a sort of hellish scream, she hurled herself, not as we expected at Hutcheson, but straight at the face of the custodian. Her claws seemed to be tearing wildly as one sees in the Chinese drawings of the dragon rampant, and as I looked I saw one of them light on the poor man's eye, and actually tear through it and down his cheek, leaving a wide band of red where the blood seemed to spurt from every vein.

With a yell of sheer terror which came quicker than even his sense of pain, the man leaped back, dropping as he did so the rope which held back the iron door. I jumped for it, but was too late, for the cord ran like lightning through the pulley-block, and the heavy mass fell forward from its own weight.

As the door closed I caught a glimpse of our poor companion's face. He seemed frozen with terror. His eyes stared with a horrible anguish as if dazed, and no sound came from his lips.

And then the spikes did their work. Happily the end was quick, for when I wrenched open the door they had pierced so deep that they had locked in the bones of the skull through which they had crushed, and actually tore him—it—out of his iron prison till, bound as he was, he fell at full length with a sickly thud upon the floor, the face turning upward as he fell.

I rushed to my wife, lifted her up and carried her out, for I feared for her very reason if she should wake from her faint to such a scene. I laid her on the bench outside and ran back. Leaning against the wooden column was the custodian moaning in pain whilst he held his reddening handkerchief to his eyes. And sitting on the head of the poor American was the cat, purring loudly as she licked the blood which trickled through the gashed socket of his eyes.

I think no one will call me cruel because I seized one of the old executioner's swords and shore her in two as she sat.

OLD HOGGEN: A MYSTERY

"IF he had half the spirit of a man in him, he would go himself," said my mother-in-law.

"Indeed, I think you might, Augustus. I know I often deny myself and make efforts to please you; and you know that my dear mamma loves crabs," said my mother-in-law's daughter.

"Far be it from me to interfere," said Cousin Jemima, as they call her, smoothing down her capstrings as she spoke. "But I do think that it would be well if Cousin Kate, who, like myself, is not at all so strong as she looks—could have something to tempt her appetite."

Cousin Jemima, who was my mother-in-law's cousin, was as robust as a Swiss guide, and had the appetite and digestion of a wild Indian. I began to get riled.

"What on earth are you all talking about?" said I. "One would think you were all suffering some terrible wrong. You want crabs—and you are actually now engaged on bolting one of the biggest crabs I ever saw. What does it all mean? Unless, indeed, you want merely to annoy me!"

Here my mother-in-law laid down her fork in a majestic way and glared at me, saying:

"If there are no crabs nearer than Bridport, then you must go there," while her daughter began to cry.

This, of course, settled the matter. When my mother-in-law has a go in at me I can—although it makes me uncomfortable and unhappy—stand it; but when her daughter cries, I am done; so I made an effort by an attempt at jocularity—feeble, though, it was—to grace my capitulation and go out with the honours of war.

"I shall get you some crabs," said I, "my dear mother-in-law, which even you will not be able to vanquish—or even, Cousin Jemima, with her feeble digestion."

They all looked very glum, so I made another effort.

"Yes," I went on. "I shall bring you some giant crabs, even if I have to find old Hoggen first."

The only answer made in words was by my mother-in-law, who cut in sharply:

"If old Hoggen was as great a brute as you, I don't wonder that he has got rid of—"

Cousin Jemima indorsed the sentiment with a series of sniffs and silences, as eloquent and expressive as the stars and negative chapters of *Tristram Shandy*. Lucy looked at me, but it was a good look, more like my wife's, and less like that of my mother-in-law's daughter than had hitherto been, so tacitly we became a linked battalion.

There was a period of silence, which was broken by my mother-in-law:

"I do not see—I fail to see why you will always introduce that repulsive subject."

As she began the battle, and as Lucy was now on my side, I did not shun the fight, but made a counter attack.

"Crabs?" I asked interrogatively, in a tone which I felt to be dangerous.

"No, not crabs—how dare you call the subject of my food—and you know how delicate an appetite I have—disgusting—"

"Well, what do you mean?" I inquired, again showing the green lamps.

"I call 'disgusting' the subject of conversation on which you always harp—that disreputable old man whom they say was murdered. I have made inquiries—many inquiries—concerning him, and I find that his life was most disreputable. Some of the details of his low amours which I have managed to find out are most improper. What do you think, Cousin Jemima—"

Here she whispered to the other old dear, who eagerly inclined her ear to listen.

"No, really! seventeen? What a wretched old man," and Cousin Jemima became absorbed in a moral reverie.

My mother-in-law went on:

"When you, Augustus, bring perpetually before our notice the name of this wicked man, you affront your wife."

Here the worm, which had hitherto been squirming about trying to imagine that it was built on the lines of a serpent, which can threaten and strike, turned, and I spoke.

"I do not think it is half so bad to mention a topic of common interest, and which is forced upon us every hour of every day since we came here, as it is for you to make such a charge. I respect and love my wife too much"—here I pulled Lucy toward me, who came willingly—"to affront her even by accident. And, moreover, I think, Madam, that it would be better if, instead of making such preposterous and monstrous charges, you would give me a little peace to my meals by holding your tongue and giving yourself an opportunity of getting tired and sick of crabs. I have not sat down to a meal since I came here that you have not spoiled it with your quarrelling. You quite upset my digestion. Can't you let me alone?"

The effect of the attack was appalling.

My mother-in-law, who by this time had finished the last morsel of the crab, sat for a moment staring and speechless, and for the only time in her life burst into tears.

Her tears were not nearly so effective upon me as Lucy's, and I sat unmoved. Cousin Jemima, with an inborn tendency to rest secure on the domineering side, said, audibly:

"Served you quite right, Cousin Kate, for interrupting the man at his supper."

Lucy said nothing, but looked at me sympathetically.

Presently my mother-in-law, with a great effort, pulled herself together and said:

"Well, Augustus, perhaps you are right. We have suffered enough about old Hoggen to make his name familiar to us."

Indeed we suffered. The whole history of old Hoggen had for some weeks past been written on our soul in the darkest shade of ink. We had come to Charmouth hoping to find in that fair spot the peace that we yearned for after the turmoil and troubles of the year. With the place we were more than satisfied, for it is a favoured spot. In quiet, lazy, Dorsetshire it lies. Close to the sea, but sheltered from its blasts. The long straggling village of substantial houses runs steeply down the hillside parallel to the seaboard. Everywhere are rivulets of sweet water, everywhere are comfort and seeming plenty. A smiling and industrious peasantry are the normal inhabitants among whom the good old customs of salutation have not died away. A town-made coat enacts a bob courtsey from the females and a salute in military fashion from the men, for the young men are all militia or volunteers.

We had been at Charmouth some three weeks. Our arrival had caused us to swell with importance, for, from the time we left Axminster in the diurnal omnibus till our being deposited at our pretty cottage, bowered in enticing greenery and rich with old world flowers, our advent seemed to excite interest and attention. Naturally I surmised that the rustic mind was overcome by the evidence of metropolitan high tone manifested in our cloths and air. Lucy put it down—in her own mind which her mother kindly interpreted for her—to the striking all-the-world-over effect of surpassing loveliness. Cousin Jemima attributed it to their respect for blood; and my mother-in-law took it as a just homage to the rare, if not unique, union of birth, grace, gentleness, breeding, talent, wisdom, culture, and power—as embodied in herself. We soon found, however, that there was a cause different from all these.

There had lately come to light certain circumstances tending to show that we are objects of suspicion rather than veneration.

Some days before our arrival great excitement had been caused in Charmouth by the disappearance, and, consequently, rumoured murder, of an old inhabitant, one Jabez Hoggen, reputed locally to be of vast wealth and miserly in the extreme. This good reputation brought him much esteem, not in Charmouth alone, but through the whole country round from Lyme Regis on the one hand, even as far as distant Bridport on the other.

Even inland the trumpet note of old Hoggen's wealth sounded to Axminster and even to Chard. This good repute of wealth was, however, the only good repute he had, for his social misdoings were so manifold and continuous as to interest even the social stars of Lyme. These are old ladies who inhabit the snug villas in the uplands at Lyme, and who claim as their special right the covered seats on the Madeira walk of that pretty town, and who are so select that they will not even associate with others except in massed groups nebulae. Old Hoggen's peccadilloes afforded them a fertile theme for gossip. There was an inexhaustible store of minute and wicked details of this famous sinner.

Year after year old Hoggen moved among the law-abiding inhabitants of Charmouth, wallowing in his wickedness and adding to his store of goods in the here and ills in the hereafter.

Strange to say, all this time not once—not even once—did the earth yawn and swallow him. On the contrary, he flourished. No matter what weather came he always benefited. Even if the rain did destroy one of his crops, it made another to flourish exceedingly. When there was storm he accumulated sea rack; when there was calm he got fish. Many of his neighbours began to have serious doubts about the earth ever yawning and swallowing at all; and even the old ladies in Lyme Regis—those who had passed the age of proposals and began to regret, or at least reconsider, their youth, sometimes thought that perhaps immorality was a little too harshly condemned after all.

Suddenly this old man disappeared, and Charmouth woke up to the fact that he was the best known, the most respected, the most important person in the place. His ill-doing sank into insignificance, and his good stood revealed in gigantic proportions. Men pointed out his public spirit, the reforms he had instituted, the powers he had developed; women called attention to the tenderness he had always exhibited to their sex, unworthy as had been the examples of the same that had darkened the horizon of his life. More than one wise matron was heard to remark that if his lot in life had been to meet one good woman, instead of those hussies, his manner of life might have been different.

It is a fact worthy of notice that in the logic of might-have-been, which is pitying woman's pathway to heaven, the major premise is pitying woman.

However, were his life good or ill, old Hoggen had disappeared: and murder was naturally suspected. Two suppositions—no one knew whence originating—were current. The most popular was that some of his unhappy companions, knowing of his wealth and greedy of his big gold watch and his diamond ring, had incited to his murder other still more disreputable companions. The alternative belief was that some of his relations—for he was believed to have some, although no one had ever seen or heard of them—had quietly removed him so that in due time they might in legal course become possessed of his heritage.

Consequent upon the latter supposition suspicion attached itself to every new-comer. It was but natural that the vulture-like relatives should appear upon the scene as soon as possible, and eager eyes scanned each fresh arrival. As I soon discovered, my respected connection by marriage, Cousin Jemima, bore a strong resemblance to the missing man, and drew around our pretty resting-place the whole curiosity of Charmouth and concentrated there the attention of the secret myrmidons of the law.

In fact, the Charmouth policeman haunted the place, and strange men in slop clothes and regulation boots came from Bridport and Lyme Regis, and even from Axminster itself.

These latter representatives of the intellectual subtlety of Devon, Dorset and Wilts were indeed men full of wile and cunning of device. The bucolic mind in moments of unbending, when frank admission of incompleteness is a tribute to good fellowship, may sometimes admit that its workings are slow, but even in the last stage of utter and conscious drunkenness one quality is insisted on—surety.

Of surety, in simple minds the correlative is tenacity of purpose and belief.

Thus it was that when once the idea of our guilt had been mooted and received, no amount of evidence, direct or circumstantial, could obliterate the idea from the minds of the rustic detectives. These astute men, one by one, each jealous of the other, and carrying on even among themselves the fiction of non-identification, began to seek the evidences of our guilt. It struck me as a curious trait in the inhabitants of the diocese of Salisbury that their primary intellectual effort had one tendency, and that all their other efforts were subordinate to this principle. It may have been that the idea arose from historical contemplation of the beauty of their cathedral and an unconscious effort to emulate the powers of its originators.

Or it may not have been.

But, at all events, their efforts took the shape of measuring. I fail myself to see how their measurements, be they never so accurate, could in anywise have helped them. Further, I cannot comprehend how the most rigid and exact scrutiny in this respect could have even suggested a combination of facts whence a spontaneous idea could have emanated. Still, they measured, never ceasing day or night for more than a week, and always surreptitiously. They measured one night the whole of the outside of our cottage. I heard them in the night, out on the roof, crawling about like gigantic cats, and, although we learned that one man had fallen off the roof and broken his arm, we were never officially informed of the fact. They made incursions into the house, under various pretexts, there to endeavour to measure the interior.

In every case a ruse was adopted. One morning, while we were out bathing, a man called to measure the gas pipes, and, after going through several of the rooms taking the dimensions of the walls, was informed by the servant that there was no gas, not only in the house, but in the village. Not being prepared with a further excuse, he said, with that nonchalance he could assume, that "it was no matter", and went away. Another time a British workman, as he styled himself, arrayed in cricket flannels and a straw hat, came to look at the kitchen boiler for the landlord, and asked that he might begin on the roof. I saw the inevitable rule and tape measure, and told him that the landlord's house was next door, and that he would find the boiler buried in the garden. He withdrew, thanking me with effusion, and making a note of the words "buried in the garden" in his notebook.

Another day a man called with fish—he had only one sole, and that he carried in his hand. The cook was out and I told him we would have it. He asked me if he might go in the garden to skin it. I told him he might, and went out. When I came back in about an hour's time, I found him there still, measuring away. He had got all the dimensions of the garden and the walls, and was now engaged on the heights of the various flowers. I asked him what the dickens he was doing there still, and why he was measuring. He answered vaguely that he was not measuring.

"Why, man alive," said I, "don't tell me such a story—I saw you at it—why, you are doing it still," as indeed he was.

He stood up and answered me:

"Well, sir, I will tell you why. I was looking to see if I could find room to bury the skin of the sole."

He had not skinned the sole, which lay on a flag in the hot sunshine, and was beginning to look glassy.

They even measured as well as they could the height of the members of the family. When any of us passed a wall where any of these men were, he immediately spotted some place on the wall of equal height, and the moment we passed, out rule and measured it.

Our cook was asked one night by a tall man to lay her head on his shoulder. She did so, as she told us afterward, being so surprised that she did not know what to do. When she came in we saw on her black stuff bonnet a series of reversed numbers in chalk dying away over the temple with 5ft. 1–2in.

Cousin Jemima, who was of a full habit of body—to say the least of it—was one evening stopped in the lane by two men, who put their arms round her waist from opposite sides. She distinctively said that they had something that looked like a long rope marked in yards, or, as she persisted, in chains, which, when she had escaped from them, they examined with seeming anxiety, and made some entry in books which they carried, laughing all the time heartily and digging each other in the ribs as they pointed at her.

Our dog was often measured, and one afternoon there was a terrible caterwauling, which we found to arise from a respectable man trying to weigh our cat in an ouncel, borrowed from a neighbouring shop.

My mother-in-law, who had no suspicion whatever that she was an object of suspicion, waxed at times furiously indignant at the rudeness of the loiterers round our door, and now and again comported herself so violently as to cause them serious fright. I was unaware during the time of my courtship that this remarkable woman possessed such a power of invective. She certainly proved herself a consummate actress in concealing it as she did: for during that time of rapture and agony I enjoyed the contemplation and experienced the practical outcome of a sympathy and sweetness as ripe as unalloyed. My wife and I both understand the motives of the local detectives, and always recognised them under their disguises. It was a never-ending source of mirth to us to enjoy the spectacle of Cousin Jemima's ungratified curiosity, and of my mother-in-law's periodic anger. For the purposes of our own amusement we filled up the daily blanks caused by the slackness of the executive in keeping perpetually before them the theme of old Hoggen. I amused myself by keeping a little notebook in which I jotted down all kinds of odd measurements for the purpose of leaving it about some time to puzzle the detectives.

Thus it came about that the repulsive individuality of old Hoggen became, in a manner, of interest to us, and his name to be interwoven in the web of our daily converse.

I knew that to mention old Hoggen to my mother-in-law, when previously influenced by hunger or any collateral vexation, would have the effect of a red rag on a bull, and, as has been seen, I was not disappointed.

Now, however, that supper was over and the crab had been all consumed, I found myself pledged to discover by the morrow a full supply of that succulent food. I did not let the matter distress me, as I anticipated a delightful walk by the shore to Bridport, a walk which I had not yet undertaken. In the morning I awoke early, just a little after daybreak, and, leaving my wife asleep, started on my walk.

The atmosphere of the early dawn was delightful and refreshing, and the sight of the moving sea filled me with a great pleasure, notwithstanding the fact that an ominous shower on the water and a cold wind foretold a coming storm.

At this part of the Dorset coast the sea makes perpetual inroads on the land. As all the country is undulating, the shore presents from the sea an endless succession of steep cliffs, some of which rise by comparison to a scale of moderate grandeur.

The cliffs are either of blue clay or sandstone, which soft or friable material perpetually gives way under the undermining influence of the tides assisted by the exfiltration of the springs, causing an endless series of moraines. The beach is either of fine gravel or of shingle, save at places where banks of half formed rock full of fossils run into the sea.

The shingle, which forms the major portion of the road, makes walking at times trying work.

I passed by the target for a rifle practice, and the spot reserved tacitly as the bathing place for gentlemen, and so on under the first headland, the summit of whose bare yellow cliff is fringed with dark pine trees bent eastwards by the prevailing westerly breeze.

Here the shingle began to get heavier. It had been driven by successive tides and storms into a mass like a snow drift, and it was necessary to walk along the top of the ridge whence the pebbles rolled down every step.

The wind had now begun to rise, and as I went onward the waves increased in force till the whole shore was strewn with foam swept from the crests of the waves. Sometimes great beds of seaweed—a rare commodity on the Dorset coast—rose and fell as the waves rolled in and broke.

On I went as sturdily as I could. The blue black earth of the Charmouth cliffs had now given place to sandstone, and great boulders shaped like mammoth bones—as indeed they probably were, cumbered the foreshore. I stopped to examine some of these, ostensibly from scientific interest, but in reality to rest myself. I was now getting a little tired, and more than a little hungry, for when starting I had determined to eat my breakfast at Bridport, and to test the culinary capabilities of the place.

As I sat on the stones looking seaward I noticed something washing in and out among the boulders. On examination it proved to be a hat—a human hat. I hooked it in with a piece of driftwood. I turned it over, and in turning it saw something white stuck within the leather lining. Gingerly enough I made an examination, and found the white mass to be some papers, on the outside of one of which was the name "J. Hoggen".

"Hullo!" said I to myself. "Here is some news of old Hoggen at last." I took the papers out, carefully squeezed the wet out of them, as well as I could between flat stones, and put them in the pocket of my shooting jacket. I placed the hat on a boulder and looked round to see if I could find any further signs of the missing man. All the while the breeze was freshening and the waves came rolling in in increasing volume.

Again I saw, some twenty yards out, something black floating, bobbing up and down with each wave. After a while I made it out to be the body of a man. By this time my excitement had grown to intensity, and I could hardly await the incoming of the body borne by the waves.

On and on it came, advancing a little with each wave, till at last it got so close that reaching out I hooked part of the clothing with my piece of timber, and pulled the mass close to the shore.

Then I took hold of the collar of the coat and pulled. The cloth, rotten with the sea water, tore away, and left the piece in my hand.

With much effort—for I had to be very careful—I brought the body up on the beach, and began to make an accurate examination of it.

While doing so I found in the pocket a tape measure, and it occurred to me that I must fulfil all the requirements of the local police, and so began to take dimensions of the corpse.

I measured the height, the length of the limbs, of the hands and feet. I took the girth of the shoulders and the waist, and, in fact, noted in my pocketbook a sufficiency of detail to justify a tailor in commencing sartorial operations on a full scale. Some of the dimensions struck me at the time as rather strange, but having verified the measurements I noted them down.

On examination of the cloths and pockets I found the massive gold watch hanging on the chain and the big diamond ring, to whose power of inspiring greed local opinion had attributed the murder. These I put in my pocket together with the purse, studs, papers and money of the dead man. In making the examination the coat became torn, revealing a mass of bank notes between cloth and lining: in fact, the whole garment was quilted with them. There was also a small note case containing the necessary papers for a voyage to Queensland by a ship leaving Southampton the previous week.

These discoveries I thought so valuable that I felt it my duty to try to bring the body to the nearest place of authority, which I considered would probably be Chidiock, a village on the Bridport road which I had seen upon the map.

It was now blowing a whole gale, and the waves broke on the beach in thunder, dragging down the shingle in their ebb with a loud screaming. The rain fell in torrents, and the increasing of the storm decided me in my intention to carry the body with me.

I lifted it across my shoulder with some difficulty, for at each effort the clothes, already torn in the extrication of paper money, fell to pieces. However, at last I got it on my shoulder, face downwards, and started. I had hardly taken a step when, with an impulse which I could not restrain, I let it slip—or, rather, threw it—to the ground.

It had seemed to me to be alive. I certainly felt a movement. As it lay all in a heap on the beach, with the drenching rain sweeping the pale face, I grew ashamed of my impulse, and, with another, effort, took it up and started again.

Again there was the same impulse, with the same cause—the body seemed alive. This time, however, I was prepared, and held on, and after a while the idea wore away.

Presently I came to a place where a mass of great boulders strewed the shore. The stepping from one to another shook me and my burden, and as I jumped from the last of the rocks to the smooth sand which lay beyond I felt a sudden diminution of weight. As my load overbalanced, I fell on the sand higgledy-piggledy with my burden.

Old Hoggen had parted in the middle.

As may be imagined, I was not long getting up. On a survey of the wreck I saw, to my intense astonishment, some large crabs walking out of the body. This, then, explained the strange movement of the corpse. It occurred to me that the presence of these fishes was incontrovertible proof that crabs did exist between Bridport and Lyme Regis, and not without a thought of Cousin Jemima and my mother-in-law, I lifted two or three and put them in the big pocket of my shooting coat.

Then I began to consider whether I should leave the departed Hoggen where he was or bring him on.

For a while I weighed the arguments pro and con, and finally concluded to bring him on with me, or it, or them, or whatever the fragments could be called. It was not an alluring task, in any aspect, and it was by a great effort that I undertook the duty.

I gathered the things together, and a strange looking heap they made—waxen limbs protruding from a wet heap of dishevelled rags. Then I began to lift them. It had been a task of comparative ease carrying the body over my shoulder, but now I had to pick up separate pieces and carry them altogether in my hands and under my arms. Often I had laughed, as I went through Victoria Street, to see people of both sexes, worthy, but deficient of organising power and system, coming forth from the co-operative stores bearing hosts of packages purchased without system in the various departments. Such a one I now felt myself to be. Do what I would, I could not hold all at one time, the various segments of my companion. Just as I had carefully tucked the moieties of old Hoggen under my arms, I spied some of his clothing on the shore, and in trying to raise these also lost a portion of my load. What added to the aggravation of the situation was that the wear and tear began to tell upon the person of the defunct. Thus while I was lifting the upper section an arm came away, and from the lower a foot.

However, with a supreme effort I bundled the pieces together, and, lifting the mass in my arms, proceeded on my way. But now the storm was raging in full force, and I saw that I must hurry or the advancing waves, every moment rushing closer to the cliffs, would cut me off. I could see, through the blinding rain, a headland before me, and knew that if I could once pass it I would be in comparative safety.

So I hurried on as fast as I could, sometimes losing a portion of my burden, but never being able to wait to pick it up. Had my thoughts and ejaculations been recorded they would have been somewhat as follows:

"There goes a hand; it was lucky I took off the ring."

"Half the coat; well that I found the bank notes."

"There goes the waistcoat; a fortunate thing I have the watch."

"A leg off—my! Will I ever get him home?"

"Another leg."

"An arm gone."

"His grave will be a mile long."

"We must consecrate the shore that he may lay in hallowed ground."

"The lower trunk gone, too. Poor fellow; no one can hit him now below the belt."

"An arm gone, too; he would not be able to defend himself if they did."

"Murder! but he's going fast."

"The clothes all gone, too—I had better have left him where he was."

"Ugh! there goes the trunk; nothing left now but the head."

"Ugh! that was a close shave anyhow. Never mind, I will keep you safe."

I clung tight to the head, which was now my sole possession of the corpse.

It was mighty hard to hold it, for it was as slippery as glass, and the tight holding of it cramped my efforts and limited me as I leaped from rock to rock or dashed through the waves, which now touched in their onward rush to the base of the cliff.

At last, through the blinding rain, I saw the headland open, and with a great rush through the recoil of a big wave I rounded it and rested for a moment to breathe on the wide shore beyond.

Then I tried for a while to collect my scattered faculties, such being the only part of the goods scattered in the last half-hour which could be collected.

I felt ruefully that my effort to bring to the rites of burial the body of old Hoggen had been a mistaken one. All had gone save the head which lay on the sand, and whose eyes actually seemed to wink at me as the flakes of the spume settled over the eyes, dissolving as the bubbles burst. The property was, I felt, safe enough. I put my hand into the pocket of my shooting coat but in an instant drew it out again with a scream of pain, for it had been severely nipped. I had forgotten the crabs.

Very carefully I took out one of these fish and held him legs upward, he making frantic efforts to seize me with his claws. He seemed a greedy one, indeed, for he was trying to eat the diamond ring which he had got half within that mysterious mouth which is covered with a flap like that over the lock of a portmanteau. Hence also projected part of the watch chain. I found that the brute had actually swallowed the watch, and it was with some difficulty that I relieved from his keeping both it and the ring. I took care to place the valuable property in the other pocket where the crabs were not.

Then I took up my head—or, rather old Hoggen's—and started on my way, carrying the final relic under my arm.

The storm began to decrease, and died away as quickly as it had arisen, so that, before I had traversed half the long stretch of sand that lay before me, instead of storm there was marked calm, and for blinding rain an almost insupportable heat.

I struggled on over the sand, and at length found an opening in the dirt—which, on coming close, I found to be caused by a small stream which had worn a deep cleft in the blue-black earthy rock, and, falling and tumbling from above, became lost in the beach.

There was a look about the sand here that seemed to me to be somewhat peculiar. Its surface was smooth and shining, with a sort of odd dimple here and there. It looked so flat and inviting after my scramble over the rock and shingle and plodding through the deep sand, that with joy I hurried toward it—and at once began to sink.

By the odd shiver that traversed it I knew that I was being engulfed in a quicksand.

It was a terrible position.

I had already sunk over my knees and knew that unless aid came I was utterly lost. I would at that moment have welcomed even Cousin Jemima.

It is the misfortune of such people as her that they never do make an appearance at a favourable time—such as this.

But there was no help—on one side lay the sea with never a sail in sight, and the waves still angry from the recent storm tumbling in sullenly upon the shore—on the other side was a wilderness of dark cliff; and along the shore on either way an endless waste of sand.

I tried to shout, but the misery and terror of the situation so overcame me that my voice clung to my jaws, and I could make no sound. I still kept old Hoggen's head under my arm. In moments of such danger the mind is quick to grasp an offered chance, and it suddenly occurred to me that, if I could get a foothold even for a moment, I might still manage to extricate myself. I was as yet but on the edge of the quicksand, and but a little help would suffice. With the thought came also the means—old Hoggen's head.

No sooner thought than done.

I laid the head on the sand before me, and pressing on it with my hands, felt that I was relieving my feet of part of their weight. With an effort I lifted one leg and placed the foot on the head now imbedded some inches in the treacherous sand. Then pressing all my weight on this foot made a great effort, and tearing up the imbedded foot leaped to the firm sand, where I slipped and fell and for a few minutes panted with exhaustion.

I was saved, but old Hoggen's head was gone forever.

Then I went toward the cliff, cautiously feeling my way, testing every spot on which my foot must rest, before trusting my weight to it. I gained the cliff, and resting on its firm base passed behind the fatal quicksand and went on my course to the stable strand beyond.

On I plodded till at last I came near a few houses built in a green cleft, whence through the cliffs a tiny stream, on whose banks stood the pretty village of Chidiock, fell into the sea.

There was a coast guard station here, with a little rope-railed plot, where before the row of trim houses the flagstaff rose.

As I drew near a coastguard and a policeman rushed toward me from behind a shed and grasped me on either side, holding me tight with a vigour which I felt to be quite disproportionate to the necessity of the occasion.

With the instinct of conscious innocence I struggled with them.

"Let me go!" I cried. "Let me go—what do you mean? Let me go I say!"

"Come now—none of this," said the policeman.

I still struggled.

"Better keep quiet!" said the coastguard. "It's no use struggling."

"I will not keep quiet," I cried, struggling more frantically than ever.

The policeman looked at me right savagely and gave my neckcloth a twist which nearly strangled me. "Tell you what," he said sternly, "if you struggle any more, I'll whale you over the head with my baton."

I did not struggle any more.

"Now," said he, "remember that I caution you that anything you say or do will be afterward used in evidence against you."

I thought a policy of conciliation was now best; so with what heartiness I could assume I said:

"My good fellow, you really make a mistake. Why you seize me I do not know."

"We know," he interrupted, with a hard laugh, "and if you say you don't know, why then you're a liar!"

I felt choking with anger. To be held is bad enough, but when the additional insult of calling one a liar is added, rage may surely be excused. My impulse on hearing the insult was to break free and strike the man, but he knew my intention and held me tighter.

"Take care!" he said, holding up his baton.

I took care.

"I ask you formally," I said, with all my dignity, "on what authority you treat me thus?"

"On this authority!" he answered, holding up his baton, and again laughing with his harsh, exasperating cachinnation. He playfully twirled his baton as if to impress on me a sense of his proficiency in its use.

He then produced a pair of handcuffs, which were put on me. I struggled very hard, but the two men were too much for me, and I had to succumb.

He then began to search me. First he put his hand into the pocket of my shooting coat and pulled out the watch and chain. He looked at it with exultation.

"That is old Hoggen's watch," I said.

"I know it is," he answered, at the same time pulling out a notebook and writing down my words. Next he produced the diamond ring, and the purse.

"That also," said I, "and that!" and again he wrote down my words—this time in silence. Then he put in his hand again and drew it out, saying:

"Only wet paper!"

He next put his hand into the other pocket, but drew it out again in an instant—not in silence this time.

"Curse the thing! What is it?"

I smiled as he lifted a crab out of the pocket with great carefulness and replaced it. When he had got thus far:

"Now, young fellow," said he, "what have you got to say for yourself?"

For the last few minutes a very unpleasant thought had in my mind been growing to colossal proportions. It was evident that I was arrested for the murder of old Hoggen, and here I was arrested when in possession of his property, but with no witness to prove my innocence, and with no trace of the lost man himself to substantiate my story. I began to be a little frightened as to the result.

"What I have to tell you is very strange," said I. "I left Charmouth early this morning to walk to Bridport to get some crabs for my mother-in-law."

"Why, you have got crabs with you," said the policeman.

"I got them on the shore beyond," said I, pointing westward.

"Come! stow that!" said the policeman. "That won't wash here. There isn't a crab to be found on the shore between Bridport and Lyme."

"That's true, anyhow. Every fool knows that!" added the coastguard. I went on:

"I found the body of old Hoggen floating in the water. I tried to carry it on here, but the storm came, and it was as much as I could do to escape. Besides, the body all fell in pieces, and at last—"

"A nice story that!" said the policeman. "But if it fell to bits, why didn't you bring one on with you?"

"I tried some, but they fell to bits."

"The head didn't," said he, "why did you not bring it? Eh?"

"I did bring it," said I, "but I got into the quicksand and it was lost."

The coastguard struck in.

"There is only one bit of quicksand on all this coast, they say, for I never see it myself. Why, man alive, it doesn't show once in twenty years."

"And the crabs?" asked the policeman.

"They were in old Hoggen's body!"

"And what were you doing with them?"

"I was bringing them to my mother-in-law."

"Oh, the filthy scoundrel!" ejaculated the coastguard.

"Did you carry them through the quicksand?" inquired the policeman.

"I did," said I, "and when I got out I found that the big fellow had eaten the watch and was trying to swallow the ring."

The policeman and the coastguard seized me roughly, the latter saying:

"Come, take him off. He's the plumpest liar I ever seen."

"Let us finish the search first," said the policeman, as he renewed his investigations.

The thought that I was in a really suspicious position now began to make me most uncomfortable. "My poor wife! My poor wife!" I kept saying to myself.

The policeman, in his zeal, again put his hand into the pocket with the crabs, and drew it out with a yell. Then he took out the biggest crab, which, by the way, as is sometimes the case, had one claw very much larger than the other. The left claw was the larger. He threw the crab on the shore, and was about to stamp on it, when the coast guard put him back, saying:

"Avast, there, mate. Crabs isn't so plenty here, that we walk on them. None here between Bridport and Lyme."

The policeman continued his search. He took the mass of wet papers and notes from the other pocket, and threw them on the ground, and went on diving into the recesses of the pockets. The coastguard was evidently struck with something, for he stooped and looked at the papers, turned them over, and fell down on his knees beside them with a loud cry. Then, in an excited whisper he called out:

"Look here! mate, look here! It's all money. It's thousands of pounds."

The constable also dropped beside the papers, and over the mass the two men stood gazing at each other with excited faces.

"Take care of it—take care!" said the policeman.

"You bet!" said the other shortly.

"What a fortune!"

The two men looked at each other, and then at me furtively, and somehow I felt that they had in common some vile instinct by which I was felt to be in the way. I remained, therefore, as passive as I could.

The two men eyed the papers. Said the coastguard:

"Where are the other things?"

"Here!" said the policeman, slapping his pocket.

"Better put them all together."

"Not at all. They are quite safe with me."

The men looked at each other and seemed mutually to understand, for, without a word, the policeman took the watch and the ring and the purse from his pocket and laid them on the shore.

Both men eyed the lot greedily. Suddenly the policeman looked round and ran down the beach like a maniac shouting, "Stop thief! Stop thief!" At the very edge of the water he stopped and lifted the crab which had been making its escape. He brought it back and laid it on its back beside the other things. As he eyed the heap suspiciously as if to see that nothing had been removed, he said, shaking his fist at the crab:

"You infernal brute, you may have been stealing something." The accent with which he said the word "you" was evidently meant as a caution and suspicion of the coastguard. The latter took it as such, for he said angrily:

"Stow that!"

The two men then proceeded to search me further. They took from me everything which could by any torturing of greed have been construed into a valuable. They opened a seam of my coat and turned out the lining.

Then, drawing away, they whispered a little together, and, returning to me, tied my legs together, put a gag in my mouth, and carried me round the point of a rock where we were out of sight of any chance comer. Then they brought hither the valuables, and, sitting down, began to reckon the worth of the lot.

One by one they opened the bank notes, and laid them flat. They were of all dates and numbers, and I felt as I looked that, from this fact, if once lost, there could be no possibility of tracing them. They laid the gold in a heap with the watch and ring, and put all the papers by themselves.

There was an immense amount of money—in gold only some seventy pounds, but in notes 57,300 pounds.

When the two men had figured it all out, they looked at me with a look that made my blood run cold—for it meant murder.

Again they looked at each other, and, with a whisper, withdrew to a little distance.

I turned partly on my side, so that I could watch them. There was no difficulty in this, and the fact of its being so added to my fear, for I knew that their being without fear of my taking notes of their movements meant that their minds were made up.

A short time sufficed them, and they turned again toward me. As they came, however, the bell of the old church at Chidiock began to ring. It was still but early morning and the bell was for matins.

The coastguard stopped—some memory stirred within him, and with it came a doubt. He paused a moment and spoke:

"Mate."

The policeman realised the intention of mercy in the faltering tone, and answered as roughly and harshly as he could, turning quickly, almost threateningly, as he spoke.

"Well!"

"Mate, must we kill him? Wouldn't it do if he kept quiet, and let us get off with the money? No one knows of the thing—why need they ever know?"

"He won't keep quiet," said the other. "Better cut his throat, and bury him here in the sand."

The sailor looked at me, and, reading the inquiry in his eyes, I answered as well as I could with mine:

"I will be quiet!"

It was as plain as daylight that my life hung on the alternative, so I did not hesitate or falter.

I compounded a felony with a glance.

Notwithstanding my acquiescence, a violent discussion arose between the two men—the preserver of the peace being the more dangerous of the two.

The coastguard urged and argued that it were useless to commit a murder when the end they desired was insured. The policeman stuck persistently to his one point that it were safer to cut my throat.

To me the anguish was intense. All the misdeeds of my life rose before me, and also every reason why life should be dear. I implored the sailor with my eyes to let me speak, and after a little while he removed the gag, after cautioning me that if I spoke above a whisper, my first syllable should be my last.

I whispered but one argument.

"If you kill me, I shall be sought after. You are safer as you are with my promise not to inform on you."

The argument was cogent, and told, as sound logic usually does. So, after a terrible threatening in case of my breaking my pledge, they untied my legs and took off the handcuffs.

Then they brought me into a boathouse by the beach and there brushed me and removed any traces of travel or violence. Next they put me into a pony cart that stood ready by the side of the laneway leading to Chidiock, and drove me into Charmouth, depositing me at my own door. We did not meet a single person by the way.

The last words I heard were the whispered caution of the policeman:

"No one has seen you or us. Go back to your bed and pretend you were never out," and then they drove off again.

I took the advice, slipped off my boots and stole upstairs. My wife was still sleeping, so I undressed and got into bed. Lest I should wake her, I pretended to sleep, and soon, despite my mental agitation, slept, too.

I was awakened by my wife, who was up and dressed.

"Why, Augustus, you are desperately sleepy this morning. It is after ten, and breakfast is over long ago. Cousin Jemima would not wait. However, your breakfast is kept hot."

I awoke to broad consciousness, but thought it wiser to feign heaviness.

"Never mind—I'll get up presently."

"But, my dear, you must get up now or you will miss the 'bus to Bridport. Remember, you promised to get some crabs for Cousin Jemima!"

"Oh, bother Cousin Jemima. There has been enough about crabs for one night." I said this with a sudden impulse and then stopped.

"Well, dear. I hope you have not had indigestion, too. Cousin Jemima says she has been very poorly and that it must have been from eating the new bread."

"Indeed!" said I, adding to myself, "I'm glad she suffered, too, for it was all through her that I had that terrible ordeal to go through."

I got up and went down stairs. All was usual; and presently I began to think I must have been dreaming. The idea grew; and the more I thought the matter over the more unreal and dreamlike it all seemed.

While, however, I was finishing my breakfast the servant came in and said that there were two men at the door who had crabs to sell.

"Send them away at once," I called out, angrily, "I want no crabs."

The servant went, and returned shortly, saying: "If you please, sir, the men say that they hope you will buy a crab; they have one which was got between Bridport and Lyme."

This statement rather staggered me, for I felt a kind of dread that my late assailants had come to look me up. I told the servant I would see to the matter, and went out myself to the door. There stood two men—but not the least like the others. The coastguard was a small man with a big beard, and the policeman was a large man, clean shaven. Of these two, one was large, and the other small, but the large man had a bushy beard, and the small one was clean shaven. I thought that both men looked at me very hard, so I pretended not to notice anything except the subject of barter, and said as unconcernedly as I could.

"Well, my men, so I hear you have crabs to sell; let me look at them."

The big man answered: "We have only one left. Here it is!" and, looking at me very searchingly, he produced from a basket a crab with a big left claw and a small right one. I could not help a start of surprise which did not pass unnoticed, so I thought it better to be more unconcerned still, and said:

"No; that's not good enough. I think I do not care for it."

As I spoke, my wife approached the door, coming home, and with her were my mother-in-law and Cousin Jemima.

The men did not notice them, but the big man said to me, civilly enough:

"All right, sir. It does not matter, but I thought it well to show it to you."

As he was putting the crab back in the basket, Cousin Jemima saw it, and came forward quickly.

"What is that, Augustus? Not a crab that you are sending away? You wretch!" the last words *sotto voce*.

After a little haggling she purchased the crab, which, strangely enough, the men seemed unwilling to sell her, and for which I had the additional pleasure of paying.

Cousin Jemima took the crab in triumph to the kitchen, and the men went away toward Axmouth.

When I went back to the sitting room, I was assailed on all sides. Cousin Jemima, in tears, said that I had behaved like a brute—that I was sending away the only crab seen for days, just to vex and disappoint her.

My mother-in-law surmised that I did so because I wished to have to go over to Bridport, where, unnoticed, I might play billiards and get tipsy, if not meet some "creature". Her daughter, to a small degree, shared in her feelings—particularly the latter.

I maintained a strictly negative position.

In the course of the day the wife of the parson, George Edward Ancey, came to tea—her husband was a justice of the peace, and, as a perpetual resident, was practically the magistrate of the place. In the course of conversation she remarked that George Edward had been very much upset and worried in the morning. That two cases of insubordination had been before him. One was a coastguard, who had affronted his chief boatman before the other men, and who, on being severely censured, resigned on the spot, and had already left the village. The other was a policeman, who had refused to go on duty, and who had been accordingly summarily dismissed. Mr. Ancey regretted his departure, for he had been looked upon as the most trustworthy and active officer in the place.

When these small facts came to my knowledge, I felt more than ever in a perplexity, for their combination and the accurate manner in which they fitted into the history of the morning seemed conclusive proof that the whole thing was not a dream.

Before supper time I went for a walk. As I was going out my wife said:

"Be sure to be home in time, Gus. There is a crab for supper and Cousin Jemima is going to dress it herself—"

A walk on the beach did me good, for it cooled my brain, and in the serener atmosphere of the evening I began to believe again that the whole episode of finding old Hoggen was a dream—a nightmare.

I returned home in a more cheerful humour and, conscious of security and immunity from fear, felt kindly even to Cousin Jemima and tolerant of her foibles.

At the very threshold of my home my good resolution was tried.

On a chair in the hall sat Cousin Jemima awaiting my arrival, the very picture of grim, aggressive dissatisfaction. As I came in she sniffed—I saw that something was wrong and waited—she followed me into the dining room where, supper having been just served, my wife and her mother were seated.

"I said we would not wait a single moment for you, after your conduct," said the latter.

"What's up now?" said I.

"What's up, indeed!"—this with indignant sarcasm. "A nice gentlemanly trick to play upon two ladies whose appetites are not good."

"O-h-h," said I, with what I certainly intended to be utmost sarcasm spoken in the most polished way, "then you allude to something I have done by letter."

"By letter? certainly not! What are you talking of?"

"You said I had played a trick on two ladies whose appetites were not good, and I presume I must have done so by letter. Do you not see? The some one must be at a long distance from this, for I know no one here answering the description."

"You brute!" was the comment of Cousin Jemima, while my mother-in-law said nothing, but glared at her daughter, who smiled.

I sat down and tried to make matters a little pleasanter.

"Come, now, mother," I said, "tell me what I have done and what it is all about."

"The crab," said Cousin Jemima, in tones at once sepulchral and hysterical.

"Well, what about it?"

"You did it on purpose."

"What did I do? I am all in surprise."

Here my wife struck in.

"The fact is, dear, that the crab was a fraud, and mamma and Cousin Jemima, seeing that you were talking to the men, imagine that you got the whole thing up for a joke—that it was, in fact, what you call a 'plant.'"

"My dear, I am no nearer to the fact than I was. How was the crab a fraud?"

"Well, you see there was something very queer about it. It was quite fresh, you know, and all that, but it had been opened and was all cut to little bits with knives and then put back again, just as if some one had been searching it."

Here was a staggering proof that I had not dreamed. I almost gasped for breath and felt that I turned white.

The three women noticed the change.

"Are you ill, dear?" said my wife.

"He might well be," said her mother.

"Served him right!" said Cousin Jemima.

I recovered myself in a moment, and laughed as well as I could.

"You are a parcel of silliness, and I know nothing about it. Why, it was you, Cousin Jemima, who bought the crab."

After a while the conversation changed to other topics. I was now beset by a most extraordinary doubt. Was my whole adventure a dream, or was it not?

I cannot tell.

Some three months after our return to town we read in the *South Dorset News*, which some of our seaside friends sent us regularly, the following paragraph:

The Mystery of Mr. Hoggen.

"The strange mystery regarding the late Mr. Jabez Hoggen—the Charmouth millionaire—whose disappearance set Dorset and neighbouring counties in a blaze, has at last been cleared up. Our readers will of course remember the disappearance early in August last of Mr. Hoggen, whose wealth and eccentricity were fruitful topics of conversation not only in the quiet village of Charmouth, his native place—but through all the neighbouring country. Lyme, on the one hand, and Bridport on the other, and the inland town of Axminster and Chard, were well acquainted with the name of the wealthy eccentric. Mr. Hoggen was very retired and uncommunicative, and it so came to pass that when his disappearance became known not a single person could even guess at any motive or cause for such a fact. No one was in his confidence. It was for a time generally supposed that he had been murdered for the sake of his reputed wealth, and suspicion was by the police baselessly attached to certain of the summer visitors to our pleasant Dorset coast. Our contemporary, the *Bridport Banner*, with that gross bad taste which, equally with its mendacity, characterises its utterances, suggested—if we remember aright, the ribald shrieking forced on our ears by some drunken Conservative reeking with the scurrilous falsity of some paltry true blue meeting—for we do not read the rag—that perhaps Mr. Hoggen had in his old age seen the error of his ways, and, overcome with the remorse for his adherence to the principles of liberalism, committed suicide. Time had given the lie, as it ever does, to such paltry attacks upon the noble dead. It has come to light that Mr. Hoggen took a passage in the name of Smith for Queensland on the *Tamar Indien*, sailing from Southampton on the 26th of August. We are justified in supposing that the poor gentleman, oppressed with the decadent spirit which allows such vile rags as the conservative organs to flourish in this once pure soil, and longing for the purer atmosphere where the pollution of atmosphere conservatism is not left in sorrow his native shore. He was recognised on board by a native of Charmouth— one Miles Ruddy, a steward on the *Tamar Indien*. It appears that he was much upset by the recognition. The following evening, as the bell was sounding for the putting out of the ship's lights, a splash was heard, and the dread cry 'man overboard' was raised. Every effort was made to save the life of the human creature, whose head was seen for a few minutes bobbing up and down among the foam that marked the mighty vessel's track. But without avail. He never rose, and the ship was compelled to proceed on her course. A muster of the crew and passengers showed that the missing man was Jabez Smith, or, more properly, Jabez Hoggen. The depositions of the captain and officers of the ship and of several of the chief passengers regarding the event have been registered at Queensland, and we hasten to lay the facts just arrived by the mail before our readers."

A little time passed, and in some two months there appeared in the same print the following paragraph:

Strange History of Two Charmouth Men.

"The Australian mail just in brings from Victoria the details, as far as they are known, of a romance, unhappily tragic, concerning two late inhabitants of Charmouth. It appears that the two men, but a few months ago well known in our pleasant Dorset village, one having been a policeman and the other a coastguard, had but lately arrived in Melbourne. At first they did not seem of much account, but before long met with a lucky stroke of fortune—alas! fatal to them. After but a short absence, presumably in the northern gold fields, they had evidently made some wonderfully lucky discoveries of gold pockets, for on their return they made such purchases of land and houses as showed that they must have been at the time possessed of great wealth. Suddenly they had quarrelled, for some unknown reason, sold again their property and together disappeared up country. A few days later their bodies, greatly mutilated, were discovered among the charred ruins of a deserted camp. They had either fought and killed each other, or they had been murdered. The fire of the camp had spread and partially consumed the bodies, so that nothing definite could be ascertained. In this romantic story we may read as we run of the vanity of wealth."

When I read the paragraph I felt my mind relieved, for here was assurance to me that I had not dreamed.

One evening long afterward I told my wife and her mother and Cousin Jemima the whole story.

My wife came and put her arms round me and whispered:

"Augustus, dear—you may have dreamed—I hope so, but, thank God! you are spared to us."

My mother-in-law said:

"I think you might have managed to keep some of the money, but you never do as you ought in such things. At any rate, you might have told us before this, but I suppose you have so much to conceal that things like this get lost among them."

Cousin Jemima, after frowning a while and pursing her lips as if thinking, said, sniffing:

"I believe it's all a lie!"

"My dear Cousin Jemima!" I remonstrated.

"Well! suppose it's not," she answered, sharply, "at any rate, you took the crabs from old Hoggen's body and brought them here—no you didn't bring them here, but you let me buy them—to eat! Ugh!! You brute!!!"

I am still in doubt about the whole affair.

Was it a dream?

I do not know!

A DREAM OF RED HANDS

THE first opinion given to me regarding Jacob Settle was a simple descriptive statement, "He's a down-in-the-mouth chap": but I found that it embodied the thoughts and ideas of all his fellow-workmen. There was in the phrase a certain easy tolerance, an absence of positive feeling of any kind, rather than any complete opinion, which marked pretty accurately the man's place in public esteem. Still, there was some dissimilarity between this and his appearance which unconsciously set me thinking, and by degrees, as I saw more of the place and the workmen, I came to have a special interest in him. He was, I found, for ever doing kindnesses, not involving money expenses beyond his humble means, but in the manifold ways of forethought and forbearance and self-repression which are of the truer charities of life. Women and children trusted him implicitly, though, strangely enough, he rather shunned them, except when anyone was sick, and then he made his appearance to help if he could, timidly and awkwardly. He led a very solitary life, keeping house by himself in a tiny cottage, or rather hut, of one room, far on the edge of the moorland. His existence seemed so sad and solitary that I wished to cheer it up, and for the purpose took the occasion when we had both been sitting up with a child, injured by me through accident, to offer to lend him books. He gladly accepted, and as we parted in the grey of the dawn I felt that something of mutual confidence had been established between us.

The books were always most carefully and punctually returned, and in time Jacob Settle and I became quite friends. Once or twice as I crossed the moorland on Sundays I looked in on him; but on such occasions he was shy and ill at ease so that I felt diffident about calling to see him. He would never under any circumstances come into my own lodgings.

One Sunday afternoon, I was coming back from a long walk beyond the moor, and as I passed Settle's cottage stopped at the door to say "How do you do?" to him. As the door was shut, I thought that he was out, and merely knocked for form's sake, or through habit, not expecting to get any answer. To my surprise, I heard a feeble voice from within, though what was said I could not hear. I entered at once, and found Jacob lying half-dressed upon his bed. He was as pale as death, and the sweat was simply rolling off his face. His hands were unconsciously gripping the bed-clothes as a drowning man holds on to whatever he may grasp. As I came in he half arose, with a wild, hunted look in his eyes, which were wide open and staring, as though something of horror had come before him; but when he recognised me he sank back on the couch with a smothered sob of relief and closed his eyes. I stood by him for a while, quite a minute or two, while he gasped. Then he opened his eyes and looked at me, but with such a despairing, woeful expression that, as I am a living man, I would have rather seen that frozen look of horror. I sat down beside him and asked after his health. For a while he would not answer me except to say that he was not ill; but then, after scrutinising me closely, he half arose on his elbow and said—

"I thank you kindly, sir, but I'm simply telling you the truth. I am not ill, as men call it, though God knows whether there be not worse sicknesses than doctors know of. I'll tell you, as you are so kind, but I trust that you won't even mention such a thing to a living soul, for it might work me more and greater woe. I am suffering from a bad dream."

"A bad dream!" I said, hoping to cheer him; "but dreams pass away with the light—even with waking." There I stopped, for before he spoke I saw the answer in his desolate look round the little place.

"No! no! that's all well for people that live in comfort and with those they love around them. It is a thousand times worse for those who live alone and have to do so. What cheer is there for me, waking here in the silence of the night, with the wide moor around me full of voices and full of faces that make my waking a worse dream than my sleep? Ah, young sir, you have no past that can send its legions to people the darkness and the empty space, and I pray the good God that you may never have!" As he spoke, there was such an almost irresistible gravity of conviction in his manner that I abandoned my remonstrance about his solitary life. I felt that I was in the presence of some secret influence which I could not fathom. To my relief, for I knew not what to say, he went on—

"Two nights past have I dreamed it. It was hard enough the first night, but I came through it. Last night the expectation was in itself almost worse than the dream—until the dream came, and then it swept away every remembrance of lesser pain. I stayed awake till just before the dawn, and then it came again, and ever since I have been in such an agony as I am sure the dying feel, and with it all the dread of to-night." Before he had got to the end of the sentence my mind was made up, and I felt that I could speak to him more cheerfully.

"Try and get to sleep early to-night—in fact, before the evening has passed away. The sleep will refresh you, and I promise you there will not be any bad dreams after to-night." He shook his head hopelessly, so I sat a little longer and then left him.

When I got home I made my arrangements for the night, for I had made up my mind to share Jacob Settle's lonely vigil in his cottage on the moor. I judged that if he got to sleep before sunset he would wake well before midnight, and so, just as the bells of the city were striking eleven, I stood opposite his door armed with a bag, in which were my supper, an extra large flask, a couple of candles, and a book. The moonlight was bright, and flooded the whole moor, till it was almost as light as day; but ever and anon black clouds drove across the sky, and made a darkness which by comparison seemed almost tangible. I opened the door softly, and entered without waking Jacob, who lay asleep with his white face upward. He was still, and again bathed in sweat. I tried to imagine what visions were passing before those closed eyes which could bring with them the misery and woe which were stamped on the face, but fancy failed me, and I waited for the awakening. It came suddenly, and in a fashion which touched me to the quick, for the hollow groan that broke from the man's white lips as he half arose and sank back was manifestly the realisation or completion of some train of thought which had gone before.

"If this be dreaming," said I to myself, "then it must be based on some very terrible reality. What can have been that unhappy fact that he spoke of?"

While I thus spoke, he realised that I was with him. It struck me as strange that he had no period of that doubt as to whether dream or reality surrounded him which commonly marks an expected environment of waking men. With a positive cry of joy, he seized my hand and held it in his two wet, trembling hands, as a frightened child clings on to someone whom it loves. I tried to soothe him—

"There, there! it is all right. I have come to stay with you to-night, and together we will try to fight this evil dream." He let go my hand suddenly, and sank back on his bed and covered his eyes with his hands.

"Fight it?—the evil dream! Ah! no, sir no! No mortal power can fight that dream, for it comes from God—and is burned in here;" and he beat upon his forehead. Then he went on—

"It is the same dream, ever the same, and yet it grows in its power to torture me every time it comes."

"What is the dream?" I asked, thinking that the speaking of it might give him some relief, but he shrank away from me, and after a long pause said—

"No, I had better not tell it. It may not come again."

There was manifestly something to conceal from me—something that lay behind the dream, so I answered—

"All right. I hope you have seen the last of it. But if it should come again, you will tell me, will you not? I ask, not out of curiosity, but because I think it may relieve you to speak." He answered with what I thought was almost an undue amount of solemnity—

"If it comes again, I shall tell you all."

Then I tried to get his mind away from the subject to more mundane things, so I produced supper, and made him share it with me, including the contents of the flask. After a little he braced up, and when I lit my cigar, having given him another, we smoked a full hour, and talked of many things. Little by little the comfort of his body stole over his mind, and I could see sleep laying her gentle hands on his eyelids. He felt it, too, and told me that now he felt all right, and I might safely leave him; but I told him that, right or wrong, I was going to see in the daylight. So I lit my other candle, and began to read as he fell asleep.

By degrees I got interested in my book, so interested that presently I was startled by its dropping out of my hands. I looked and saw that Jacob was still asleep, and I was rejoiced to see that there was on his face a look of unwonted happiness, while his lips seemed to move with unspoken words. Then I turned to my work again, and again woke, but this time to feel chilled to my very marrow by hearing the voice from the bed beside me—

"Not with those red hands! Never! never!" On looking at him, I found that he was still asleep. He woke, however, in an instant, and did not seem surprised to see me; there was again that strange apathy as to his surroundings. Then I said:

"Settle, tell me your dream. You may speak freely, for I shall hold your confidence sacred. While we both live I shall never mention what you may choose to tell me."

"I said I would; but I had better tell you first what goes before the dream, that you may understand. I was a schoolmaster when I was a very young man; it was only a parish school in a little village in the West Country. No need to mention any names. Better not. I was engaged to be married to a young girl whom I loved and almost reverenced. It was the old story. While we were waiting for the time when we could afford to set up house together, another man came along. He was nearly as young as I was, and handsome, and a gentleman, with all a gentleman's attractive ways for a woman of our class. He would go fishing, and she would meet him while I was at my work in school. I reasoned with her and implored her to give him up. I offered to get married at once and go away and begin the world in a strange country; but she would not listen to anything I could say, and I could see that she was infatuated with him. Then I took it on myself to meet the man and ask him to deal well with the girl, for I thought he might mean honestly by her, so that there might be no talk or chance of talk on the part of others. I went where I should meet him with none by, and we met!" Here Jacob Settle had to pause, for something seemed to rise in his throat, and he almost gasped for breath. Then he went on—

"Sir, as God is above us, there was no selfish thought in my heart that day, I loved my pretty Mabel too well to be content with a part of her love, and I had thought of my own unhappiness too often not to have come to realise that, whatever might come to her, my hope was gone. He was insolent to me—you, sir, who are a gentleman, cannot know, perhaps, how galling can be the insolence of one who is above you in station—but I bore with that. I implored him to deal well with the girl, for what might be only a pastime of an idle hour with him might be the breaking of her heart. For I never had a thought of her truth, or that the worst of harm could come to her—it was only the unhappiness to her heart I feared. But when I asked him when he intended to marry her his laughter galled me so that I lost my temper and told him that I would not stand by and see her life made unhappy. Then he grew angry too, and in his anger said such cruel things of her that then and there I swore he should not live to do her harm. God knows how it came about, for in such moments of passion it is hard to remember the steps from a word to a blow, but I found myself standing over his dead body, with my hands crimson with the blood that welled from his torn throat. We were alone and he was a stranger, with none of his kin to seek for him and murder does not always out—not all at once. His bones may be whitening still, for all I know, in the pool of the river where I left him. No one suspected his absence, or why it was, except my poor Mabel, and she dared not speak. But it was all in vain, for when I came back again after an absence of months—for I could not live in the place—I learned that her shame had come and that she had died in it. Hitherto I had been borne up by the thought that my ill deed had saved her future, but now, when I learned that I had been too late, and that my poor love was smirched with that man's sin, I fled away with the sense of my useless guilt upon me more heavily than I could bear. Ah! sir, you that have not done such a sin don't know what it is to carry it with you. You may think that custom makes it easy to you, but it is not so. It grows and grows with every hour, till it becomes intolerable, and with it growing, too, the feeling that you must for ever stand outside Heaven. You don't know what that means, and I pray God that you never may. Ordinary men, to whom all things are possible, don't often, if ever, think of Heaven. It is a name, and nothing more, and they are content to wait and let things be, but to those who are doomed to be shut out for ever you cannot think what it means, you cannot guess or measure the terrible endless longing to see the gates opened, and to be able to join the white figures within.

"And this brings me to my dream. It seemed that the portal was before me, with great gates of massive steel with bars of the thickness of a mast, rising to the very clouds, and so close that between them was just a glimpse of a crystal grotto, on whose shining walls were figured many white-clad forms with faces radiant with joy. When I stood before the gate my heart and my soul were so full of rapture and longing that

I forgot. And there stood at the gate two mighty angels with sweeping wings, and, oh! so stern of countenance. They held each in one hand a flaming sword, and in the other the latchet, which moved to and fro at their lightest touch. Nearer were figures all draped in black, with heads covered so that only the eyes were seen, and they handed to each who came white garments such as the angels wear. A low murmur came that told that all should put on their own robes, and without soil, or the angels would not pass them in, but would smite them down with the flaming swords. I was eager to don my own garment, and hurriedly threw it over me and stepped swiftly to the gate; but it moved not, and the angels, loosing the latchet, pointed to my dress, I looked down, and was aghast, for the whole robe was smeared with blood. My hands were red; they glittered with the blood that dripped from them as on that day by the river bank. And then the angels raised their flaming swords to smite me down, and the horror was complete—I awoke. Again, and again, and again, that awful dream comes to me. I never learn from the experience, I never remember, but at the beginning the hope is ever there to make the end more appalling; and I know that the dream does not come out of the common darkness where the dreams abide, but that it is sent from God as a punishment! Never, never shall I be able to pass the gate, for the soil on the angel garments must ever come from these bloody hands!"

I listened as in a spell as Jacob Settle spoke. There was something so far away in the tone of his voice—something so dreamy and mystic in the eyes that looked as if through me at some spirit beyond—something so lofty in his very diction and in such marked contrast to his workworn clothes and his poor surroundings that I wondered if the whole thing were not a dream.

We were both silent for a long time. I kept looking at the man before me in growing wonderment. Now that his confession had been made, his soul, which had been crushed to the very earth, seemed to leap back again to uprightness with some resilient force. I suppose I ought to have been horrified with his story, but, strange to say, I was not. It certainly is not pleasant to be made the recipient of the confidence of a murderer, but this poor fellow seemed to have had, not only so much provocation, but so much self-denying purpose in his deed of blood that I did not feel called upon to pass judgment upon him. My purpose was to comfort, so I spoke out with what calmness I could, for my heart was beating fast and heavily—

"You need not despair, Jacob Settle. God is very good, and his mercy is great. Live on and work on in the hope that some day you may feel that you have atoned for the past." Here I paused, for I could see that sleep, natural sleep this time, was creeping upon him. "Go to sleep," I said; "I shall watch with you here, and we shall have no more evil dreams to-night."

He made an effort to pull himself together, and answered—

"I don't know how to thank you for your goodness to me this night, but I think you had best leave me now. I'll try and sleep this out; I feel a weight off my mind since I have told you all. If there's anything of the man left in me, I must try and fight out life alone."

"I'll go to-night, as you wish it," I said; "but take my advice, and do not live in such a solitary way. Go among men and women; live among them. Share their joys and sorrows, and it will help you to forget. This solitude will make you melancholy mad."

"I will!" he answered, half unconsciously, for sleep was overmastering him.

I turned to go, and he looked after me. When I had touched the latch I dropped it, and, coming back to the bed, held out my hand. He grasped it with both his as he rose to a sitting posture, and I said my good-night, trying to cheer him—

"Heart, man, heart! There is work in the world for you to do, Jacob Settle. You can wear those white robes yet and pass through that gate of steel!"

Then I left him.

A week after I found his cottage deserted, and on asking at the works was told that he had "gone north," no one exactly knew whither.

Two years afterwards, I was staying for a few days with my friend Dr. Munro in Glasgow. He was a busy man, and could not spare much time for going about with me, so I spent my days in excursions to the Trossachs and Loch Katrine and down the Clyde. On the second last evening of my stay I came back somewhat later than I had arranged, but found that my host was late too. The maid told me that he had been sent for to the hospital—a case of accident at the gas-works, and the dinner was postponed an hour; so telling her I would stroll down to find her master and walk back with him, I went out. At the hospital I found him washing his hands preparatory to starting for home. Casually, I asked him what his case was.

"Oh, the usual thing! A rotten rope and men's lives of no account. Two men were working in a gasometer, when the rope that held their scaffolding broke. It must have occurred just before the dinner hour, for no one noticed their absence till the men had returned. There was about seven feet of water in the gasometer, so they had a hard fight for it, poor fellows. However, one of them was alive, just alive, but we have had a hard job to pull him through. It seems that he owes his life to his mate, for I have never heard of greater heroism. They swam together while their strength lasted, but at the end they were so done up that even the lights above, and the men slung with ropes, coming down to help them, could not keep them up. But one of them stood on the bottom and held up his comrade over his head, and those few breaths made all the difference between life and death. They were a shocking sight when they were taken out, for that water is like a purple dye with the gas and the tar. The man upstairs looked as if he had been washed in blood. Ugh!"

"And the other?"

"Oh, he's worse still. But he must have been a very noble fellow. That struggle under the water must have been fearful; one can see that by the way the blood has been drawn from the extremities. It makes the idea of the *Stigmata* possible to look at him. Resolution like this could, you would think, do anything in the world. Ay! it might almost unbar the gates of Heaven. Look here, old man, it is not a very pleasant sight, especially just before dinner, but you are a writer, and this is an odd case. Here is something you would not like to miss, for in all human probability you will never see anything like it again." While he was speaking he had brought me into the mortuary of the hospital.

On the bier lay a body covered with a white sheet, which was wrapped close round it.

"Looks like a chrysalis, don't it? I say, Jack, if there be anything in the old myth that a soul is typified by a butterfly, well, then the one that this chrysalis sent forth was a very noble specimen and took all the sunlight on its wings. See here!" He uncovered the face. Horrible, indeed, it looked, as though stained with blood. But I knew him at once, Jacob Settle! My friend pulled the winding sheet further down.

The hands were crossed on the purple breast as they had been reverently placed by some tender-hearted person. As I saw them, my heart throbbed with a great exultation, for the memory of his harrowing dream rushed across my mind. There was no stain now on those poor, brave hands, for they were blanched white as snow.

And somehow as I looked I felt that the evil dream was all over. That noble soul had won a way through the gate at last. The white robe had now no stain from the hands that had put it on.

THE MAN FROM SHORROX'

"THROTH, yer 'ann'rs, I'll tell ye wid pleasure; though, trooth to tell, it's only poor wurrk telling the same shtory over an' over agin. But I niver object to tell it to rale gintlemin, like yer 'ann'rs, what don't forget that a poor man has a mouth on to him as much as Creeshus himself has.

"The place was a market-town in Kilkenny—or maybe King's County or Queen's County. At all evints, it was wan of them counties what Cromwell—bad cess to him!—gev his name to. An' the house was called after him that was the Lord Liftinint an' invinted the polis—God forgive him! It was kep' be a man iv the name iv Misther Mickey Byrne an' his good lady—at laste it was till wan dark night whin the bhoys mistuk him for another gintleman, an unknown man, what had bought a contagious property—mind ye the impidence iv him. Mickey was comin' back from the Curragh Races wid his skin that tight wid the full of the whisky inside of him that he couldn't open his eyes to see what was goin' on, or his mouth to set the bhoys right afther he had got the first tap on the head wid wan of the blackthorns what they done such jobs wid. The poor bhoys was that full of sorra for their mishap whin they brung him home to his widdy that the crather hadn't the hearrt to be too savere on thim. At the first iv course she was wroth, bein' only a woman afther all, an' weemin not bein' gave to rayson like min is. Millia murdher! but for a bit she was like a madwoman, and was nigh to have cut the heads from aff av thim wid the mate chopper, till, seein' thim so white and quite, she all at wance flung down the chopper an' knelt down be the corp.

"'Lave me to me dead,' she sez. 'Oh min! it's no use more people nor is needful bein' made unhappy over this night's terrible wurrk. Mick Byrne would have no man worse for him whin he was living, and he'll have harm to none for his death! Now go; an', oh bhoys, be dacent and quite, an' don't thry a poor widdied sowl too hard!'

"Well, afther that she made no change in things ginerally, but kep' on the hotel jist the same; an' whin some iv her friends wanted her to get help, she only sez:

"'Mick an' me run this house well enough; an' whin I'm thinkin' of takin' help I'll tell yez. I'll go on be meself, as I mane to, till Mick an' me comes together agin.'

"An', sure enough, the ould place wint on jist the same, though, more betoken, there wasn't Mick wid his shillelagh to kape the pace whin things got pretty hot on fair nights, an' in the gran' ould election times, when heads was bruk like eggs—glory be to God!

"My! but she was the fine woman, was the Widdy Byrne! A gran' cra-thur intirely: a fine upshtandin' woman, nigh as tall as a modherate-sized man, wid a forrm on her that'd warrm yer hearrt to look at, it sthood out that way in the right places. She had shkin like satin, wid a warrm flush in it, like the sun shinin' on a crock iv yesherday's crame; an' her cheeks an' her neck was that firrm that ye couldn't take a pinch iv thim—though sorra wan iver dar'd to thry, the worse luck! But her hair! Begor, that was the finishing touch that set all the min crazy. It was jist wan mass iv red, like the hearrt iv a burnin' furze-bush whin the smoke goes from aff iv it. Musha! but it'd make the blood come up in yer eyes to see the glint iv that hair wid the light shinin' on it. There was niver a man, what was a man at all at all, iver kem in be the door that he didn't want to put his two arrms round the widdy an' giv' her a hug immadiate. They was fine min too, some iv thim—and warrm men—big graziers from Kildare,

and the like, that counted their cattle be scores, an' used to come ridin' in
to market on huntin' horses what they'd refuse hundhreds iv pounds for
from officers in the Curragh an' the quality. Begor, but some iv thim an'
the dhrovers was rare min in a fight. More nor wance I seen them, forty,
maybe half a hundred, strong, clear the market-place at Banagher or
Athy. Well do I remember the way the big, red, hairy wrists iv thim'd go
up in the air, an' down'd come the springy ground-ash saplins what they
carried for switches. The whole lot iv thim wanted to come coortin' the
widdy; but sorra wan iv her'd look at thim. She'd flirt an' be coy an' taze
thim and make thim mad for love iv her, as weemin likes to do. Thank
God for the same! for mayhap we min wouldn't love thim as we do only
for their thricky ways; an' thin what'd become iv the counthry wid nothin'
in it at all except single min an' ould maids jist dyin', and growin' crabbed
for want iv childher to kiss an' tache an' shpank an' make love to? Shure,
yer 'ann'rs, 'tis childher as makes the hearrt iv man green, jist as it is fresh
wather that makes the grass grow. Divil a shtep nearer would the widdy
iver let mortial man come. 'No,' she'd say; 'whin I see a man fit to fill
Mick's place, I'll let yez know iv it; thank ye kindly'; an' wid that she'd
shake her head till the beautiful red hair iv it'd be like shparks iv fire—an'
the min more mad for her nor iver.

"But, mind ye, she wasn't no shpoil-shport; Mick's wife knew more
nor that, an' his widdy didn't forgit the thrick iv it. She'd lade the laugh
herself if 'twas anything a dacent woman could shmile at; an' if it wasn't,
she'd send the girrls aff to their beds, an' tell the min they might go on
talkin' that way, for there was only herself to be insulted; an' that'd shut
thim up pretty quick I'm tellin' yez. But av any iv thim'd thry to git
affectionate, as min do whin they've had all they can carry, well, thin she
had a playful way iv dalin' wid thim what'd always turn the laugh agin'
thim. She used to say that she larned the beginnin' iv it at the school
an' the rest iv it from Mick. She always kep by her on the counther iv
the bar wan iv thim rattan canes wid the curly ends, what the soldiers

carries whin they can't borry a whip, an' are goin' out wid their cap on
three hairs, an' thim new oiled, to scorch the girrls. An' thin whin any iv
the shuitors'd get too affectionate she'd lift the cane an' swish them wid
it, her laughin' out iv her like mad all the time. At first wan or two iv
the min'd say that a kiss at the widdy was worth a clip iv a cane; an' wan
iv thim, a warrm horse-farmer from Poul-a-Phoka, said he'd complate
the job av she was to cut him into ribbons. But she was a handy woman
wid the cane—which was shtrange enough, for she had no childer to be
practisin' on—an' whin she threw what was left iv him back over the bar,
wid his face like a gridiron, the other min what was laughin' along wid
her tuk the lesson to hearrt. Whiniver afther that she laid her hand on
the cane, no matther how quitely, there'd be no more talk iv thryin' for
kissin' in that quarther.

"Well, at the time I'm comin' to there was great divarshuns intirely
goin' on in the town. The fair was on the morra, an' there was a power
iv people in the town; an' cattle, an' geese, an' turkeys, an' butther, an'
pigs, an' vegetables, an' all kinds iv divilment, includin' a berryin'—the
same bein' an ould attorney-man, savin' yer prisince; a lone man widout
friends, lyin' out there in the gran' room iv the hotel what they call the
'Queen's Room.' Well, I needn't tell yer 'ann'rs that the place was pretty
full that night. Musha, but it's the fleas thimselves what had the bad time
iv it, wid thim crowded out on the outside, an' shakin', an' thrimblin' wid
the cowld. The widdy, av coorse, was in the bar passin' the time iv the
day wid all that kem in, an' keepin' her eyes afore an' ahint her to hould
the girrls up to their wurrk an' not to be thriflin' wid the min. My! but
there was a power iv min at the bar that night; warrm farmers from four
counties, an' graziers wid their ground-ash plants an' big frieze coats,
an' plinty iv commercials, too. In the middle iv it all, up the shtreet at a
hand gallop comes an Athy carriage wid two horses, an' pulls up at the
door wid the horses shmokin'. An' begor', the man in it was smokin' too,
a big cygar nigh as long as yer arrm. He jumps out an' walks up as bould

as brass to the bar, jist as if there was niver a livin' sowl but himself in the place. He chucks the widdy undher the chin at wanst, an', taking aff his hat, sez:

"'I want the best room in the house. I travel for Shorrox', the greatest long-cotton firrm in the whole worrld, an' I want to open up a new line here! The best is what I want, an' that's not good enough for me!'

"Well, gintlemin, ivery wan in the place was spacheless at his impidence; an', begor! that was the only time in her life I'm tould whin the widdy was tuk back. But, glory be, it didn't take long for her to recover herself, an' sez she quitely:

"'I don't doubt ye, sur! The best can't be too good for a gintleman what makes himself so aisy at home!' an' she shmiled at him till her teeth shone like jools.

"God knows, gintlemin, what does be in weemin's minds whin they're dalin' wid a man! Maybe it was that Widdy Byrne only wanted to kape the pace wid all thim min crowdin' roun' her, an' thim clutchin' on tight to their shticks an' aiger for a fight wid any man on her account. Or maybe it was that she forgive him his impidence; for well I know that it's not the most modest man, nor him what kapes his distance, that the girrls, much less the widdies, likes the best. But anyhow she spake out iv her to the man from Manchesther:—

"'I'm sorry, sur, that I can't give ye the best room—what we call the best—for it is engaged already.'

"'Then turn him out!' sez he.

"'I can't,' she says—'at laste not till to-morra; an' ye can have the room thin iv ye like.'

"There was a kind iv a sort iv a shnicker among some iv the min, thim knowin' iv the corp, an' the Manchesther man tuk it that they was laughin' at him; so he sez:

"'I'll shleep in that room to-night; the other gintleman can put up wid me iv I can wid him. Unless,' sez he, oglin' the widdy, 'I can have the place iv the masther iv the house, if there's a priest or a parson handy in this town—an' sober,' sez he.

"Well, tho' the widdy got as red as a Claddagh cloak, she jist laughed an' turned aside, sayin':

"'Throth, sur, but it's poor Mick's place ye might have, an' welkim, this night.'

"'An' where might that be now, ma'am?' sez he, lanin' over the bar; an' him would have chucked her under the chin agin, only that she moved her head away that quick.

"'In the churchyard!' she sez. 'Ye might take Mick's place there, av ye like, an' I'll not be wan to say ye no.'

"At that the min round all laughed, an' the man from Manchesther got mad, an' shpoke out, rough enough too it seemed:

"'Oh, he's all right where he is. I daresay he's quiter times where he is than whin he had my luk out. Him an' the devil can toss for choice in bein' lonely or bein' quite.'

"Wid that the widdy blazes up all iv a suddint, like a live sod shtuck in the thatch, an' sez she:

"'Who are ye that dares to shpake ill iv the dead, an' to couple his name wid the divil, an' to his widdy's very face? It's aisy seen that poor Mick is gone!' an' wid that she threw her apron over her head an' sot down an' rocked herself to and fro, as widdies do whin the fit is on thim iv missin' the dead.

"There was more nor wan man there what'd like to have shtud opposite the Manchesther man wid a bit iv a blackthorn in his hand; but they knew the widdy too well to dar to intherfere till they were let. At length wan iv thim—Mr. Hogan, from nigh Portarlington, a warrm man, that'd put down a thousand pounds iv dhry money any day in the week—kem over to the bar an' tuk aff his hat, an' sez he:

"Mrs. Byrne, ma'am, as a friend of poor dear ould Mick, I'd be glad to take his quarrel on meself on his account, an' more than proud to take it on his widdy's, if, ma'am, ye'll only honour me be saying the wurrd.'

"Wid that she tuk down the apron from aff iv her head an' wiped away the tears in her jools iv eyes wid the corner iv it.

"'Thank ye kindly,' sez she; 'but, gintlemin, Mick an' me run this hotel long together, an' I've run it alone since thin, an' I mane to go on runnin' it be meself, even if new min from Manchesther itself does be bringin' us new ways. As to you, sur,' sez she, turnin' to him, 'it's powerful afraid I am that there isn't accommodation here for a gintlemin what's so requireful. An' so I think I'll be askin' ye to find convanience in some other hotel in the town.'

"Wid that he turned on her an' sez, 'I'm here now, an' I offer to pay me charges. Be the law ye can't refuse to resave me or refuse me lodgmint, especially whin I'm on the primises.'

"So the Widdy Byrne drewed herself up, an' sez she, 'Sur, ye ask yer legal rights; ye shall have them. Tell me what it is ye require.'

"Sez he sthraight out: 'I want the best room.'

"'I've tould you already,' sez she, 'there's a gintleman in it.'

"'Well,' sez he, 'what other room have ye vacant?'

"'Sorra wan at all,' sez she. 'Every room in the house is tuk. Perhaps, sur, ye don't think or remimber that there's a fair on to-morra.'

"She shpoke so polite that ivery man in the place knew there was somethin' comin'—later on. The Manchesther man felt that the laugh was on him; but he didn't want for impidence, so he up, an' sez he:

"'Thin, if I have to share wid another, I'll share wid the best! It's the Queen's Room I'll be shleepin' in this night.'

"Well, the min shtandin' by wasn't too well plazed wid what was going on; for the man from Manchesther he was plumin' himself for all the worrld like a cock on a dunghill. He laned agin over the bar an' began makin' love to the widdy hot an' fast. He was a fine, shtout-made man, wid a bull neck on to him an' short hair, like wan iv thim 'two-to-wan-bar-wans' what I've seen at Punchestown an' Fairy House an' the Galway races. But he seemed to have no manners at all in his coortin', but done it as quick an' business-like as takin' his commercial ordhers. It was like this: 'I want to make love; you want to be made love to, bein' a woman. Hould up yer head!'

"We all could see that the widdy was boilin' mad; but, to do him fair, the man from Manchesther didn't seem to care what any wan thought. But we all seen what he didn't see at first, that the widdy began widout thinkin' to handle the rattan cane on the bar. Well, prisintly he began agin to ask about his room, an' what kind iv a man it was that was to share it wid him.

"So sez the widdy, 'A man wid less wickedness in him nor you have, an' less impidence.'

"'I hope he's a quite man,' sez he.

"So the widdy began to laugh, an' sez she: 'I'll warrant he's quite enough.'

"'Does he shnore? I hate a man—or a woman ayther—what shnores.'

"'Throth,' sez she, 'there's no shnore in him'; an' she laughed agin.

"Some iv the min round what knew iv the ould attorney-man—saving yer prisince—began to laugh too; and this made the Manchesther man suspicious. When the likes iv him gets suspicious he gets rale nasty; so he sez, wid a shneer:

"'You seem to be pretty well up in his habits, ma'am!'

"The widdy looked round at the graziers, what was clutchin' their ash plants hard, an' there was a laughin' divil in her eye that kep' thim quite; an' thin she turned round to the man, and sez she:

"'Oh, I know that much, anyhow, wid wan thing an' another, begor!'

"But she looked more enticin' nor iver at that moment. For sure the man from Manchesther thought so, for he laned nigh his whole body over the counther, an' whispered somethin' at her, puttin' out his hand as he did so, an' layin' it on her neck to dhraw her to him. The widdy seemed to know what was comin', an' had her hand on the rattan; so whin he was draggin' her to him an' puttin' out his lips to kiss her—an' her first as red as a turkey-cock an' thin as pale as a sheet—she ups wid the cane and gev him wan skelp across the face wid it, shpringin' back as she done so. Oh jool! but that was a skelp! A big wale iv blood riz up as quick as the blow was shtruck, jist as I've seen on the pigs' backs whin they do be prayin' aloud not to be tuk where they're wanted.

"'Hands off, Misther Impidence!' sez she. The man from Manchesther was that mad that he ups wid the tumbler forninst him an' was goin' to throw it at her, whin there kem an odd sound from the graziers—a sort of 'Ach!' as whin a man is workin' a sledge, an' I seen the ground-ash plants an' the big fists what held thim, and the big hairy wrists go up in the air. Begor, but polis thimselves wid bayonets wouldn't care to face thim like that! In the half of two twos the man from Manchesther would have been cut in ribbons, but there came a cry from the widdy what made the glasses ring:

"'Shtop! I'm not goin' to have any fightin' here; an' besides, there's bounds to the bad manners iv even a man from Shorrox'. He wouldn't dar to shtrike me—though I have no head! Maybe I hit a thought too hard; but I had rayson to remimber that somethin' was due on Mick's account too. I'm sorry, sur,' sez she to the man, quite polite, 'that I had to defind meself; but whin a gintleman claims the law to come into a house, an' thin assaults th' owner iv it, though she has no head, it's more restrainful he should be intirely!'

"'Hear, hear!' cried some iv the min, an' wan iv thim sez 'Amen,' sez he, an' they all begin to laugh. The Manchesther man he didn't know what to do; for begor he didn't like the look of thim ash plants up in the air, an' yit he was not wan to like the laugh agin' him or to take it aisy. So he turns to the widdy an' he lifts his hat an' sez he wid mock politeness:

"'I must complimint ye, ma'am, upon the shtrength iv yer arrm, as upon the mildness iv yer disposition. Throth, an' I'm thinkin' that it's misther Mick that has the best iv it, wid his body lyin' paceful in the churchyard, anyhow; though the poor sowl doesn't seem to have much good in changin' wan devil for another!' An' he looked at her rale spiteful.

"Well, for a minit her eyes blazed, but thin she shmiled at him, an' made a low curtsey, an' sez she—oh! mind ye, she was a gran' woman at givin' back as good as she got—

"'Thank ye kindly, sur, for yer polite remarks about me arrm. Sure me poor dear Mick often said the same; only he said more an' wid shuparior knowledge! "Molly," sez he—"I'd mislike the shtrength iv yer arrm whin ye shtrike, only that I forgive ye for it whin it comes to the huggin'!" But as to poor Mick's prisint condition I'm not goin' to argue wid ye, though I can't say that I forgive ye for the way you've shpoke iv him that's gone. Bedad, it's fond iv the dead y'are, for ye seem onable to kape thim out iv yer mouth. Maybe ye'll be more respectful to thim before ye die!'

"'I don't want no sarmons!' sez he, wery savage. 'Am I to have me room to-night, or am I not?'

"'Did I undherstand ye to say,' sez she, 'that ye wanted a share iv the Queen's Room?'

"'I did! an' I demand it.'

"'Very well, sur,' sez she very quitely, 'ye shall have it!' Jist thin the supper war ready, and most iv the min at the bar thronged into the coffee-room, an' among thim the man from Manchesther, what wint bang up to the top iv the table an sot down as though he owned the place, an' him niver in the house before. A few iv the bhoys shtayed a minit to say another word to the widdy, an' as soon as they was alone Misther Hogan up, an' sez he:

"'Oh, darlint! but it's a jool iv a woman y' are! Do ye raly mane to put him in the room wid the corp?'

"'He said he insisted on being in that room!' she says, quite sarious; an' thin givin' a look undher her lashes at the bhoys as made thim lep, sez she:

"'Oh! min, an ye love me give him his shkin that full that he'll tumble into his bed this night wid his sinses obscurified. Dhrink toasts till he mis-remimbers where he is! Whist! Go, quick, so that he won't suspect nothin'!'

"That was a warrm night, I'm telling ye! The man from Shorrox' had wine galore wid his mate; an' afther, whin the plates an' dishes was tuk away an' the nuts was brought in, Hogan got up an' proposed his health, an' wished him prosperity in his new line. Iv coorse he had to dhrink that; an' thin others got up, an' there was more toasts dhrunk than there was min in the room, till the man, him not bein' used to whisky punch, began to git onsartin in his shpache. So they gev him more toasts—'Ireland as a nation,' an' 'Home Rule,' an' 'The mimory iv Dan O'Connell,' an' 'Bad luck to Boney,' an' 'God save the Queen,' an' 'More power to Manchesther,' an' other things what they thought would plaze him, him bein' English. Long hours before it was time for the house to shut, he was as dhrunk as a whole row of fiddlers, an' kep shakin' hands wid ivery man an' promisin' thim to open a new line in Home Rule, an' sich nonsinse. So they tuk him up to the door iv the Queen's Room an' left him there.

"He managed to undhress himself all except his hat, and got into bed wid the corp iv th' ould attorney-man, an' thin an' there fell asleep widout noticin' him.

"'Well, prisintly he woke wid a cowld feelin' all over him. He had lit no candle, an' there was only the light from the passage comin' in through the glass over the door. He felt himself nigh failin' out iv the bed wid him almost on the edge, an' the cowld shtrange gintleman lyin' shlap on the broad iv his back in the middle. He had enough iv the dhrink in him to be quarrelsome.

"'I'll throuble ye,' sez he, 'to kape over yer own side iv the bed—or I'll soon let ye know the rayson why.' An' wid that he give him a shove. But iv coorse the ould attorney-man tuk no notice whatsumiver.

"'Y'are not that warrm that one'd like to lie contagious to ye,' sez he. 'Move over, I say, to yer own side!' But divil a shtir iv the corp.

"Well, thin he began to get fightin' angry, an' to kick an' shove the corp; but not gittin' any answer at all at all, he turned round an' hit him a clip on the side iv the head.

"'Git up,' he sez, 'iv ye're a man at all, an' put up yer dooks.'

"Then he got more madder shtill, for the dhrink was shtirrin' in him, an' he kicked an' shoved an' grabbed him be the leg an' the arrm to move him.

"'Begor!' sez he, 'but ye're the cowldest chap I iver kem anigh iv. Musha! but yer hairs is like icicles.'

"Thin he tuk him be the head, an' shuk him an' brung him to the bedside, an' kicked him clane out on to the flure on the far side iv the bed.

"'Lie there,' he sez, 'ye ould blast furnace! Ye can warrm yerself up on the flure till to-morra.'

"Be this time the power iv the dhrink he had tuk got ahoult iv him agin, an' he fell back in the middle iv the bed, wid his head on the pilla an' his toes up, an' wint aff ashleep, like a cat in the frost.

"By-an'-by, whin the house was about shuttin' up, the watcher from th' undher-taker's kem to sit be the corp till the mornin', an' th' attorney him bein' a Protestan' there was no candles. Whin the house was quite, wan iv the girrls, what was coortin' wid the watcher, shtole into the room.

"'Are ye there, Michael?' sez she.

"'Yis, me darlint!' he sez, comin' to her; an' there they shtood be the door, wid the lamp in the passage shinin' on the red heads iv the two iv thim.

"'I've come,' sez Katty, 'to kape ye company for a bit, Michael; for it's crool lonesome worrk sittin' there alone all night. But I mustn't shtay long, for they're all goin' to bed soon, when the dishes is washed up.'

"'Give us a kiss,' sez Michael.

"'Oh, Michael!' sez she: 'kissin' in the prisince iv a corp! It's ashamed iv ye I am.'

"Sorra cause, Katty. Sure, it's more respectful than any other way. Isn't it next to kissin' in the chapel?—an' ye do that whin ye're bein' married.

If ye kiss me now, begor but I don't know as it's mortial nigh a weddin' it is! Anyhow, give us a kiss, an' we'll talk iv the rights an' wrongs iv it aftherwards.'

"Well, somehow, yer 'ann'rs, that kiss was bein' gave—an' a kiss in the prisince iv a corp is a sarious thing an' takes a long time. Thim two was payin' such attintion to what was going on betune thim that they didn't heed nothin', whin suddint Katty stops, and sez:

"'Whist! what is that?'

"Michael felt creepy too, for there was a quare sound comin' from the bed. So they grabbed one another as they shtud in the doorway an' looked at the bed almost afraid to breathe till the hair on both iv thim began to shtand up in horror; for the corp rose up in the bed, an' they seen it pointin' at thim, an' heard a hoarse voice say,—

"'It's in hell I am!—Divils around me! Don't I see thim burnin' wid their heads like flames? an' it's burnin' I am too—burnin', burnin', burnin'! Me throat is on fire, an' me face is burnin'! Wather! wather! Give me wather, if only a dhrop on me tongue's tip!'

"Well, thin Katty let one screetch out iv her, like to wake the dead, an' tore down the passage till she kem to the shtairs, and tuk a flyin' lep down an' fell in a dead faint on the mat below; and Michael yelled 'murdher' wid all his might.

"It wasn't long till there was a crowd in that room, I tell ye; an' a mighty shtrange thing it was that sorra wan iv the graziers had even tuk his coat from aff iv him to go to bed, or laid by his shtick. An' the widdy too, she was as nate an' tidy as iver, though seemin' surprised out iv a sound shleep, an' her clothes onto her, all savin' a white bedgown, an' a candle in her hand. There was some others what had been in bed, min an' wimin wid their bare feet an' slippers on to some iv thim, wid their bracers down their backs, an' their petticoats flung on anyhow. An' some iv thim in big nightcaps, an' some wid their hair all screwed up in knots wid little wisps iv paper, like farden screws iv Limerick twist or Lundy

Foot snuff. Musha! but it was the ould weemin what was afraid iv things what didn't alarrm the young wans at all. Divil resave me! but the sole thing they seemed to dhread was the min—dead or alive it was all wan to thim—an' 'twas ghosts an' corpses an' mayhap divils that the rest was afeard iv.

"Well, whin the Manchester man seen thim all come tumblin' into the room he began to git his wits about him; for the dhrink was wearin' aff, an' he was thryin' to remimber where he was. So whin he seen the widdy he put his hand up to his face where the red welt was, an' at wance seemed to undhershtand, for he got mad agin an' roared out:

"'What does this mane? Why this invasion iv me chamber? Clear out the whole kit, or I'll let yez know!' Wid that he was goin' to jump out of bed, but the moment they seen his toes the ould weemin let a screech out iv thim, an' clung to the min an' implored thim' to save thim from murdher—an' worse. An' there was the Widdy Byrne laughin' like mad; an' Misther Hogan shtepped out, an' sez he:

"'Do jump out, Misther Shorrox! The boys has their switches, an' it's a mighty handy costume ye're in for a leatherin'!'

"So wid that he jumped back into bed an' covered the clothes over him.

"'In the name of God,' sez he, 'what does it all mane?'

"'It manes this,' sez Hogan, goin' round the bed an' draggin' up the corp an' layin' it on the bed beside him. 'Begorra! but it's a cantankerous kind iv a scut y'are. First nothin' will do ye but sharin' a room wid a corp; an' thin ye want the whole place to yerself.'

"'Take it away! Take it away,' he yells out.

"'Begorra,' sez Mister Hogan, 'I'll do no such thing. The gintleman ordhered the room first, an' it's he has the right to ordher you to be brung out!'

"'Did he shnore much, sur?' says the widdy; an' wid that she burst out laughin' an' cryin' all at wanst. 'That'll tache ye to shpake ill iv the dead agin!' An' she flung her petticoat over her head an' run out iv the room.

"Well, we turned the min all back to their own rooms; for the most part iv thim had plenty iv dhrink on board, an' we feared for a row. Now that the fun was over, we didn't want any unplisintness to follow. So two iv the graziers wint into wan bed, an' we put the man from Manchesther in th' other room, an' gev him a screechin' tumbler iv punch to put the hearrt in him agin.

"I thought the widdy had gone to her bed; but whin I wint to put out the lights I seen one in the little room behind the bar, an' I shtepped quite, not to dishturb her, and peeped in. There she was on a low shtool rockin' herself to an' fro, an' goin' on wid her laughin' an' cryin' both together, while she tapped wid her fut on the flure. She was talkin' to herself in a kind iv a whisper, an' I heerd her say:

"'Oh, but it's the crool woman I am to have such a thing done in me house—an' that poor sowl, wid none to weep for him, knocked about that a way for shport iv dhrunken min—while me poor dear darlin' himself is in the cowld clay!—But oh! Mick, Mick, if ye were only here! Wouldn't it be you—you wid the fun iv ye an' yer merry hearrt—that'd be plazed wid the doin's iv this night!'"

THE BURIAL OF THE RATS

L EAVING Paris by the Orleans road, cross the Enceinte, and, turning to the right, you find yourself in a somewhat wild and not at all savoury district. Right and left, before and behind, on every side rise great heaps of dust and waste accumulated by the process of time.

Paris has its night as well as its day life, and the sojourner who enters his hotel in the Rue de Rivoli or the Rue St. Honore late at night or leaves it early in the morning, can guess, in coming near Montrouge—if he has not done so already—the purpose of those great waggons that look like boilers on wheels which he finds halting everywhere as he passes.

Every city has its peculiar institutions created out of its own needs; and one of the most notable institutions of Paris is its rag-picking population. In the early morning—and Parisian life commences at an early hour—may be seen in most streets standing on the pathway opposite every court and alley and between every few houses, as still in some American cities, even in parts of New York, large wooden boxes into which the domestics or tenement-holders empty the accumulated dust of the past day. Round these boxes gather and pass on, when the work is done, to fresh fields of labour and pastures new, squalid, hungry-looking men and women, the implements of whose craft consist of a coarse bag or basket slung over the shoulder and a little rake with which they turn over and probe and examine in the minutest manner the dustbins. They pick up and deposit in their baskets, by aid of their rakes, whatever they may find, with the same facility as a Chinaman uses his chopsticks.

Paris is a city of centralisation—and centralisation and classification are closely allied. In the early times, when centralisation is becoming a fact, its forerunner is classification. All things which are similar or analogous become grouped together, and from the grouping of groups rises one whole or central point. We see radiating many long arms with innumerable tentaculæ, and in the centre rises a gigantic head with a comprehensive brain and keen eyes to look on every side and ears sensitive to hear—and a voracious mouth to swallow.

Other cities resemble all the birds and beasts and fishes whose appetites and digestions are normal. Paris alone is the analogical apotheosis of the octopus. Product of centralisation carried to an *ad absurdum*, it fairly represents the devil fish; and in no respects is the resemblance more curious than in the similarity of the digestive apparatus.

Those intelligent tourists who, having surrendered their individuality into the hands of Messrs. Cook or Gaze, "do" Paris in three days, are often puzzled to know how it is that the dinner which in London would cost about six shillings, can be had for three francs in a café in the Palais Royal. They need have no more wonder if they will but consider the classification which is a theoretic speciality of Parisian life, and adopt all round the fact from which the chiffonier has his genesis.

The Paris of 1850 was not like the Paris of to-day, and those who see the Paris of Napoleon and Baron Hausseman can hardly realise the existence of the state of things forty-five years ago.

Amongst other things, however, which have not changed are those districts where the waste is gathered. Dust is dust all the world over, in every age, and the family likeness of dust-heaps is perfect. The traveller, therefore, who visits the environs of Montrouge can go back in fancy without difficulty to the year 1850.

In this year I was making a prolonged stay in Paris. I was very much in love with a young lady who, though she returned my passion, so far yielded to the wishes of her parents that she had promised not to see me or to correspond with me for a year. I, too, had been compelled to accede to these conditions under a vague hope of parental approval. During the term of probation I had promised to remain out of the country and not to write to my dear one until the expiration of the year.

Naturally the time went heavily with me. There was no one of my own family or circle who could tell me of Alice, and none of her own folk had, I am sorry to say, sufficient generosity to send me even an occasional word of comfort regarding her health and well-being. I spent six months wandering about Europe, but as I could find no satisfactory distraction in travel, I determined to come to Paris, where, at least, I would be within easy hail of London in case any good fortune should call me thither before the appointed time. That "hope deferred maketh the heart sick" was never better exemplified than in my case, for in addition to the perpetual longing to see the face I loved there was always with me a harrowing anxiety lest some accident should prevent me showing Alice in due time that I had, throughout the long period of probation, been faithful to her trust and my own love. Thus, every adventure which I undertook had a fierce pleasure of its own, for it was fraught with possible consequences greater than it would have ordinarily borne.

Like all travellers I exhausted the places of most interest in the first month of my stay, and was driven in the second month to look for amusement whithersoever I might. Having made sundry journeys to the better-known suburbs, I began to see that there was a *terra incognita*, in so far as the guide book was concerned, in the social wilderness lying between these attractive points. Accordingly I began to systematise my researches, and each day took up the thread of my exploration at the place where I had on the previous day dropped it.

In process of time my wanderings led me near Montrouge, and I saw that hereabouts lay the Ultima Thule of social exploration—a country as little known as that round the source of the White Nile. And so I determined to investigate philosophically the chiffonier—his habitat, his life, and his means of life.

The job was an unsavoury one, difficult of accomplishment, and with little hope of adequate reward. However, despite reason, obstinacy prevailed, and I entered into my new investigation with a keener energy than I could have summoned to aid me in any investigation leading to any end, valuable or worthy.

One day, late in a fine afternoon, toward the end of September, I entered the holy of holies of the city of dust. The place was evidently the recognised abode of a number of chiffoniers, for some sort of arrangement was manifested in the formation of the dust-heaps near the road. I passed amongst these heaps, which stood like orderly sentries, determined to penetrate further and trace dust to its ultimate location.

As I passed along I saw behind the dust-heaps a few forms that flitted to and fro, evidently watching with interest the advent of any stranger to such a place. The district was like a small Switzerland, and as I went forward my tortuous course shut out the path behind me.

Presently I got into what seemed a small city or community of chiffoniers. There were a number of shanties or huts, such as may be met with in the remote parts of the Bog of Allan—rude places with wattled walls, plastered with mud and roofs of rude thatch made from stable refuse—such places as one would not like to enter for any consideration, and which even in water-colour could only look picturesque if judiciously treated. In the midst of these huts was one of the strangest adaptations—I cannot say habitations—I had ever seen. An immense old wardrobe, the colossal remnant of some boudoir of Charles VII. or Henry II., had been converted into a dwelling-house. The double doors lay open, so that the entire menage was open to public view. In the open half of the wardrobe was a common sitting-room of some four feet by six, in which sat, smoking their pipes round a charcoal brazier, no fewer than six old soldiers of the First Republic, with their uniforms torn and worn threadbare. Evidently they were of the *mauvais sujet* class; their blear eyes and limp jaws told plainly of a common love of absinthe; and their eyes had that haggard, worn look which stamps the drunkard at his worst, and that look of slumbering ferocity which follows hard in the wake of drink. The other side stood as of old, with its shelves intact, save that they were cut to half their depth, and in each shelf of which there were six, was a bed made with rags and straw. The half-dozen of worthies who inhabited this structure looked at me curiously as I passed; and when I looked back after going a little way I saw their heads together in a whispered conference. I did not like the look of this at all, for the place was very lonely, and the men looked very, very villainous. However, I did not see any cause for fear, and went on my way, penetrating further and further into the Sahara. The way was tortuous to a degree, and from going round in a series of semi-circles, as one goes in skating with the Dutch roll, I got rather confused with regard to the points of the compass.

When I had penetrated a little way I saw, as I turned the corner of a half-made heap, sitting on a heap of straw an old soldier with threadbare coat.

"Hallo!" said I to myself; "the First Republic is well represented here in its soldiery."

As I passed him the old man never even looked up at me, but gazed on the ground with stolid persistency. Again I remarked to myself: "See what a life of rude warfare can do! This old man's curiosity is a thing of the past."

When I had gone a few steps, however, I looked back suddenly, and saw that curiosity was not dead, for the veteran had raised his head and was regarding me with a very queer expression. He seemed to me to look very like one of the six worthies in the press. When he saw me looking he dropped his head; and without thinking further of him I went on my way, satisfied that there was a strange likeness between these old warriors.

Presently I met another old soldier in a similar manner. He, too, did not notice me whilst I was passing.

By this time it was getting late in the afternoon, and I began to think of retracing my steps. Accordingly I turned to go back, but could see a number of tracks leading between different mounds and could not ascertain which of them I should take. In my perplexity I wanted to see someone of whom to ask the way, but could see no one. I determined to go on a few mounds further and so try to see someone—not a veteran.

I gained my object, for after going a couple of hundred yards I saw before me a single shanty such as I had seen before—with, however, the difference that this was not one for living in, but merely a roof with three walls open in front. From the evidences which the neighbourhood exhibited I took it to be a place for sorting. Within it was an old woman wrinkled and bent with age; I approached her to ask the way.

She rose as I came close and I asked her my way. She immediately commenced a conversation; and it occurred to me that here in the very centre of the Kingdom of Dust was the place to gather details of the history of Parisian rag-picking—particularly as I could do so from the lips of one who looked like the oldest inhabitant.

I began my inquiries, and the old woman gave me most interesting answers—she had been one of the ceteuces who sat daily before the guillotine and had taken an active part among the women who signalised themselves by their violence in the revolution. While we were talking she said suddenly: "But m'sieur must be tired standing," and dusted a rickety old stool for me to sit down. I hardly liked to do so for many reasons; but the poor old woman was so civil that I did not like to run the risk of hurting her by refusing, and moreover the conversation of one who had been at the taking of the Bastille was so interesting that I sat down and so our conversation went on.

While we were talking an old man—older and more bent and wrinkled even than the woman—appeared from behind the shanty. "Here is

Pierre," said she. "M'sieur can hear stories now if he wishes, for Pierre was in everything, from the Bastille to Waterloo." The old man took another stool at my request and we plunged into a sea of revolutionary reminiscences. This old man, albeit clothed like a scare-crow, was like any one of the six veterans.

I was now sitting in the centre of the low hut with the woman on my left hand and the man on my right, each of them being somewhat in front of me. The place was full of all sorts of curious objects of lumber, and of many things that I wished far away. In one corner was a heap of rags which seemed to move from the number of vermin it contained, and in the other a heap of bones whose odour was something shocking. Every now and then, glancing at the heaps, I could see the gleaming eyes of some of the rats which infested the place. These loathsome objects were bad enough, but what looked even more dreadful was an old butcher's axe with an iron handle stained with clots of blood leaning up against the wall on the right hand side. Still these things did not give me much concern. The talk of the two old people was so fascinating that I stayed on and on, till the evening came and the dust-heaps threw dark shadows over the vales between them.

After a time I began to grow uneasy, I could not tell how or why, but somehow I did not feel satisfied. Uneasiness is an instinct and means warning. The psychic faculties are often the sentries of the intellect; and when they sound alarm the reason begins to act, although perhaps not consciously.

This was so with me. I began to bethink me where I was and by what surrounded, and to wonder how I should fare in case I should be attacked; and then the thought suddenly burst upon me, although without any overt cause, that I was in danger. Prudence whispered: "Be still and make no sign," and so I was still and made no sign, for I knew that four cunning eyes were on me. "Four eyes—if not more." My God, what a horrible thought! The whole shanty might be surrounded on three sides with villains! I might be in the midst of a band of such desperadoes as only half a century of periodic revolution can produce.

With a sense of danger my intellect and observation quickened, and I grew more watchful than was my wont. I noticed that the old woman's eyes were constantly wandering toward my hands. I looked at them too, and saw the cause—my rings. On my left little finger I had a large signet and on the right a good diamond.

I thought that if there was any danger my first care was to avert suspicion. Accordingly I began to work the conversation round to rag-picking—to the drains—of the things found there; and so by easy stages to jewels. Then, seizing a favourable opportunity, I asked the old woman if she knew anything of such things. She answered that she did, a little. I held out my right hand, and, showing her the diamond, asked her what she thought of that. She answered that her eyes were bad, and stooped over my hand. I said as nonchalantly as I could: "Pardon me! You will see better thus!" and taking it off handed it to her. An unholy light came into her withered old face, as she touched it. She stole one glance at me swift and keen as a flash of lightning.

She bent over the ring for a moment, her face quite concealed as though examining it. The old man looked straight out of the front of the shanty before him, at the same time fumbling in his pockets and producing a screw of tobacco in a paper and a pipe, which he proceeded to fill. I took advantage of the pause and the momentary rest from the searching eyes on my face to look carefully round the place, now dim and shadowy in the gloaming. There still lay all the heaps of varied reeking foulness; there the terrible blood-stained axe leaning against the wall in the right hand corner, and everywhere, despite the gloom, the baleful glitter of the eyes of the rats. I could see them even through some of the chinks of the boards at the back low down close to the ground. But stay! these latter eyes seemed more than usually large and bright and baleful!

For an instant my heart stood still, and I felt in that whirling condition of mind in which one feels a sort of spiritual drunkenness, and as though the body is only maintained erect in that there is no time for it to fall before recovery. Then, in another second, I was calm—coldly calm, with all my energies in full vigour, with a self-control which I felt to be perfect and with all my feeling and instincts alert.

Now I knew the full extent of my danger: I was watched and surrounded by desperate people! I could not even guess at how many of them were lying there on the ground behind the shanty, waiting for the moment to strike. I knew that I was big and strong, and they knew it, too. They knew also, as I did, that I was an Englishman and would make a fight for it; and so we waited. I had, I felt, gained an advantage in the last few seconds, for I knew my danger and understood the situation. Now, I thought, is the test of my courage—the enduring test: the fighting test may come later!

The old woman raised her head and said to me in a satisfied kind of way:

"A very fine ring, indeed—a beautiful ring! Oh, me! I once had such rings, plenty of them, and bracelets and earrings! Oh! for in those fine days I led the town a dance! But they've forgotten me now! They've forgotten me! They? Why they never heard of me! Perhaps their grandfathers remember me, some of them!" and she laughed a harsh, croaking laugh. And then I am bound to say that she astonished me, for she handed me back the ring with a certain suggestion of old-fashioned grace which was not without its pathos.

The old man eyed her with a sort of sudden ferocity, half rising from his stool, and said to me suddenly and hoarsely:

"Let me see!"

I was about to hand the ring when the old woman said:

"No! no, do not give it to Pierre! Pierre is eccentric. He loses things; and such a pretty ring!"

"Cat!" said the old man, savagely. Suddenly the old woman said, rather more loudly than was necessary:

"Wait! I shall tell you something about a ring." There was something in the sound of her voice that jarred upon me. Perhaps it was my hypersensitiveness, wrought up as I was to such a pitch of nervous excitement, but I seemed to think that she was not addressing me. As I stole a glance round the place I saw the eyes of the rats in the bone heaps, but missed the eyes along the back. But even as I looked I saw them again appear. The old woman's "Wait!" had given me a respite from attack, and the men had sunk back to their reclining posture.

"I once lost a ring—a beautiful diamond hoop that had belonged to a queen, and which was given to me by a farmer of the taxes, who afterwards cut his throat because I sent him away. I thought it must have been stolen, and taxed my people; but I could get no trace. The police came and suggested that it had found its way to the drain. We descended—I in my fine clothes, for I would not trust them with my beautiful ring! I know more of the drains since then, and of rats, too! but I shall never forget the horror of that place—alive with blazing eyes, a wall of them just outside the light of our torches. Well, we got beneath my house. We searched the outlet of the drain, and there in the filth found my ring, and we came out.

"But we found something else also before we came! As we were coming toward the opening a lot of sewer rats—human ones this time—came toward us. They told the police that one of their number had gone into the drain, but had not returned. He had gone in only shortly before we had, and, if lost, could hardly be far off. They asked help to seek him, so we turned back. They tried to prevent me going, but I insisted. It was a new excitement, and had I not recovered my ring? Not far did we go till we came on something. There was but little water, and the bottom of the drain was raised with brick, rubbish, and much matter of the kind. He had made a fight for it, even when his torch had gone out. But they were too many for him! They had not been long about it! The bones were still warm; but they were picked clean. They had even eaten their own dead ones and there were bones of rats as well as of the man. They took it cool enough those other—the human ones—and joked of their comrade when they found him dead, though they would have helped him living. Bah! what matters it—life or death?"

"And had you no fear?" I asked her.

"Fear!" she said with a laugh. "Me have fear? Ask Pierre! But I was younger then, and, as I came through that horrible drain with its wall of greedy eyes, always moving with the circle of the light from the torches, I did not feel easy. I kept on before the men, though! It is a way I have! I never let the men get it before me. All I want is a chance and a means! And they ate him up—took every trace away except the bones; and no one knew it, nor no sound of him was ever heard!" Here she broke into a chuckling fit of the ghastliest merriment which it was ever my lot to hear and see. A great poetess describes her heroine singing: "Oh! to see or hear her singing! Scarce I know which is the divinest."

And I can apply the same idea to the old crone—in all save the divinity, for I scarce could tell which was the most hellish—the harsh, malicious, satisfied, cruel laugh, or the leering grin, and the horrible square opening of the mouth like a tragic mask, and the yellow gleam of the few discoloured teeth in the shapeless gums. In that laugh and with that grin and the chuckling satisfaction I knew as well as if it had been spoken to me in words of thunder that my murder was settled, and the murderers only bided the proper time for its accomplishment. I could read between the lines of her gruesome story the commands to her accomplices. "Wait," she seemed to say, "bide your time. I shall strike the first blow. Find the weapon for me, and I shall make the opportunity! He shall not escape! Keep him quiet, and then no one will be wiser. There will be no outcry, and the rats will do their work!"

It was growing darker and darker; the night was coming. I stole a glance round the shanty, still all the same! The bloody axe in the corner, the heaps of filth, and the eyes on the bone heaps and in the crannies of the floor.

Pierre had been still ostensibly filling his pipe; he now struck a light and began to puff away at it. The old woman said:

"Dear heart, how dark it is! Pierre, like a good lad, light the lamp!"

Pierre got up and with the lighted match in his hand touched the wick of a lamp which hung at one side of the entrance to the shanty, and which had a reflector that threw the light all over the place. It was evidently that which was used for their sorting at night.

"Not that, stupid! Not that! The lantern!" she called out to him.

He immediately blew it out, saying: "All right, mother, I'll find it," and he hustled about the left corner of the room—the old woman saying through the darkness:

"The lantern! the lantern! Oh! That is the light that is most useful to us poor folks. The lantern was the friend of the revolution! It is the friend of the chiffonier! It helps us when all else fails."

Hardly had she said the word when there was a kind of creaking of the whole place, and something was steadily dragged over the roof.

Again I seemed to read between the lines of her words. I knew the lesson of the lantern.

"One of you get on the roof with a noose and strangle him as he passes out if we fail within."

As I looked out of the opening I saw the loop of a rope outlined black against the lurid sky. I was now, indeed, beset!

Pierre was not long in finding the lantern. I kept my eyes fixed through the darkness on the old woman. Pierre struck his light, and by its flash I saw the old woman raise from the ground beside her where it had mysteriously appeared, and then hide in the folds of her gown, a long sharp knife or dagger. It seemed to be like a butcher's sharpening iron fined to a keen point.

The lantern was lit.

"Bring it here, Pierre," she said. "Place it in the doorway where we can see it. See how nice it is! It shuts out the darkness from us; it is just right!"

Just right for her and her purposes! It threw all its light on my face, leaving in gloom the faces of both Pierre and the woman, who sat outside of me on each side.

I felt that the time of action was approaching; but I knew now that the first signal and movement would come from the woman, and so watched her.

I was all unarmed, but I had made up my mind what to do. At the first movement I would seize the butcher's axe in the right-hand corner and fight my way out. At least, I would die hard. I stole a glance round to fix its exact locality so that I could not fail to seize it at the first effort, for then, if ever, time and accuracy would be precious.

Good God! It was gone! All the horror of the situation burst upon me; but the bitterest thought of all was that if the issue of the terrible position should be against me Alice would infallibly suffer. Either she would believe me false—and any lover, or any one who has ever been one, can imagine the bitterness of the thought—or else she would go on loving long after I had been lost to her and to the world, so that her life would be broken and embittered, shattered with disappointment and despair. The very magnitude of the pain braced me up and nerved me to bear the dread scrutiny of the plotters.

I think I did not betray myself. The old woman was watching me as a cat does a mouse; she had her right hand hidden in the folds of her gown, clutching, I knew, that long, cruel-looking dagger. Had she seen any disappointment in my face she would, I felt, have known that the moment had come, and would have sprung on me like a tigress, certain of taking me unprepared.

I looked out into the night, and there I saw new cause for danger. Before and around the hut were at a little distance some shadowy forms;

they were quite still, but I knew that they were all alert and on guard. Small chance for me now in that direction.

Again I stole a glance round the place. In moments of great excitement and of great danger, which is excitement, the mind works very quickly, and the keenness of the faculties which depend on the mind grows in proportion. I now felt this. In an instant I took in the whole situation. I saw that the axe had been taken through a small hole made in one of the rotten boards. How rotten they must be to allow of such a thing being done without a particle of noise.

The hut was a regular murder-trap, and was guarded all around. A garroter lay on the roof ready to entangle me with his noose if I should escape the dagger of the old hag. In front the way was guarded by I know not how many watchers. And at the back was a row of desperate men—I had seen their eyes still through the crack in the boards of the floor, when last I looked—as they lay prone waiting for the signal to start erect. If it was to be ever, now for it!

As nonchalantly as I could I turned slightly on my stool so as to get my right leg well under me. Then with a sudden jump, turning my head, and guarding it with my hands, and with the fighting instinct of the knights of old, I breathed my lady's name, and hurled myself against the back wall of the hut.

Watchful as they were, the suddenness of my movement surprised both Pierre and the old woman. As I crashed through the rotten timbers I saw the old woman rise with a leap like a tiger and heard her low gasp of baffled rage. My feet lit on something that moved, and as I jumped away I knew that I had stepped on the back of one of the row of men lying on their faces outside the hut. I was torn with nails and splinters, but otherwise unhurt. Breathless I rushed up the mound in front of me, hearing as I went the dull crash of the shanty as it collapsed into a mass.

It was a nightmare climb. The mound, though but low, was awfully steep, and with each step I took the mass of dust and cinders tore down with me and gave way under my feet. The dust rose and choked me; it was sickening, fœtid, awful; but my climb was, I felt, for life or death, and I struggled on. The seconds seemed hours; but the few moments I had in starting, combined with my youth and strength, gave me a great advantage, and, though several forms struggled after me in deadly silence which was more dreadful than any sound, I easily reached the top. Since then I have climbed the cone of Vesuvius, and as I struggled up that dreary steep amid the sulphurous fumes the memory of that awful night at Montrouge came back to me so vividly that I almost grew faint.

The mound was one of the tallest in the region of dust, and as I struggled to the top, panting for breath and with my heart beating like a sledge-hammer, I saw away to my left the dull red gleam of the sky, and nearer still the flashing of lights. Thank God! I knew where I was now and where lay the road to Paris!

For two or three seconds I paused and looked back. My pursuers were still well behind me, but struggling up resolutely, and in deadly silence. Beyond, the shanty was a wreck—a mass of timber and moving forms. I could see it well, for flames were already bursting out; the rags and straw had evidently caught fire from the lantern. Still silence there! Not a sound! These old wretches could die game, anyhow.

I had no time for more than a passing glance, for as I cast an eye round the mound preparatory to making my descent I saw several dark forms rushing round on either side to cut me off on my way. It was now a race for life. They were trying to head me on my way to Paris, and with the instinct of the moment I dashed down to the right-hand side. I was just in time, for, though I came as it seemed to me down the steep in a few steps, the wary old men who were watching me turned back, and one, as I rushed by into the opening between the two mounds in front, almost struck me a blow with that terrible butcher's axe. There could surely not be two such weapons about!

Then began a really horrible chase. I easily ran ahead of the old men, and even when some younger ones and a few women joined in the hunt I easily distanced them. But I did not know the way, and I could not even guide myself by the light in the sky, for I was running away from it. I had heard that, unless of conscious purpose, hunted men turn always to the left, and so I found it now; and so, I suppose, knew also my pursuers, who were more animals than men, and with cunning or instinct had found out such secrets for themselves: for on finishing a quick spurt, after which I intended to take a moment's breathing space, I suddenly saw ahead of me two or three forms swiftly passing behind a mound to the right.

I was in the spider's web now indeed! But with the thought of this new danger came the resource of the hunted, and so I darted down the next turning to the right. I continued in this direction for some hundred yards, and then, making a turn to the left again, felt certain that I had, at any rate, avoided the danger of being surrounded.

But not of pursuit, for on came the rabble after me, steady, dogged, relentless, and still in grim silence.

In the greater darkness the mounds seemed now to be somewhat smaller than before, although—for the night was closing—they looked bigger in proportion. I was now well ahead of my pursuers, so I made a dart up the mound in front.

Oh joy of joys! I was close to the edge of this inferno of dust-heaps. Away behind me the red light of Paris in the sky, and towering up behind rose the heights of Montmartre—a dim light, with here and there brilliant points like stars.

Restored to vigour in a moment, I ran over the few remaining mounds of decreasing size, and found myself on the level land beyond. Even then, however, the prospect was not inviting. All before me was dark and dismal, and I had evidently come on one of those dank, low-lying waste places which are found here and there in the neighbourhood of great cities. Places of waste and desolation, where the space is required for the ultimate agglomeration of all that is noxious, and the ground is so poor as to create no desire of occupancy even in the lowest squatter. With eyes accustomed to the gloom of the evening, and away now from the shadows of those dreadful dust-heaps, I could see much more easily than I could a little while ago. It might have been, of course, that the glare in the sky of the lights of Paris, though the city was some miles away, was reflected here. Howsoever it was, I saw well enough to take bearings for certainly some little distance around me.

In front was a bleak, flat waste that seemed almost dead level, with here and there the dark shimmering of stagnant pools. Seemingly far off on the right, amid a small cluster of scattered lights, rose a dark mass of Fort Montrouge, and away to the left in the dim distance, pointed with stray gleams from cottage windows, the lights in the sky showed the locality of Bicêtre. A moment's thought decided me to take to the right and try to reach Montrouge. There at least would be some sort of safety, and I might possibly long before come on some of the cross roads which I knew. Somewhere, not far off, must lie the strategic road made to connect the outlying chain of forts circling the city.

Then I looked back. Coming over the mounds, and outlined black against the glare of the Parisian horizon, I saw several moving figures, and still a way to the right several more deploying out between me and my destination. They evidently meant to cut me off in this direction, and so my choice became constricted; it lay now between going straight ahead or turning to the left. Stooping to the ground, so as to get the advantage of the horizon as a line of sight, I looked carefully in this direction, but could detect no sign of my enemies. I argued that as they had not guarded or were not trying to guard that point, there was evidently danger to me there already. So I made up my mind to go straight on before me.

It was not an inviting prospect, and as I went on the reality grew worse. The ground became soft and oozy, and now and again gave way beneath me in a sickening kind of way. I seemed somehow to be going down, for I saw round me places seemingly more elevated than where I was, and this in a place which from a little way back seemed dead level. I looked around, but could see none of my pursuers. This was strange, for all along these birds of the night had followed me through the darkness as well as though it was broad daylight. How I blamed myself for coming out in my light-coloured tourist suit of tweed. The silence, and my not being able to see my enemies, whilst I felt that they were watching me, grew appalling, and in the hope of some one not of this ghastly crew hearing me I raised my voice and shouted several times. There was not the slightest response; not even an echo rewarded my efforts. For a while I stood stock still and kept my eyes in one direction. On one of the rising places around me I saw something dark move along, then another, and another. This was to my left, and seemingly moving to head me off.

I thought that again I might with my skill as a runner elude my enemies at this game, and so with all my speed darted forward.

Splash!

My feet had given way in a mass of slimy rubbish, and I had fallen headlong into a reeking, stagnant pool. The water and the mud in which my arms sank up to the elbows was filthy and nauseous beyond description, and in the suddenness of my fall I had actually swallowed some of the filthy stuff, which nearly choked me, and made me gasp for breath. Never shall I forget the moments during which I stood trying to recover myself almost fainting from the fœtid odour of the filthy pool, whose white mist rose ghostlike around. Worst of all, with the acute despair of the hunted animal when he sees the pursuing pack closing on him, I saw before my eyes whilst I stood helpless the dark forms of my pursuers moving swiftly to surround me.

It is curious how our minds work on odd matters even when the energies of thought are seemingly concentrated on some terrible and pressing need. I was in momentary peril of my life: my safety depended on my action, and my choice of alternatives coming now with almost every step I took, and yet I could not but think of the strange dogged persistency of these old men. Their silent resolution, their steadfast, grim, persistency even in such a cause commanded, as well as fear, even a measure of respect. What must they have been in the vigour of their youth. I could understand now that whirlwind rush on the bridge of Arcola, that scornful exclamation of the Old Guard at Waterloo! Unconscious cerebration has its own pleasures, even at such moments; but fortunately it does not in any way clash with the thought from which action springs.

I realised at a glance that so far I was defeated in my object, my enemies as yet had won. They had succeeded in surrounding me on three sides, and were bent on driving me off to the left-hand, where there was already some danger for me, for they had left no guard. I accepted the alternative—it was a case of Hobson's choice and run. I had to keep the lower ground, for my pursuers were on the higher places. However, though the ooze and broken ground impeded me my youth and training made me able to hold my ground, and by keeping a diagonal line I not only kept them from gaining on me but even began to distance them. This gave me new heart and strength, and by this time habitual training was beginning to tell and my second wind had come. Before me the ground rose slightly. I rushed up the slope and found before me a waste of watery slime, with a low dyke or bank looking black and grim beyond. I felt that if I could but reach that dyke in safety I could there, with solid ground under my feet and some kind of path to guide me, find with comparative ease a way out of my troubles. After a glance right and left and seeing no one near, I kept my eyes for a few minutes to their rightful work of aiding my feet whilst I crossed the swamp. It was rough, hard work, but there was little danger, merely toil; and a short time took me to the dyke. I rushed up the slope exulting; but here again I met a new shock. On either side of me rose a number of crouching figures. From right and left they rushed at me. Each body held a rope.

The cordon was nearly complete. I could pass on neither side, and the end was near.

There was only one chance, and I took it. I hurled myself across the dyke, and escaping out of the very clutches of my foes threw myself into the stream.

At any other time I should have thought that water foul and filthy, but now it was as welcome as the most crystal stream to the parched traveller. It was a highway of safety!

My pursuers rushed after me. Had only one of them held the rope it would have been all up with me, for he could have entangled me before I had time to swim a stroke; but the many hands holding it embarrassed and delayed them, and when the rope struck the water I heard the splash well behind me. A few minutes' hard swimming took me across the stream. Refreshed with the immersion and encouraged by the escape, I climbed the dyke in comparative gaiety of spirits.

From the top I looked back. Through the darkness I saw my assailants scattering up and down along the dyke. The pursuit was evidently not ended, and again I had to choose my course. Beyond the dyke where I stood was a wild, swampy space very similar to that which I had crossed. I determined to shun such a place, and thought for a moment whether I would take up or down the dyke. I thought I heard a sound—the muffled sound of oars, so I listened, and then shouted.

No response; but the sound ceased. My enemies had evidently got a boat of some kind. As they were on the up side of me I took the down path and began to run. As I passed to the left of where I had entered the water I heard several splashes, soft and stealthy, like the sound a rat makes as he plunges into the stream, but vastly greater; and as I looked I saw the dark sheen of the water broken by the ripples of several advancing heads. Some of my enemies were swimming the stream also.

And now behind me, up the stream, the silence was broken by the quick rattle and creak of oars; my enemies were in hot pursuit. I put my best leg foremost and ran on. After a break of a couple of minutes I looked back, and by a gleam of light through the ragged clouds I saw several dark forms climbing the bank behind me. The wind had now begun to rise, and the water beside me was ruffled and beginning to break in tiny waves on the bank. I had to keep my eyes pretty well on the ground before me, lest I should stumble, for I knew that to stumble was death. After a few minutes I looked back behind me. On the dyke were only a few dark figures, but crossing the waste, swampy ground were many more. What new danger this portended I did not know—could only guess. Then as I ran it seemed to me that my track kept ever sloping away to the right. I looked up ahead and saw that the river was much wider than before, and that the dyke on which I stood fell quite away, and beyond it was another stream on whose near bank I saw some of the dark forms now across the marsh. I was on an island of some kind.

My situation was now indeed terrible, for my enemies had hemmed me in on every side. Behind came the quickening roll of the oars, as though my pursuers knew that the end was close. Around me on every side was desolation; there was not a roof or light, as far as I could see. Far off to the right rose some dark mass, but what it was I knew not. For a moment I paused to think what I should do, not for more, for my pursuers were drawing closer. Then my mind was made up. I slipped down the bank and took to the water. I struck out straight ahead, so as to gain the current by clearing the backwater of the island for such I presume it was, when I had passed into the stream. I waited till a cloud came driving across the moon and leaving all in darkness. Then I took off my hat and laid it softly on the water floating with the stream, and a second after dived to the right and struck out under water with all my might. I was, I suppose half a minute under water, and when I rose came up as softly as I could, and turning, looked back. There went my light brown hat floating merrily away. Close behind it came a rickety old boat, driven furiously by a pair of oars. The moon was still partly obscured by the drifting clouds, but in the partial light

I could see a man in the bows holding aloft ready to strike what appeared to me to be that same dreadful pole-axe which I had before escaped. As I looked the boat drew closer, closer, and the man struck savagely. The hat disappeared. The man fell forward, almost out of the boat. His comrades dragged him in but without the axe, and then as I turned with all my energies bent on reaching the further bank, I heard the fierce whirr of the muttered "Sacre!" which marked the anger of my baffled pursuers.

That was the first sound I had heard from human lips during all this dreadful chase, and full as it was of menace and danger to me it was a welcome sound for it broke that awful silence which shrouded and appalled me. It was as though an overt sign that my opponents were men and not ghosts, and that with them I had, at least, the chance of a man, though but one against many.

But now that the spell of silence was broken the sounds came thick and fast. From boat to shore and back from shore to boat came quick question and answer, all in the fiercest whispers. I looked back—a fatal thing to do—for in the instant someone caught sight of my face, which showed white on the dark water, and shouted. Hands pointed to me, and in a moment or two the boat was under weigh, and following hard after me. I had but a little way to go, but quicker and quicker came the boat after me. A few more strokes and I would be on the shore, but I felt the oncoming of the boat, and expected each second to feel the crash of an oar or other weapon on my head. Had I not seen that dreadful axe disappear in the water I do not think that I could have won the shore. I heard the muttered curses of those not rowing and the laboured breath of the rowers. With one supreme effort for life or liberty I touched the bank and sprang up it. There was not a single second to spare, for hard behind me the boat grounded and several dark forms sprang after me. I gained the top of the dyke, and keeping to the left ran on again. The boat put off and followed down the stream. Seeing this I feared danger in this direction, and quickly turning, ran down the dyke on the other side, and after passing a short stretch of marshy ground gained a wild, open flat country and sped on.

Still behind me came on my relentless pursuers. Far away, below me, I saw the same dark mass as before, but now grown closer and greater. My heart gave a great thrill of delight, for I knew that it must be the fortress of Bicêtre, and with new courage I ran on. I had heard that between each and all of the protecting forts of Paris there are strategic ways, deep sunk roads, where soldiers marching should be sheltered from an enemy. I knew that if I could gain this road I would be safe, but in the darkness I could not see any sign of it, so, in blind hope of striking it, I ran on.

Presently I came to the edge of a deep cut, and found that down below me ran a road guarded on each side by a ditch of water fenced on either side by a straight, high wall.

Getting fainter and dizzier, I ran on; the ground got more broken—more and more still, till I staggered and fell, and rose again, and ran on in the blind anguish of the hunted. Again the thought of Alice nerved me. I would not be lost and wreck her life: I would fight and struggle for life to the bitter end. With a great effort I caught the top of the wall. As, scrambling like a catamount, I drew myself up, I actually felt a hand touch the sole of my foot. I was now on a sort of causeway, and before me I saw a dim light. Blind and dizzy, I ran on, staggered, and fell, rising, covered with dust and blood.

"Halt la!"

The words sounded like a voice from heaven. A blaze of light seemed to enwrap me, and I shouted with joy.

"Qui va la?" The rattle of musketry, the flash of steel before my eyes. Instinctively I stopped, though close behind me came a rush of my pursuers.

Another word or two, and out from a gateway poured, as it seemed to me, a tide of red and blue, as the guard turned out. All around seemed blazing with light, and the flash of steel, the clink and rattle of arms, and the loud, harsh voices of command. As I fell forward, utterly exhausted, a soldier caught me. I looked back in dreadful expectation, and saw the mass of dark forms disappearing into the night. Then I must have fainted. When I recovered my senses I was in the guard room. They gave me brandy, and after a while I was able to tell them something of what had passed. Then a commissary of police appeared, apparently out of the empty air, as is the way of the Parisian police officer. He listened attentively, and then had a moment's consultation with the officer in command. Apparently they were agreed, for they asked me if I were ready now to come with them.

"Where to?" I asked, rising to go.

"Back to the dust-heaps. We shall, perhaps, catch them yet!"

"I shall try!" said I.

He eyed me for a moment keenly, and said suddenly:

"Would you like to wait a while or till to-morrow, young Englishman?" This touched me to the quick, as, perhaps, he intended, and I jumped to my feet.

"Come now!" I said; "now! now! An Englishman is always ready for his duty!"

The commissary was a good fellow, as well as a shrewd one; he slapped my shoulder kindly. "Brave garçon!" he said. "Forgive me, but I knew what would do you most good. The guard is ready. Come!"

And so, passing right through the guard room, and through a long vaulted passage, we were out into the night. A few of the men in front had powerful lanterns. Through courtyards and down a sloping way we passed out through a low archway to a sunken road, the same that I had seen in my flight. The order was given to get at the double, and with a quick, springing stride, half run, half walk, the soldiers went swiftly along. I felt my strength renewed again—such is the difference between hunter and hunted. A very short distance took us to a low-lying pontoon bridge across the stream, and evidently very little higher up than I had struck it.

Some effort had evidently been made to damage it, for the ropes had all been cut, and one of the chains had been broken. I heard the officer say to the commissary:

"We are just in time! A few more minutes, and they would have destroyed the bridge. Forward, quicker still!" and on we went. Again we reached a pontoon on the winding stream; as we came up we heard the hollow boom of the metal drums as the efforts to destroy the bridge was again renewed. A word of command was given, and several men raised their rifles.

"Fire!" A volley rang out. There was a muffled cry, and the dark forms dispersed. But the evil was done, and we saw the far end of the pontoon swing into the stream. This was a serious delay, and it was nearly an hour before we had renewed ropes and restored the bridge sufficiently to allow us to cross.

We renewed the chase. Quicker, quicker we went towards the dust-heaps.

After a time we came to a place that I knew. There were the remains of a fire—a few smouldering wood ashes still cast a red glow, but the bulk of the ashes were cold. I knew the site of the hut and the hill behind it up which I had rushed, and in the flickering glow the eyes of the rats still shone with a sort of phosphorescence. The commissary spoke a word to the officer, and he cried:

"Halt!"

The soldiers were ordered to spread around and watch, and then we commenced to examine the ruins. The commissary himself began to lift away the charred boards and rubbish. These the soldiers took and piled together. Presently he started back, then bent down and rising beckoned me.

"See!" he said.

It was a gruesome sight. There lay a skeleton face downwards, a woman by the lines—an old woman by the coarse fibre of the bone.

Between the ribs rose a long spike-like dagger made from a butcher's sharpening knife, its keen point buried in the spine.

"You will observe," said the commissary to the officer and to me as he took out his note book, "that the woman must have fallen on her dagger. The rats are many here—see their eyes glistening among that heap of bones—and you will also notice"—I shuddered as he placed his hand on the skeleton—"that but little time was lost by them, for the bones are scarcely cold!"

There was no other sign of any one near, living or dead; and so deploying again into line the soldiers passed on. Presently we came to the hut made of the old wardrobe. We approached. In five of the six compartments was an old man sleeping—sleeping so soundly that even the glare of the lanterns did not wake them. Old and grim and grizzled they looked, with their gaunt, wrinkled, bronzed faces and their white moustaches.

The officer called out harshly and loudly a word of command, and in an instant each one of them was on his feet before us and standing at "attention!"

"What do you here?"

"We sleep," was the answer.

"Where are the other chiffoniers?" asked the commissary.

"Gone to work."

"And you?"

"We are on guard!"

"Peste!" laughed the officer grimly, as he looked at the old men one after the other in the face and added with cool deliberate cruelty, "Asleep on duty! Is this the manner of the Old Guard? No wonder, then, a Waterloo!"

By the gleam of the lantern I saw the grim old faces grow deadly pale, and almost shuddered at the look in the eyes of the old men as the laugh of the soldiers echoed the grim pleasantry of the officer.

I felt in that moment that I was in some measure avenged.

For a moment they looked as if they would throw themselves on the taunter, but years of their life had schooled them and they remained still.

"You are but five," said the commissary; "where is the sixth?" The answer came with a grim chuckle.

"He is there!" and the speaker pointed to the bottom of the wardrobe. "He died last night. You won't find much of him. The burial of the rats is quick!"

The commissary stooped and looked in. Then he turned to the officer and said calmly:

"We may as well go back. No trace here now; nothing to prove that man was the one wounded by your soldiers' bullets! Probably they murdered him to cover up the trace. See!" again he stooped and placed his hands on the skeleton. "The rats work quickly and they are many. These bones are warm!"

I shuddered, and so did many more of those around me.

"Form!" said the officer, and so in marching order, with the lanterns swinging in front and the manacled veterans in the midst, with steady tramp we took ourselves out of the dust-heaps and turned backward to the fortress of Bicêtre.

My year of probation has long since ended, and Alice is my wife. But when I look back upon that trying twelvemonth one of the most vivid incidents that memory recalls is that associated with my visit to the City of Dust.